Praise for the
Forensic Handwriting Mysteries
by Sheila Lowe

Dead Write

"Lowe's list of credible suspects and well-placed red herrings keep us guessing about the villain's identity till the end, and then, with only a few pages remaining, she delivers one more shocking 'Kapow!' . . . Lowe's expertise as a handwriting expert gives her books authenticity. From tics, t-bars, and twisted loops, to dot grinding and word crowding, readers get a fascinating insider look at the tools and techniques used in graphology."
—Los Angeles Chronicle

"Lowe manages to keep the reader in suspense and wondering not only who did it, but how and why, up to nearly the last page. There're some interesting surprises and some near misses to keep you glued to your favorite reading spot until the last page."   Gumshoe

"[A] solid mystery featuring an engaging amateur sleuth, fascinating tidbits about handwriting analysis, and top-notch writing."   —Cozy Library

Written in Blood

"A fascinating and complex murder mystery that keeps readers involved and guessing till the exciting climax."
—American Chronicle

"Readers will relish Sheila Lowe's fine tale."
—Genre Go Round Reviews

continued . . .

Also by Sheila Lowe

Forensic Handwriting Mysteries

Poison Pen
Written in Blood
Dead Write

Nonfiction Works

The Complete Idiot's Guide to Handwriting Analysis
Handwriting of the Famous & Infamous

Last Writes

A FORENSIC HANDWRITING MYSTERY

SHEILA LOWE

AN OBSIDIAN MYSTERY

OBSIDIAN

Published by New American Library, a division of
Penguin Group (USA) Inc., 375 Hudson Street,
New York, New York 10014, USA
Penguin Group (Canada), 90 Eglinton Avenue East, Suite 700, Toronto,
Ontario M4P 2Y3, Canada (a division of Pearson Penguin Canada Inc.)
Penguin Books Ltd., 80 Strand, London WC2R 0RL, England
Penguin Ireland, 25 St. Stephen's Green, Dublin 2,
Ireland (a division of Penguin Books Ltd.)
Penguin Group (Australia), 250 Camberwell Road, Camberwell, Victoria 3124,
Australia (a division of Pearson Australia Group Pty. Ltd.)
Penguin Books India Pvt. Ltd., 11 Community Centre, Panchsheel Park,
New Delhi - 110 017, India
Penguin Group (NZ), 67 Apollo Drive, Rosedale, North Shore 0632,
New Zealand (a division of Pearson New Zealand Ltd.)
Penguin Books (South Africa) (Pty.) Ltd., 24 Sturdee Avenue,
Rosebank, Johannesburg 2196, South Africa

Penguin Books Ltd., Registered Offices:
80 Strand, London WC2R 0RL, England

First published by Obsidian, an imprint of New American Library,
a division of Penguin Group (USA) Inc.

First Printing, July 2010
10 9 8 7 6 5 4 3 2 1

Acknowledgments

Heartfelt thanks to all the usual suspects: Bob Bealmear, Bruce Cook, Gwen Freeman, Bob Joseph, Raul Melendez, Barbara Petty, and Ellen Larson for their unflinching critiques. Thanks for making me a better writer. And on the technical side, thanks to Doug Lyle for answering my interminable medical questions. For law enforcement help: Bob Brounsten, Robin Burcell, George Fong, and Ernesto Pittino, I deeply appreciate your willingness to be there for me as needed.

Rita Frayer and Lynn Ryder were the winning bidders for character names on behalf of the Ventura County Professional Women's Network. Thanks for supporting a great organization.

Chapter 1

The angelic face gazed past the camera with serious eyes the color of spring violets and a rosebud mouth turned down. The child in the picture was hardly more than a toddler—around two, two and a half, Claudia Rose guessed—but there was a grown-up wistfulness in the way her chin rested on her dimpled hand.

Studying the photograph, Claudia fancied she could see life experience in those eyes, experience that extended far beyond the scant few months the little girl had been on earth. *An old soul*, she thought as she returned the photograph to the child's mother.

Erin Powers replaced the photo in an envelope and stuffed it into an inside pocket of the battered leather bag at her feet. More saddlebag than purse, its faded sides bulged with unseen items. "We've always known Kylie was special. As soon as we saw those eyes, we said God has a plan for her. I've *got* to get her back." Erin's head was bowed, her slender shoulders shaking as she choked back a sob. "Please, please tell me you'll help me find them."

Claudia's friend Kelly Brennan leaned over and put an arm around the half sister she hadn't seen in almost twenty years. It had been only a couple of hours since Erin had showed up without warning at her door, and Kelly wore a bemused expression, as if she were still getting used to the idea. But the surprise of her sister's arrival was supplanted by an even greater one: Kelly learned that she had a young niece, Kylie. A niece who was missing.

Claudia's eyes returned to the sheet of notebook paper in her hand. "The handwriting is a little disturbing," she said. "I'm glad you asked me to come and look at it." She searched for diplomatic words that wouldn't add to Erin's distress, but they weren't easy to find. Red flags sprouted from the brief note.

Hand-printed in black ink, the note read: DON'T BOTHER LOOKING. THERE MIGHT BE SUFFERING BUT NOT AS BAD AS YOU THINK. GOD'S WILL BE DONE.

Below the words, the signature was just a scribble, which Erin identified as that of her husband, Rodney Powers.

The three women were gathered around a small wrought iron table on the plant-filled patio of Kelly's condo. But no one was paying attention to the lush colors of morning glory or the scent of star jasmine filling the sun-warmed air.

"I thought he'd just taken her for a walk." Tears welled up in Erin's eyes and spilled onto her pale cheeks. "I had a bad night and I woke up this morning with a headache. So I slept late because I thought they'd be right back, but they didn't come back, and when I got up and went into the kitchen—" Her voice broke again and she buried her face in the tissue Kelly pressed into her hand.

"It's okay, honey." Kelly gave her sister's arm an awkward pat and threw Claudia a helpless glance. "The only family news I ever get is from my brothers, and you know how rarely I hear from them." She turned back to Erin with a regretful sigh. "I can't believe how completely I lost track of you. It's been ages since I heard anything."

The sisters shared a genetic history, but there the relationship ended. Claudia had been present when Kelly said goodbye to Erin, to her family. It was a memory that she found could still produce a sharp pang: Erin, four years old. A shy little girl sucking her thumb. Their three brothers madly waving goodbye from the back of an old pickup truck piled high with boxes and furniture. Their mother driving away without a backward glance, leaving her eldest child behind to live with Claudia's family.

Kelly added, "The last I heard, you'd joined a cult—"

Erin pulled away from her. "It's not a cult!"

Behind Erin's head, Kelly rolled her eyes. "Okay, sorry. New religion."

"Why don't you tell us what happened with your husband?" Claudia interjected before an argument could break out. Kelly's emotions could flare unexpectedly, and Claudia would rather not find out whether Erin had inherited the same trait.

Erin began to explain how she'd found the note from her husband on the kitchen table. "Rod left it propped against my coffee mug," she said, sniffling miserably into the tissue. "We've been staying at a cabin near Big Bear for the last few weeks. I—I didn't know what to do; we don't know anyone around there. I called Sean."

"You've stayed in touch with our brothers?" Kelly asked. "I guess I shouldn't be surprised. You're a lot closer in age to the boys than to me."

"I talk with Sean a couple times a year maybe. He lets me know if he hears anything from Mom. She calls him once in a while."

Claudia sensed Kelly stiffen. Erin didn't know that she had just wandered into dangerous territory. She was unaware of the tacit agreement that Kelly's mother was a topic to be avoided if at all possible.

"Those would be the times when she wants to hit him up for money," Kelly muttered.

Erin made a sound of distress. "Fine, Kelly, I get it that you hate Mom, but she's not—"

"Let's not go there, Erin. You and Sean weren't around when I was raising Mickey and Pat. Mom was out hurling herself at as many bars as would take the grocery money. It's only thanks to sheer luck and the goodwill of people like Claudia's parents and some of the other neighbors pitching in that the rest of us didn't starve or get split up and put into foster care long before you were ever born."

Erin's eyes widened. "But she's— I didn't know it was going on that long."

"I'll just *bet* you didn't."

The sudden burst of hostility charged the air and Claudia found her neck and shoulders aching from the tension. As she reached up to massage the taut muscles, another flash of memory washed over her: the day the Brennan family moved into the rattiest house on the block.

The hand-lettered cardboard For Rent sign had finally disappeared from the front yard of the old Drew house across the street and a few doors down from Claudia's parents' home. The sign had stood there since the previous Christmas when the widowed Mr. Drew had suffered a massive stroke. His children, who apparently had their own busy lives and couldn't be persuaded to take him in, had moved him into a nursing home, where he died six weeks later. A Realtor hammered the For Rent sign into the grass the day after the funeral.

On that Saturday, the weekend before Claudia was due to enter kindergarten, the weeds in the yard of the Drew house were taller than the flowers they choked. The concrete driveway was cracked and stained with the oil of the 1952 Dodge Coronet that had previously rested there, probably since before she was born, and had now been towed away.

Squeezing herself behind an ancient elm in her parents' garden, six-year-old Claudia watched two sweaty men in sleeveless T-shirts unload a moving van stacked with furniture shabby enough to match the house. A car pulled into the driveway. She could still remember being impressed by the woman who climbed out of the driver's seat. Ruby red halter top, shorts that showed off long, tanned legs. Georgia Brennan, Claudia later learned. The mother.

Three children spilled out of the car. Two small boys and a little girl around Claudia's own age. They had been out of the car only moments before the girl was running around the yard in a futile attempt to corral the boys.

"Kelly Ann Brennan!" the mother screeched, oblivious of curtains twitching in disapproval in windows across the street. "Can't you do anything right, you lazy girl? You're about as useless as your father was. Didn't I tell you to watch your brothers?" The mother's voice reached a pitch that could set dogs howling. "You get those boys inside right now and wash them up. And don't let me see or hear a peep from any of you till dinner. You hear me, Kelly Ann? Do you *hear* me? What did I just say?"

That night, Claudia's own mother held forth over dinner about what she termed "that unladylike caterwauling." It was the first of her many commentaries on the Brennan family matriarch.

On Monday, when she and Kelly met on their way to the first day of school, Claudia had invited her new friend over to play with her Barbie dolls. Kelly looked like she desperately wanted to say yes, but instead she told Claudia that she had to go straight home and take care of her brothers because her mother would be passed out on the couch. At the time, Claudia hadn't understood what that meant, but over the years there were many occasions where she saw for herself.

Before Kelly turned sixteen, two more fatherless Brennan kids—Erin and Sean—were crammed into the two-bedroom house. But by then, Kelly spent most of her free time at Claudia's home anyway. She made her escape from the sardine can with great relief when Claudia's parents invited her to live with them full-time until the girls completed high school.

When Georgia Brennan informed her eldest daughter that she was moving her four younger children to Banning, where housing was far cheaper, Kelly had said nothing. Banning was only about a ninety-minute drive from their current home in Santa Monica, but it might as well have been a thousand miles away.

Returning her attention to the present, Claudia realized that the uncomfortable silence between the sisters was unbroken. She cleared her throat and prepared to mediate. "Why don't we get back to the little girl who's missing? That's where we need to focus our attention."

Kelly's cheeks puffed as she blew out a long breath. "You're so right, Claud. The only thing we should concentrate on is making sure my niece is safe."

"You're gonna help me, aren't you, Kelly?" Erin looked young and vulnerable as she made her appeal. "Sean said you're a really smart attorney and you'd know what to do."

"He said that because I kept him out of jail when he got arrested for dealing pot. But that's another story. I think we have to take this note to the police. This line about 'the suffering' is scaring the crap out of me."

"We can ask Joel about it," Claudia suggested. "He can tell us who to talk to."

Kelly made a gun finger and pointed it at her. "Obvious choice. But first, I think we need some more information about what kind of person Rodney is."

"There's a lot of information in this handwriting sample," Claudia said. "And as I said earlier, some of it is troublesome."

Kelly said, "If you were to write up a report on it, we might be able to get a judge to—"

"Wait," Erin interrupted. "Who's Joel?"

"He's my guy—my—" *Boyfriend* felt slightly ridiculous at forty. Significant Other was worse. "He's a detective with LAPD."

Erin looked doubtful. "I'm not so sure we should—I mean, I don't want Rod to get in any trouble. I don't think he would actually *hurt* Kylie."

"Well, pardon me," Kelly said, throwing up her hands. "But what about what he wrote in this note? Holy Christ, Erin, if you don't think Kylie is in trouble, what the hell are you here for?"

"I didn't know what else to do." Erin rubbed her hands over her face, which was pretty, even without the benefit of any makeup. "He didn't take Tickle with them. That's what really got me worried."

"*Tickle?* Who, or *what* is Tickle?"

Erin leaned down, unzipped her bag again and reached inside. When she withdrew her hand, she was holding a fuzzy brown stuffed bunny that had seen a lot of wear. "Kylie never, ever goes anywhere without Tickle. That means she had to be asleep when Rod took her. She's probably come totally unglued by now."

The three women looked at each other with sober faces, fully comprehending the importance of the stuffed toy to a small child.

"What the hell was Rod thinking, Erin?" Kelly asked. "Don't you have any idea at all why he would take Kylie like this? What do you think he plans to do with her?"

Erin shook her head. "I don't know, Kelly, I just don't know."

"Why don't you tell us what led up to it," Claudia encouraged her. "Something like this doesn't happen in a vacuum. What's been going on lately between you?"

Erin began to speak, slowly at first, drawing the words out as if she were reluctant to part with them. "We've been arguing on and off for a couple of days. He never said anything about leaving, though. I never guessed he would take the baby! Can't you do something, Kelly?"

"Is he Kylie's father?" Kelly asked.

"Of course he is," Erin said indignantly.

"And you're legally married?"

"Yes! We've been married almost six years."

"You got married at eighteen?" Kelly looked as if she was going to explode, but she forced herself to stay on track. "Has he ever abused her or you? Hit you or . . . ?"

"No, of course he's never done anything like that. We're God-fearing people. He's a little older than me, but Rod's been a good husband. We did missionary work together for three years before I got pregnant."

"Even missionaries can get into trouble," Kelly pointed out. "How much older than you is he?"

Erin answered reluctantly. "He's thirty-eight."

Kelly did a quick calculation in her head. "Fourteen years is more than just *a bit* older, honey child. Okay, like Claudia said, we'll start by talking to Joel about taking the note to the police; see if he thinks they would view it as a threat since there's a child involved."

"I'll call him right now," Claudia said, taking out her cell phone.

Kelly rose and stretched her arms high above her head. "Erin, let's go to the kitchen while she's making the call. I could use a cold one."

Claudia watched them go, hoping her friend was talking about iced tea or a soda. Kelly had been working hard at staying sober and for the past several months had been successful. She hoped the stress of Erin's situation wouldn't push her into changing that.

After a disappointing chat with Jovanic, Claudia joined the sisters in the kitchen.

"He said that as Kylie's father, Rodney has a legal right to take her. I asked him about the possibility of issuing an Amber Alert, but he said under the circumstances, they can't. The wording of the note is ambiguous. It's not a direct threat, so there's no evidence that he intends to harm her."

"Damn." The ice cubes clinked against the glass as Kelly handed Claudia a diet cola. She turned to the refrigerator and got out a bag of French rolls, mayonnaise and mustard, sliced meats and cheese, arranged them on the kitchen counter. Claudia had a feeling that it wasn't because Kelly was in the mood for lunch; she just needed something to do, to help her contain the agitation that her busy hands telegraphed.

She returned to the refrigerator, dug in the crisper drawer and found a tomato and lettuce. Went back for a jar of pickles. Went back again, but found nothing more. "Let's talk about the handwriting," she said, busying herself with her sandwich making. "You saw danger signs, didn't you, Claud?"

Claudia chose her words with care. "There are indications of some . . . problems. But I'd like to enlarge the note on the computer so I can look at it in more detail." There was no point in offering a hasty opinion that could lead to mistakes. She added, "If you would scan it and e-mail it to me, Kel, I'll have a proper look at it when I get home. Six-hundred DPI would be high enough resolution to show the fine points when I blow it up."

She asked Erin to let her see the note again. The block printing Rodney Powers had penned on the scrap of lined paper told her that the writer had high control needs. He could be opinionated and more than a little self-important. It wouldn't be easy to get to know him— or to break through his defenses if he didn't want to believe something, regardless of how hard one tried to convince him.

Flipping the paper over, she ran her fingers across the back, feeling ridges where the pen had dug hard into the paper on the other side. She glanced over at Erin, who was watching her closely. "Do you know what kind of surface he wrote on?" she asked. "Do you think he might have put a magazine under the paper, or something like that?"

"We don't read outsider magazines," Erin said. "We just took our Bibles. I'm pretty sure he wrote it on the kitchen table. That's where I found it."

Without comparing the note to additional samples of Rodney Powers's handwriting, there was no way to know for certain whether the degree of emotional depth indicated by the considerable pen pressure was his habit, but of one thing Claudia was certain: when he wrote the note Rodney had been laboring under powerful emotions.

"He's stubborn," she mused aloud. "Needs to feel he's in control. I believe he would have planned this ahead. This is not the type of person who would act on the spur of the moment without first knowing what he was going to do and how he was going to accomplish it. He's not someone who easily caves under pressure."

She glanced over at Erin, who was twisting her tissue to shreds. "Who do you know that he might have gone to for help? It would be hard for a man to handle a small child on his own."

Erin shook her head. "Not Rod. He's crazy about Kylie. He spends more time with her than I do. He knows how to handle her. Anyway, he was raised TBL. He doesn't know any outsiders."

"TBL? What's that?"

"Our church, The Temple of Brighter Light. We don't associate with anyone who's not a member. Well, unless it's for a good reason, like this, of course. That's why I'm sure Rod doesn't know anyone outside well enough that he could ask for help."

Kelly left her sandwich-making for a moment to wipe her hands on a kitchen towel. She tossed the towel onto the washing machine on the porch, then turned to her sister. "Erin, if you're both so heavily involved in the church, how about your pastor? Wouldn't Rodney listen to him?"

Erin looked as though she might begin to weep again. "Brother Harold would be so disappointed in him. I don't want to tell him about Rod leaving. That's why I have to find him and Kylie myself. With your help, I mean."

"If you don't associate with outsiders, can you think of anyone *inside* the church he might have turned to?" Claudia said. "Someone he has a close relationship with?"

"*All* the TBL members are close. It's the most supportive, wonderful bunch of people you could ever meet. I've been a member since I was fifteen."

Kelly said, "I was in the middle of a divorce back then. I was pretty messed up, but one of the boys told me that you'd run away from home."

It was a period in their lives that Claudia remembered well. Kelly, inconsolable when her second brief marriage ended, had gone on a bender that lasted months; a month more in rehab. Surprising that any of the details of Erin's split from the family had stuck.

"Don't worry about it, Kelly," Erin said. "You and the older boys were all gone by then, so it was pretty much just Sean and me. Mom kept taking off for days at a time, but nobody knew, we never told anyone. At school they said I was a delinquent, so I decided to become one." Her laugh sounded hollow. "Unfortunately for me, living on the streets of Banning was even worse than being home, so I ended up hitchhiking to Hollywood."

Kelly turned away from them and started layering slices of turkey and provolone on the French rolls, assembling sandwiches as if her life depended on it. But not before Claudia noticed the tears of regret that brightened her eyes.

"I'm so sorry, Erin," Kelly said in a trembly voice. "I abandoned you, too. But after I got out of that house I didn't want to ever look back. I wanted to believe you were going to be treated better than I was. I made myself think that way. I'm just so freaking sorry I failed you."

"It's okay, you don't have to feel bad. It all worked out for the best." Erin gave a weak smile. "It was actually exciting and fun for a while, but I got tired of that life really fast. There are hundreds of runaways in Hollywood. They have this amazing network, sharing what they've got with each other and helping each other survive. Their methods may not be exactly conventional, but they sure are effective."

Kelly was busy getting plates out of the cabinet, so Claudia asked, "Dare I ask what happened next?"

"God sent me to the TBL shelter, Teens for the Lord."

Suddenly, Erin's face was shining and her prettiness became more apparent. "It was so awesome. It was a day that Brother Harold 'just happened' to be preaching there. But I know that was no coincidence; it had the hand of God written all over it. They do so much good at the shelter."

"Tell us about this Brother Harold. You mentioned him earlier."

"He's our spiritual leader at TBL. He and Sister Grace—she was in charge at the shelter—they talked to me about the end of time, which was pretty terrifying until they showed me how I could be saved. They invited me to go back to the Ark with them,"

"You mean like Noah's ark?" Kelly interrupted. "You live on a boat?"

Erin gave her head an impatient shake. "No, it doesn't *look* like the Bible ark. It's the best! Sort of our own little world that keeps TBL separate from the outsiders. In Bible times, God told Noah to build an ark to save his family from the flood. *Our* Ark is to keep the TBL family safe until the end-of-time days, which is coming soon."

"Back up a minute," Claudia said. "This Brother Harold took you there to live when you were fifteen?" She did her best to look neutral, but she knew her skepticism must show on her face.

"Brother Harold and Sister Grace—she was his wife, but she had cancer and the Lord took her to be with him about five years ago." Then Erin's mouth dropped open as she got the implication. "Hey, wait a minute, there was nothing inappropriate going on. It's just, I wasn't going to go back home, no way, no how. So when they invited me to the Ark, I said I'd go with them and try it out. Right away, I knew I was in the right place. I finally had a *real* family." She shot an uneasy glance at her older sister. "I mean, at the Ark we eat all our meals together—real food, not Chicken McNuggets or a box of macaroni-and-cheese every other night."

"It's okay, hon." Kelly looked unusually chastened. "I understand. Our family wasn't exactly *Leave It to Beaver.*"

For the first time, Erin seemed to relax a little as she extolled the virtues of her substitute family. "The brothers and sisters at the Ark couldn't have been more kind and loving. They were willing to work with me and help me clean up my act, get off drugs. I started going to school again—we have our own private classes at the Ark. There are regular school lessons, plus I trained to become a missionary. They taught me how to talk to other people about what we believe in, to help them be saved, too. It was really hard at first, talking to strangers who didn't want to listen. But now I can talk to just about anyone."

"A minute ago, you said something about the end-of-time days," Claudia said. "What's that about?"

Behind her sister's back, Claudia could see Kelly shaking her head, discouraging her, but Erin's face lit up as she jumped at the chance to explain the beliefs that she had adopted. "We're living in the End of Time days right now!"

"End of Time *daze,*" Kelly muttered.

Erin ignored the jibe and continued. "The earth is about to be destroyed—"

"What does that *mean?*" Claudia asked. "Destroyed how?"

"We're gonna see a whole series of natural disasters. Everyone who doesn't know how to be saved will be destroyed with the earth, and it's gonna happen really soon. This time we're living in, it's like, well, it's like just before your alarm clock goes off in the morning—you know how you wake up just before the alarm? That's where we are now, the alarm is about to go off. If you want to be saved, you have to pay attention *right now*, and wake up." She nodded in earnest as she spoke, as if encouraging her listeners to think hard about what she was saying.

Kelly brushed aside the sermon. "Look, Erin, I want to know what happened with Rodney that would make him do something so drastic and so rash as to take Kylie."

Erin's beatific look faded fast. Her lower lip quivered and her eyes filled. "I told you, we'd been fighting."

"Yes, you did. So, what was the fight about?"

The tears dried as fast as they'd started and Erin's tone sharpened. "What does it matter what we fought about? It's personal. The important thing is, he took my Kylie away, and I want her back."

"Erin," Claudia said. "If you want our help, we need to know what happened. Why don't you want to tell us what you were fighting about?"

"Because you won't understand if I tell you, I know you won't. Why isn't it good enough just to know we had an argument?" Erin said it like a petulant child, peeved about not getting away with avoiding something unpleasant.

"We can't help you if we don't have all the facts," Claudia pressed.

"Just tell us the truth," Kelly added. "We're not going to judge you. You don't have to hide anything, just tell us what happened. And don't bother to bullshit a bullshitter, Erin. Believe me, there's nothing you can say that I haven't said or done a thousand times over. Maybe if we know what we're dealing with, we can come up with a plan to get my niece back."

Erin looked from one to the other of them with

the distrust of a wounded animal in the forest. When she realized that neither was going to back down, she shrugged, giving up on the debate. "Okay, fine. But don't say I didn't warn you. I know how you outsiders are; your minds are totally made up and closed."

Kelly and Claudia exchanged a surprised glance, their eyes telegraphing the same message—*What's going on here?*

"Like I told you, we were in the mountains," Erin said. "We were there because we enrolled Kylie in a super-special TBL program. It's called Jephthah's Daughters. It's one of those things that comes up only once in a lifetime. It was getting to be time for her to go into the program and we were there in the mountains, getting her ready for it."

"Let's go back to the patio," Kelly suggested, picking up her sandwich. "This is getting interesting."

When they were settled around the table once again, Kelly said. "Okay, *whose* daughters?"

Claudia said, "Jephthah's. I remember the story from Sunday school because at the time, it scared the hell out of me. Jephthah was a judge in ancient Israel. He asked God to help him win a big battle, and in return, he offered to sacrifice the first person who came out of his house to greet him when he got home."

"Oh, hell no," Kelly said. "I don't like the sound of this."

Erin nodded, looking gratified that Claudia was familiar with the name. She took up the story. "The Lord gave Jephthah the victory. When he got home, the first person to come out of the house was his only daughter, who he loved with his whole soul."

"Holy shit."

Throwing her sister a glare of disapproval for her use

of profanity, Erin continued. "Jephthah was devastated. He told his daughter about the promise he'd made, but she was, like, *You have to keep the promise; you gave your word to the Lord God.* So she asked if she could have two months off to mourn her virginity, because, of course, she would never get to be married and have sex or anything. At the end of the two months, she was ready to let herself be sacrificed." Then Erin hastened to add, "Of course, the way we do it is more like a *symbolic* sacrifice. Like going to a convent."

Both Claudia and Kelly stared at her. "You're sending your three-year-old *baby* to a convent?"

"Well, that was the original plan. That's why we were in the mountains; we had the two months to get ourselves ready. But the longer we stayed there, the more I knew I couldn't do it. When I told Rod I'd changed my mind, he wouldn't listen to me. He loves Kylie, but he's been working toward becoming an elder since he was a kid, and putting her into the program would seal the deal for him. It's a really prestigious thing for a TBL member. This is a rare opportunity that only comes up once every few years." Erin huffed a big sigh. "Look, I know it's a great thing to give your child to God, but . . . I just wasn't ready to do it."

"Good choice," Kelly mumbled, stuffing potato chips into her mouth as if to gag a comment that she knew would be left better unsaid.

Claudia said, "Why couldn't Rod wait until she's old enough to have a say in the matter?"

Erin's eyes went to the bits of sodden tissue that dotted her jeans. She picked at the pieces, not looking up as she spoke. "It's not like that. It has to be done at a certain time. She has to go into the program on her third birthday. That's the requirement."

An awkward silence fell over them, and Claudia knew that Kelly was thinking the same thing she was. When no one spoke, she put the question into words. "When is Kylie's third birthday, Erin?"

Erin buried her face in her hands. Her words were muffled as she spoke through her fingers, but Claudia had no trouble understanding her.

"It's next Saturday."

Chapter 2

Was it the sudden breeze rippling through the patio that made Claudia's heart race, or the chill of realizing that Kylie's birthday was only five days away? Five days to find Rodney Powers and persuade him to return little Kylie to her mother. Maybe he would relent and return on his own. Then Claudia remembered the stubbornness she had seen in Rodney's handwriting and she knew that his relenting was not something they could count on.

"Are you sure that this Brother Harold person wouldn't be the best place to start?" asked Claudia. "You said Rodney wants to become an elder. Maybe you could use—"

Erin shook her head. "Wives are the helpers of their husbands. It's our job to be supportive, not contentious. Brother Harold would just tell me to follow Rod's lead. He wouldn't want me to be disobedient."

"Disobedient?" Kelly repeated in a tone of disbelief. "*Disobedient?* Erin, has anyone told you we're living in the twenty-first century? Women are not chattel anymore. That just makes me wanna barf."

Erin's chin went up. "I know what century it is, thank you so much for the information, Kelly. The point is, we interpret the Bible literally, and the wife is supposed to obey her husband, so don't give me a hard time, okay? The man is the head of the family, the responsible one. It's the wife's role to raise her children and support her husband. Besides, Brother Harold has been really good to me; I wouldn't want to—"

"Erin," Kelly broke in. "Are you *afraid* of this Harold guy?"

"Of course not!" Erin shot back. "He's our teacher, our leader. He only does what's best for us."

"How does he know what's best for you? Goddamn it, that's all about handing over responsibility to someone else. Grow up and raise your own kid! What about what's best for Kylie?"

"For Kylie, too. Brother Harold has got, like, he's got a direct line to God. He and the other elders feed us our spiritual food when we need it. We listen and learn from them, and we follow their direction."

Alarm bells were clanging in Claudia's head and she could see from Kelly's appalled expression that she was hearing them too. "But what if you don't agree?" Claudia protested. "What if you think differently from what they tell you?"

Erin smiled that irritating, tranquil smile again. It felt somehow inappropriate, given the circumstances. She said, "Why would I doubt the word of God when we're getting everything we need from the elders? It'd be foolish to engage in independent thinking."

"That sounds to me like you're quoting someone," Claudia said.

"I can't believe that you or they would think it's best to take a three-year-old away from her mother," Kelly blurted angrily.

"In Jephthah's Daughters she would be raised to be a priestess in service of the Lord God on the new earth. Tell me what's so wrong with that."

Not for the first time since Erin's arrival, Claudia found herself puzzled by Kelly's younger sister. "Erin, why are you here? You said you don't want Kylie to go into this program, and now you seem to be arguing that it's a *good* thing for her."

Erin's face crumpled. "I'm just so confused. I don't know what to think, except I've got to get my baby back before it's too late and Rod hands her over."

"That's the first credible thing you've said this morning," Kelly said.

"Have you thought about what you're going to do when we find Rodney?" asked Claudia. "Do you expect to just take Kylie back from him? Do you even have a place to take her?"

"They'll stay with me," said Kelly, turning to her sister with as serious an expression as Claudia had ever seen her wear. "Maybe I can start to make up for not being there for you when you needed me before, Erin. We'll work it out. But first, we have to find them."

"Thank you, Kelly. I'd be super grateful if you let me stay for a few days. But I can't leave the church. It's the only way we're going to be saved." Once again, Erin's eyes welled up and the tears spilled over. "I hate this! I want to do the right thing."

Claudia asked, "Are you *sure* there's nobody your husband might have told about his plans?"

Erin hesitated, looking speculative. "You know, Rod does have a close friend at the Ark. I can't imagine that James would help him do something like this, but I guess it's possible. Rod might have talked to him and told him what he was doing. We were given a cell phone so we could call in while we were away, so he *could* have called him."

"You don't even have your own cell phone?" Kelly sounded incredulous and Claudia could see her frustration building. Her own free spirit couldn't comprehend the lifestyle her younger sister had chosen.

"We don't need our own phone. We're almost always at the Ark."

"Who is this friend of Rod's, and how can we get hold of him?" Claudia asked quickly before they could get off track and start a debate about the relative merits of cell phone ownership.

Erin bit into her sandwich, chewing thoughtfully for a few moments before answering. "His name is James Miller. Rod and James have known each other all their lives; they're as close as brothers. If he was going to ask anyone for help, it would be James. You know what? . . . Oh, never mind; it wouldn't work."

"What?" Kelly demanded. "What are you thinking?"

"It's just that we're holding a rally tonight in Burbank. James is in charge of the AV, so he'll have to be there. He's the one who sets up the projector and runs the computer at all our events."

"A rally?" echoed Claudia.

"We have them every couple of months in different locations. People who are interested in getting saved come to hear Brother Harold. He opens them up to some of the TBL teachings."

"You mean they'll be recruiting new members," Claudia said.

"Well, it's more than that, but I guess you would see it that way."

"We could go, Claud." Kelly started to get excited. "We'll kick some spiritual ass."

Erin made a gulping sound as if her sister's remark shocked her. Her present self-righteousness was a far cry from the fifteen-year-old runaway who had taken refuge from the mean streets of Hollywood at the TBL Ark.

"What?" Kelly asked, feigning innocence. "I meant it in the nicest way. We'll pretend we're interested in joining, and get this James Miller to tell us what he knows."

Claudia had less enthusiasm for the idea. "That

sounds like it's easier said than done. *If* we go, let's just talk to him directly. We don't have to pretend—"

"No, Kelly's right," Erin said. "As much as I hate not being totally up front with Brother Harold, it's better if you act like you're interested. James is much more likely to talk to you that way."

"Don't worry, Erin, I'll get him to talk," Kelly said with a suggestive wiggle of her hips.

"You might want to remember, there's a child at stake here," Claudia said, irked. "The police may call Rodney's note ambiguous, but I don't like the sound of it—and remember, I'm not too crazy about the handwriting."

"But that's not how he always writes," Erin protested, making Claudia wonder why she felt the need to defend the husband who had run off with their daughter.

"He printed like that for this note, so it's significant," Claudia said.

"Well, he doesn't always print like that. What's it mean anyway?"

"The printing is done very slowly and carefully, which indicates a stronger than average need for control. Block printing makes it easier to control the pen, and that translates into controlling other aspects of life. Then there's the writing pressure." Claudia turned the paper over and showed Erin the indentations on the backside. "In general, the degree of pressure the pen exerts on the paper—in other words, how hard you press down—symbolizes how much aggression you're carrying around, and how much you act it out against the world. The pressure in this handwriting is pretty heavy, which equals a lot of aggression."

Erin reached out her hand and snatched the paper back. "It's not all that bad." She folded it into a small square and pushed it into her jeans pocket.

Kelly threw up her hands in annoyance. "Erin, I

brought Claudia into this because she's one of the top handwriting experts in the country. But she's got experience investigating crimes, too."

Erin looked startled. "Crimes? We're not talking about a crime."

"I know you must be feeling conflicted, Erin," Claudia said. "I'm sure you love your husband and don't want to think he would do anything bad. But if he doesn't always write like this, then the change tells me that he's feeling extremely anxious right now; he's behaving in ways that he might not usually. His taking off with Kylie this way is not all right, and you're going to have to face the fact that he may be planning something that—"

"No! Stop! Don't say it. Just find him. Please just find him."

Chapter 3

Erin had told them that the rally was to be held at the Marriott directly across the street from the Bob Hope Airport in Burbank, on the east side of Hollywood Way. Kelly's Toluca Lake condo was only five miles from the airport.

Kelly drove, opting for the Golden State Freeway rather than the more direct route up Hollywood Way. Late afternoon, traffic would be bad either way, but she reasoned that at least there were no traffic signals on the freeway and they had a better chance of nonstop travel. They left the freeway and made their way toward the airport.

"It's too early to go to the rally," Claudia said. "I'm craving caffeine. There's a Starbucks next door to the airport."

"There's a Starbucks every thirty feet in this town." Kelly drove past the airport entrance and parked the Mustang convertible in the lot next door, where several fast-food restaurants had sprung up. She switched off the engine and turned to Claudia. "So, Claud, tell me. Is my sister's brain squeezed all to hell?"

"You mean about this religion?"

"*Cult* is what I'd call it. It sounds so creepy—independent thinking not allowed; little girls sent to a *convent* at three years old. Holy freaking Mother of God." She opened her door and twisted to look back at Claudia. The pensiveness was gone from her eyes, replaced by mischief. "Gotta tell you, m' friend, I wouldn't say no to a nice cold martini about now." Then she laughed. "Oh, don't look so worried, Claudia. I'm just kidding. I know I have to show up for this one. You don't have to be afraid I'll sneak off to the bar."

Claudia climbed out of the Mustang and shot her a grin across the roof of the car. "Do they even have a bar at the Marriott?"

"Well, of course they have a bar there—it's a major hotel. Besides, you know that if I really wanted a drink, the absence of a bar wouldn't stop me." They started toward the Starbucks and Kelly nudged her friend with an elbow. "Hey, I'm not white-knuckling it, Claud, I'm fine. Right now, having clarity and figuring out this Rodney shit trumps everything else."

Claudia commandeered a couple of armchairs at the front of the coffeehouse. Kelly went up to the counter and placed their orders, flirting with the young barista, just to watch him squirm. She brought their drinks and Claudia shook her head, pretending despair. "You know what they call middle-aged women who flirt with boys, don't you? Cougars."

Kelly laughed and growled like a big cat. "We're only middle-aged if we live to eighty. I plan to be here for at *least* a hundred years." She turned to look out the storefront window. "You can't see the hotel at all from here."

"I wonder how many people they're expecting at the rally," Claudia said.

"The rally in the Valley. Isn't that just perfect? Could you believe some of the crap Erin was spouting? You'd think my little sister was born on a mayonnaise farm. Wives have to *obey* their husbands? I wanted to tell her 'thank you for sharing your remarkable misconceptions about the Bible.'"

"How would you know they were misconceptions?

You were way too busy playing around with the boys in Sunday school to know *what* the Bible says."

Kelly threw her a self-satisfied smirk. "You are right about that, Grasshopper, and I had a lot more fun than you did."

"I know you did. I was a nauseatingly good child," said Claudia.

"And, baby, you're making up for it now!"

"What gave me chills was Erin talking about them putting Kylie into that program."

"I can't believe anyone would send a three-year-old to a convent. That poor little—shit, now I'm weepy again." Kelly got up and grabbed a handful of napkins from the self-serve area and blew her nose. "Do you realize, the last time I saw Erin she was only a year older than Kylie is now. And now here she is, a grown woman, a total stranger. It's weird, though, as soon as I saw her, there was *something*, a connection. . . ."

"I guess that's why they say blood is thicker than water."

"Oh, thanks, that's just what I needed—a cliché."

Claudia crumpled the paper from her straw and threw it across the table, hitting Kelly's arm. "I wonder how Kylie's doing without her bunny."

Kelly batted the wrapper aside and said with pride, "*Tickle.* Isn't that adorable? That's my niece, Claud. No way am I going to see her locked up in a convent when she's still a baby. Puhlease, what kind of life is that? That's, like, *anti*-life. Erin thought she had a bad time growing up, but she's re-created the whole damn thing. Maybe it looks different on the outside, but this cult isn't really any better for her than living at home with mom was. And now she wants to give away her child? Talk about history repeating itself. In a manner of speaking anyway. What was she thinking?"

"I'm glad she changed her mind, even if Rod didn't."
Claudia removed the plastic dome from her cup so she
could lick the mountain of whipped cream on her Frap-
puccino. She wiped an errant streak of cream from her
upper lip and replaced the lid. "It's too bad Erin took
back that note Rod wrote. Can you get her to let you
scan it? I'd really like to see the handwriting enlarged."

"No problem. I have flexible ethics. If she says no, I'll
just wait till she's asleep and sneak it out of her jeans."

"What kind of father can this Powers guy be, taking
off like that with the baby? I wonder what she sees in
him."

Kelly considered her friend over the rim of her cup.
"Someone once said that people are attracted to each
other, not because they have a nice ass or a big fat bank
account, but because they're attracted to the other person's wounds."

Claudia laughed. "I'm guessing that someone was
you."

"Bury my heart at Wounded Ark. You gotta admit,
Erin is plenty wounded, and Rod probably has a shit-
load of his own wounds, growing up in that cult."

"It's nice of you to offer her your place."

"There's no way I could let her down a second time."

"Still, you didn't have to."

"I don't know what I'll do with her, but I just know she
can't be at this Ark place." Kelly frowned. "You heard
her. I think she's afraid to go back without Kylie."

"I think you may be right." Claudia freshened her lip
gloss and stuffed her paper napkin into her cup. "Are my
lips on straight? Okay, let's go rally."

Chapter 4

They found a parking place in the self-park and strolled up the circular driveway past the valets and into the hotel lobby. An electronic marquee scrolled scheduled events. The Temple of Brighter Light event was being held in the main ballroom.

After navigating to the meeting area, they found dozens of people already milling at the registration table just outside the ballroom door. Three smiling women sat there, conservatively uniformed in ecru-colored linen jackets over plain white dresses, handing out glossy brochures. They were encouraging visitors to add their names and addresses to a sign-in sheet at the end of the table.

"Watch out," Kelly hissed. "Mary Poppins at twelve o'clock."

"Keep it up, Kel, you'll get us kicked out before we find James Miller." Claudia grabbed a couple of brochures. Temple of Brighter Light propaganda. Happy, contented faces beamed from the front panel; dire warnings of the end of the world inside. On the back, information about how to join and be saved.

Claudia made for the open ballroom doors with Kelly in tow. A clean-cut young man in a neatly pressed suit blocked the entrance. "Good evening, sisters. Have you signed in yet?"

"We have to sign in to attend the meeting?" Claudia asked.

The young man showed her a friendly smile that matched the registration ladies'. "We like to know who attended and how they came to hear about us."

From her vantage point of five foot three, Kelly gazed up at him. "But we could write down anything, couldn't we? Make stuff up."

His smile never faltered. "I guess you could, sister, but if you've come here tonight because you're searching for the road to salvation, why wouldn't you want to tell the truth?"

"You've got a point there, smiley." Kelly grinned and turned to Claudia. "Come on, sistah. Seeing how you and I seriously need to get saved, we'd better take our evil, wicked, no good, very bad souls and sign in, doncha think?"

They returned to the registration desk and took their places in the lines of seekers adding their contact information to the sign-in sheet. When Claudia got to the front of the line she scrawled an illegible signature, declining to include an e-mail address. She scanned the list of names, checking out the handwriting to see what types of people had been attracted to the TBL event: a gamut of personalities from shy and retiring to gregarious to just plain odd.

Smiley seemed to have been watching for them and offered another warm welcome as he ushered them into the ballroom, where rows of chairs had been arranged in front of a curtained stage. Claudia's glance flicked over the crowd congregated in the vast assembly room. "There has to be at least a couple hundred people in here, maybe more. How in hell are we supposed to find James Miller?"

"Don't be so damned negative. Look at all the shiny TBLers busy recruiting. Ever see so many white teeth?"

Kelly leaned close and spoke in Claudia's ear. "Yoo-hoo! Message for spawn of Satan, right over here!"

Claudia ignored her banter. "What did Erin say he looked like? Mid-thirties, red hair, skinny. C'mon, let's walk around. We might learn something useful."

Kelly was right about the recruiting. At least a dozen earnest-faced young people wearing name badges were busy working the crowd. Neatly dressed in business suits and dresses like the women at the registration desk, their clothing was inexpensive and conservative. They all looked clean and well groomed, the men's hair trimmed short.

"I think these guys all have the same barber," said Claudia, strolling in the direction of the stage. "Erin said James Miller would be working the AV. Hey"—she nodded in the direction of a man in shirtsleeves working at the left of the stage, setting up electronic equipment—"what are the odds that's him?"

"Red hair. Looks like he could use a good meal," Kelly remarked. "Maybe we should go over and offer him a spiritual hamburger."

Claudia sized up the skinny arms; the large hands expertly sorting out wires and plugging them into electronic equipment. "He's a computer geek. I can picture his handwriting: absentminded professor; probably forgets to eat. I wonder what they're using the Elmo for."

"Elmo? Like the Elmo we use in court?" Kelly followed her gaze and agreed that the flat-bottomed projector the man was unfolding onto the AV cart was similar to the digital presenters used in many newer courtrooms. Unlike the older overhead projectors, which required special acetate film, the digital presenter had the capacity to project original documents onto a screen. Claudia sometimes used Elmo projectors when testifying, to demonstrate to a jury the elements of forgery in the case she was presenting.

"Should we go talk to him now?" Kelly asked.

"Let's wait until he finishes setting up. It might bug him if we interrupt while he's busy."

Kelly was about to make a retort when a teenage girl approached them with the TBL greeting, a toothy smile, full of sincerity. "Hi, there, sisters! Welcome to the meeting, I'm so glad you came tonight. How did you happen to hear about the Temple of Brighter Light? Was it from one of our flyers?"

"Hi, there, cutie," Kelly said. "What's your name? Or should I just keep calling you 'cutie'?"

The girl pointed to the white plastic badge pinned to the linen jacket she wore over her dress. Her name was engraved in blue lettering. "I'm Magdalena."

"Of course you are," Kelly said.

"Not Mary Magdalene?" Claudia added.

Magdalena smiled again, her lively eyes dancing between Kelly and Claudia, probably assessing their reason for attending the rally. She said, "No, it's just Magdalena, but you can call me Magda for short if you like."

Kelly linked arms with the girl. "Okay, Magda. So, tell me, do you live at the Ark?"

Magda looked startled, making Claudia wonder if they should have taken a less direct approach. "Uh, yes," the girl said, "I do. How did you—?"

"I've heard it's quite the place. How do you like it there?"

"I love it," she said. Her body language sent a different message.

"Why do you shake your head 'no' when you're saying you love it?" Claudia asked with a smile. "That's called cognitive dissonance."

"What does *that* mean?"

"It's a fancy expression psychologists use that means you're trying to believe in two opposite ideas at the same time. You said, *I love it*, which is a positive statement. If you meant what you were saying, your head would be nodding. But while you were speaking, you shook your head from side to side—negative. So, which is it?"

"I—well—"

"It's okay. I'm teasing," Claudia said, not wanting the girl to feel she was being judged.

"Hey, Magda," Kelly said. "See that man over there, the one who's hooking up the projector . . . ?"

Magda swung around in the direction of Kelly's pointing finger. "Brother Miller? What about him?"

"I was thinking he's kinda cute in an older-guy sort of way—you know, like *our* age, not yours."

Magdalena glanced back at James Miller, and made a face that said she seriously doubted Kelly's taste in men. She gave a little shrug. "If you say so. He's not married or anything, but you'd have to be TBL if you wanted him to ask you out."

"What if I asked *him* out?"

That drew a scandalized look. "That's not the way it works. He's a man, and that means he would have to ask you out if he was interested. Anyway, I don't think he cares about anything but his computers. He's always working on them."

"Doesn't he have any friends?"

"Of course. We're all friends at the Ark."

"But what about someone special?"

Another shrug. "I wouldn't know about that."

"Maybe you could introduce us to him."

"I don't know . . ." Magdalena suddenly seemed to remember that she was at the rally for a purpose, and that the purpose was not to hook up other TBL members with visitors. "Maybe afterward," she said, moving them back on track in a manner so practiced for one so young that she must have been trained to handle all sorts of situations.

"Have you ever heard Brother Stedman lecture?" she asked. "No? You're gonna love him, he's such an awesome speaker. Oh, look, Brother Dunn is going over to the podium. That means the program's about to start. We'd better sit down." She led them directly to three empty seats in the middle of the second row from the front. She tried to sit between them, but Kelly maneuvered so that Magdalena had to sit on her left.

To Kelly's right, Claudia dropped into her seat with more than a little exasperation. Their original plan had been to buttonhole James Miller early on and leave before the program began. But to decline Magdalena's invitation at this point would look odd. Considering the surreptitious nature of their business at the rally, it wouldn't do to make themselves conspicuous. Seated where they were now, sneaking a chat with James Miller before the program began was out of the question. They were stuck for the duration.

The man Magdalena had referred to as Brother Dunn called the meeting to order. Short and stocky in a drab brown suit, a Friar Tuck fringe of hair ringed his bald pate. Leaning heavily on the podium he cleared his throat and tapped his finger against the microphone a couple of times. The hollow echo indicated that it was turned on.

Claudia twisted in her seat to scan the rows and rows of people behind them. Standing room only. "I've never seen so many happy-looking people," she said to Kelly, nodding toward the ushers lining the walls.

"Stepfordized. Mass hypnosis. If we start to get sleepy, we make a break for it!"

"You might not be so far off. If we didn't have such

a good reason for being here, I'd be all for making that break right now."

At that moment, Brother Dunn's gaze swung around and he looked directly at them. For an uncomfortable moment Claudia considered whether there might be some way he could have heard them.

He'd have to have the hearing of a bat.

He opened his arms wide. "Welcome, welcome, everyone, welcome. Please turn off all cell phones and pagers before we begin. After all, God speaks to us directly. He doesn't use cell phones."

"But he's one hell of a Twitterer," Kelly whispered.

Claudia suppressed a grin. The lights dimmed to half brightness and the volume of a hundred conversations lowered to a hum as people hustled to find a seat. As close to the stage as Magdalena had placed them, they had a clear view of the beneficent smile Brother Dunn beamed at the audience.

"We'll open our meeting with a nondenominational prayer," he said, bowing his head. He began to intone, "Father-Mother God, we are thankful for the time you have given us to come together this evening to share our concerns about the future and to learn what you have in store for us. We ask your blessing on this assembled throng who so desperately need your help and guidance. Please open their minds and hearts and allow them to comprehend your mercy and your grace. Amen."

Someone in the crowd shouted out Amen. Others echoed. Skeptical though she was about the Temple of Brighter Light and its motives, Claudia had so far not heard anything to which she objected. Brother Dunn said a few words of welcome, then introduced Harold Stedman and stepped aside.

The thunderous applause that followed indicated to Claudia that she and Kelly were in the minority in the ballroom. Unlike them, most of the attendees seemed familiar with Harold Stedman and had returned for more of his message. She sat up straighter, curious to see the man Erin held in such great esteem; the one who had drawn this crowd.

She felt a little let down by the man who approached the podium. Not at all the handsome guru she had been half hoping for. Harold Stedman could have been anyone's grandfather. Mid- to late seventies, his egg-shaped head was smooth and bald, the blue eyes hooded, prominent nose hooked. Dark eyebrows made a startling contrast to the white beard. The charcoal gray suit with an immaculate white shirt and patterned tie gave him the look of a banker or attorney.

But as soon as Stedman started to speak, Claudia began to change her mind. His quiet voice grew in power as he warmed to his sermon.

". . . Earth has borne the brunt of man's unkindness and now is time for Earth to rebel. The Holy Bible warns that God will bring to ruin those ruining the earth. Ruination will be visited upon those who refuse to listen, but God has given to *us* the key to survival." Harold Stedman ceased speaking and gazed out over the rapt audience. When the silence had grown long, he repeated his warning: "God will bring to ruin those ruining the earth. God has given to *us* the key to survival."

Claudia hadn't counted on being mesmerized by Harold Stedman. Despite his ordinary appearance, he exuded a subtle confidence that made one want to listen. She reminded herself that looks often deceive and resolved to pay close attention to his sermon, determined to smoke out any messages hidden in the subtext. Ten minutes in, all she had detected was the sincerity of a true believer.

Stedman gave a nod to one of the ushers, who flicked

a switch. The lights dimmed further, draping the room in shadow. Behind Stedman, a theater-sized projection screen rolled down from the ceiling.

He began to speak of recent natural disasters that had occurred around the world: the 2004 massive tsunami and earthquake that killed seventy-three thousand, Hurricane Katrina in 2005, the European heat wave and North American blizzard in 2006, cyclones in Bangladesh, droughts in the American Southeast in 2007, record snowstorms in North America in 2010.

Images from one large-scale disaster after another were projected on the screen: close-ups zoomed in on the toll the devastation had taken on buildings and roadways: twisted steel girders rising from mountains of rubble; raging rivers of muck and debris rushing through downtown streets. And always, human faces distorted by unthinkable suffering and despair.

"This earth is going to be destroyed," Harold Stedman said in the powerful voice that carried throughout the silent ballroom. He paused for several seconds, waiting for his words to sink in.

"It's a pretty bold statement, isn't it?" He paused once again, letting his eyes rove the audience, resting here and there to gaze intently at a listener long enough to make them uncomfortable.

"For many people who consider themselves intelligent thinkers, all this *end-of-the-world* talk sounds like the stuff of science fiction. But the truth is, everything on earth has its cycle. There is a beginning and an ending to everything. Man has tried through science to change that, to extend life through cryogenics and whatever other means he can find. Man doesn't want to recognize that all life on this planet has its time, and that there is an end to that time."

The prophetic tone of his message chilled Claudia as

deeply as if he had the personal power to cause the act
he predicted. She envisioned him wearing a long robe
and carrying a staff, and decided it would suit him. If
Stedman had called himself Moses, she would not have
been surprised.

He continued. "Even the Garden of Eden had its cy-
cles, its seasons. That's the way God set things up. There's
a seed, the seed grows and matures into an adult, the life
cycle wanes, and what was once that seed shrivels up
and *dies.* Death is not a bad thing; it's an integral part of
the life cycle, the natural order of things. Earth has come
to the end of its life cycle, helped there too soon by the
carelessness of Man."

Claudia glanced over at Kelly and was surprised to
find her friend leaning forward in her seat, eyes riveted
on the man at the podium. She appeared to be completely absorbed in what he was saying.

In the lifetime they had known each other, she could
not remember Kelly ever having expressed any particular concern about the earth's future, or even her own. It
had always been her contention that life was a party and
she intended to enjoy it for as long as it lasted. When
it was over, she would close her eyes for the last time
and move on to the next plane of existence, wherever
and whatever it might be. But Harold Stedman radiated
credibility and Claudia suddenly understood how a less
skeptical person than she could believe he had the direct line to the Almighty that he claimed.

No wonder Erin had been drawn so thoroughly into
the Temple of Brighter Light. After the childhood ne-
glect and abuse she'd suffered at the hands of her alco-
holic mother, her need to trust in something or someone
who would take care of her had left the sensitive young
girl vulnerable. To someone looking for love, for belong-
ing, for parenting, the Temple of Brighter Light had a

natural appeal. The group had assimilated Erin, made her part of the whole, and she was happy to have been assimilated.

Harold Stedman continued to preach, constantly modulating his voice, varying the pitch and pace at just the right moments. The audience seemed spellbound.

"So, what does all this mean to you, brothers and sisters? My Heavenly Father is above me and above you. My Heavenly Father brought me here to the earth to teach you how you can be saved and not become part of the compost when he wipes clean the earth, as he is about to do very soon. You may believe, or you may not. It is your choice. *I want you to believe,* because I want to see you have a future at the feet of the Lord."

His voice had a resonant, soothing quality that began to take on an almost hypnotic cadence. Fifteen minutes into the program the crowded room began to feel stuffy. Claudia's eyelids began to droop. *A modern hotel like this one should have better air-conditioning for a group of this size,* she thought, fighting to stay awake. Or were the TBL organizers deliberately controlling the temperature?

The desire to let go and nod off grew almost overpowering. She sat up straighter in her seat and gave the skin of her left hand a painful pinch to wake herself up. She forced her mind to focus on their reason for being here at this event: little Kylie Powers.

Where might Rodney have hidden his daughter? Was it possible that he might show up here tonight, looking for help from his fellow TBL members? Neither Claudia nor Kelly would recognize him if he did. They had seen only his handwritten note and the photo of Kylie. Too bad neither of them had considered asking Erin what Rodney looked like.

While Claudia's mind drifted, Harold Stedman had

stopped talking. The lights were being turned up. Ushers were distributing index cards and pens to the audience. "What did he say?" she whispered to Kelly. "What are they doing?"

"Why, weren't you listening? We're supposed to write a confession. The worst thing you've ever done—something you're ashamed of."

"You're kidding, right?"

"No! Just write something."

Cards and pens were passed along their row. Claudia stared at the blank index card in her hand, wondering what she could write about. She had no intention of revealing anything personal to the TBL people. In the end she settled for scribbling a lie about having had an affair and signed a phony name to it. When she looked down at what she'd written she was mildly amused to note that she had unconsciously changed her regular handwriting style by switching from a right to a left slant. She turned the card facedown and handed it to the person seated next to her to pass along to the usher at the end of the row.

"What did you write about?" she whispered to Kelly.

"How bad it makes me feel for not being there for my little sister at the worst time in her life. Hell, she was only fifteen when she ran away."

"Jeeez, Kel, you really took this confession thing seriously."

"Yeah, yeah. They say confession is good for the soul, right?"

"Depends who you're confessing to. Don't go getting all caught up in this mumbo jumbo and forget why we're here."

Kelly's ready capitulation concerned Claudia. She worried that despite the difference in their ages, the same lousy upbringing as Erin had left her best friend as vulnerable as her younger sister.

"Brothers and sisters." Harold Stedman's deep voice silenced the conversations that had started up as the cards were passed back to the ushers. "We've collected the confessions and now the ushers are going to pick out a few for us to share."

A swell of anxious chatter rippled through the room. Brother Harold held up his hands, smiling in a way that jarred in the face of the audience's discomfort.

"Please, brothers and sisters, you have nothing to fear. The first step to forgiveness is public confession of one's sins. If there is anyone here who is afraid to expose himself or herself to the Lord God, let him or her leave now."

Claudia turned around, curious to see whether anyone would accept Stedman's invitation to leave. Three rows back, a man got to his feet. She could hear him muttering as he pushed his way to the aisle, caught the words *Looney Tunes*. He stalked out of the ballroom, letting the doors bang shut behind him. Several others rose, taking courage from his defection, and sheepishly trailed after him.

Harold Stedman leaned close to the microphone and said in a kind voice, "Go with God. We wish you no ill."

"I don't see him publicly confessing *his* sins," Claudia whispered to Kelly, who just shrugged. She would like to have followed the fleeing runaways who hurried through the doors, but there was a certain fascination in staying to see what happened next. Like watching a ten-car pileup happen on the I-10, knowing you couldn't stop it.

When the door had closed on the last one, Stedman waited a full minute, gazing over the audience. "Does anyone else fear to tell the truth? I sense that some of you are wavering in your faith. Please go now."

A half dozen more got up and left. After the doors had closed once again, Harold repeated his question: "Is there anyone else who fears to tell the truth?" An expectant silence fell over the crowd, a collectively held breath. When he determined that no one else was going to get up and leave, he signaled to James Miller at the computer.

The ushers had gathered around the computer station and were rapidly sorting through the cards they had collected, selecting a few and handing them to Miller. Now Claudia understood why they needed the Elmo projector. The selected index cards could be placed directly on the sensor and projected onto the screen. Her heart raced a little as she hoped her card would not be selected.

The lights were dimmed again and one of the handwritten confessions was displayed on the screen. Before she began to read the words written on the index card, Claudia noted the smallish, neat copybook writing style; the conventional, not very confident small personal pronoun *I*. The handwriting told her that the person who had written the confession would not appreciate being put on public display. Reading the content, she felt mortified on the writer's behalf.

> *"My most shameful event was when I felt sexually attracted to my brother's wife. If my husband found out, he would immediately divorce me."*

The name "Karen Harrison" had been neatly signed at the bottom.

Harold Stedman read the statement aloud. "Sister Harrison, I want you to come up here to the podium. Come up here and stand with me. Come on now, don't be afraid. Do you believe the Lord has mercy and forgives you? Where are you, sister?"

A frumpy woman around thirty in an unattractive pink-and-white-striped shirt and elastic-waist pants rose slowly from her seat. Even under the lowered lights, the flame of embarrassment could be seen burning her face.

Claudia wouldn't have thought her the type to be hankering after someone's wife. But who could say what went on in someone else's heart? That was something handwriting certainly could not reveal.

With an usher waiting to escort her to the stage, Karen Harrison inched her way to the aisle, shoulders slumped, head hung low.

Dead woman walking.

This woman's self-esteem must be the size of a peanut to allow herself to be so publicly humiliated. It seemed to Claudia that Harold Stedman was setting up those who had stayed in a way that would make it harder for them to leave. From what she knew of cult behavior, the more difficult and painful it was to join the group, the harder it was for a member to leave.

The TBL leader stepped away from the podium and went over to meet Karen Harrison as she approached the stage. She mounted the risers slowly, as if her feet were nailed to the steps. As she reached the top step, Stedman reached out and took her hands in his. He drew her the rest of the way to the stage with a smile that would melt butter. "There, now, sister. You've opened up your soul and the Lord God loves you for that. A wise man said, 'The confession of evil works is the first beginning of good works.' Do you repent of your evil works, sister?"

Karen Harrison nodded in silence and began to weep into her hands.

"This is starting to make me feel sick," Kelly whispered. "Now I wish I hadn't written what I did."

Claudia leaned close to her ear. "It's the beginning of breaking her down. That's how these people operate."

Stedman led the sobbing woman to a chair behind him on the stage and sat her down, already signaling James Miller to project the next confession before he returned to the podium.

"I'm ashamed of my mother. She's disgustingly obese and I know people are laughing behind her back. I don't want to be seen with her in public. That makes me feel guilty and a horrible person."

Claudia studied the writing on the screen. The plain printed handwriting was poorly developed, which could mean that the writer was not educated or that he was emotionally stunted.

When Harold Stedman called for the writer of the statement, a man of middle age stood right up and marched up to the stage, his head held high. Letting everyone know by his demeanor that he wasn't going to follow the humble lead of Karen Harrison.

As the man was welcomed to the stage and commended for his courage, Claudia found her attention wandering again. She was more interested in what the next handwriting might reveal. When it came, the sadness and guilt were evident in the downhill direction that the baseline took.

"I was driving drunk and killed a family. I will never forgive myself."

A man with long blond hair tied back in a ponytail joined the others on stage. Now Karen Harrison could hide behind the two men, her own confession already forgotten in the abasement of those who followed.

A few more statements projected misery of varying strengths in black and white on the big screen. Claudia felt a wave of relief that neither hers nor Kelly's were among those chosen for display.

Probably too mundane.

Small, intense looking writing with many sharp angles. The writer meant what he said.

> *"I got angry with my son and told him that I hated him and wish he'd never been born."*

> *"I took a bunch of money from the company I used to work for. I know it's wrong but I don't care. They treated me like shit, and they deserved it."*

That one had large, circular forms with hooks in the *o*'s and *a*'s and claw forms on the lowercase *d*'s. "She might be ready to confess; she might even feel guilty, but she's about as dishonest as they come," Claudia said in an undertone.

Kelly cupped her hand beside her mouth. "He'd better not pick mine."

"You and everyone else are thinking the same thing. Hey, there's another one who's lying through his teeth."

The latest index card read:

> *"I'm embarrassed to admit that my drinking and gambling is out of control."*

"Where's the lie?"

"See where it says 'I'm embarrassed.' The *I'm* turns to the left and there's a big space before he wrote *embarrassed*. He was conflicted about what he was writing because it's a lie."

Kelly gave her an admiring grin. "Claudia Rose, you are one dangerous woman."

After gathering the small crowd of penitents on the stage Harold Stedman spoke for a few minutes about how they could join the Temple of Brighter Light and be saved from their sins. Finally, he said a prayer in closing.

After the final Amen, Magdalena turned to them, her eyes bright with enthusiasm. "So, what did you think? Isn't Brother Stedman wonderful? I never get tired of hearing him speak."

Claudia drew a mental comparison between Magda and Annabelle Giordano, the fourteen-year-old girl who had recently stayed at her home for a few months while her father was fighting for custody. Magda, who was in her late teens, seemed years younger than Annabelle. There was something very 1950s about her manner and speech. Kelly's "Stepfordized" comment came back to her. It seemed an apt description.

She started to reply to Magdalena, but was interrupted by the arrival of one of the TBL ushers. He looked right at Claudia. "Would you sisters come with me, please?"

Chapter 5

"Come with you where?" Kelly demanded. "And why should we?"

Claudia watched her with admiration. When she stepped into attorney mode, Kelly seemed to grow several inches taller.

The usher said, "Brother Stedman asked me to come and get you. He's resting backstage. He'd like to meet you."

"Why would he want to meet us?" Kelly asked again. It was a good question and Claudia asked herself what they might have done to inadvertently draw attention to themselves.

The usher gave an apologetic shrug. "I'm sorry, sister, I'm just the messenger. Brother will have to tell you himself."

Seeing Magdalena's eyes widen in surprise, Claudia realized that this invitation was not a common occurrence. It occurred to her that meeting Harold Stedman could be a very good thing. They had missed the opportunity to talk to James Miller, but now were being offered the possibility of learning something from the TBL leader himself.

Claudia and Kelly followed the usher onto the stage and behind the curtains. Harold Stedman was seated at a folding card table in his shirtsleeves, eyes closed, his face slack with exhaustion. He had opened his shirt collar and loosened the knot of his tie. At their approach he opened his eyes and immediately rose and came around the table, extending his hands to welcome them.

"Thank you so much for giving me a few moments of your time," he said pleasantly. "Did you enjoy the program?"

"Your sermon was truly impressive, Mr. Stedman," Claudia said, meaning it. "You had the audience eating out of your hand—excuse the cliché."

He acknowledged the compliment with a nod. "There are so many seekers, the responsibility can sometimes be staggering. But, of course, our Heavenly Father always provides the strength to do what needs to be done."

Kelly reached out a hand and pressed it to his lapel. "Oh, you've got what it takes." Then she hardened her voice. "But did you have to humiliate those people that way?"

Claudia wanted to tell her to shut up. Alienating Harold Stedman by criticizing his methods wasn't going to help them in their quest to find Kylie Powers. She wasn't surprised when the look Stedman gave Kelly held a mild rebuke. "Humiliation is in the eye of the beholder, sister. Only those with a conscience can be humiliated, and having a conscience is a Godly virtue."

Kelly gave him a playful smile. "Shoot, you'd get *my* attention by just threatening to tell my weight out loud."

Claudia noted with interest that Stedman was not responding to Kelly the way most men did when she flirted with them. Instead, he chose to let her comment go and invited them to sit with him. Once they were settled, he turned his attention to Claudia.

"There was a reason why I wanted to speak with you. The fact is, something you said was overheard, and

I . . . well, it got me curious enough to invite you back here."

Claudia racked her brains, trying to remember whether she and Kelly had discussed Kylie or Erin since they had arrived. She didn't think so. Besides, how could she have been overheard? She had spoken only in an undertone.

The hearing of a bat.

Kelly abandoned her flirtation and returned to lawyer mode, saying out loud what Claudia was thinking: "Do you have hidden microphones, Mr. Stedman? Where are they, under the seats?"

Stedman spread his hands as if to say *you got me.* "I apologize. Unfortunately, we've had a number of problems over the years from certain elements that would dearly love to see the Temple squashed out of existence. Our little group has been active for more than fifty years, but there are some people who insist on thinking that we're up to something nefarious. They try continually to infiltrate and get the goods on us. Of course, there are no goods to get, but we do have to be careful. You understand, don't you?"

Kelly refused to be distracted. "I assume you've heard of invasion of privacy?"

Stedman turned his keen blue eyes on her. From where Claudia sat, they seemed able to penetrate like a laser, through skin and bone to the heart and its motivation.

"I completely understand your concerns, sister," he said. "But as you may know, in a public forum such as this evening's, privacy is not protected."

Kelly lifted her chin, preparing to argue. "That's debatable. It's clearly illegal to surreptitiously eavesdrop on someone's private conversation."

"That may be true when they have an expectation of

privacy." The lines around Stedman's eyes creased as he broke into a smile. "You'll have to trust me on this, my dear. I've discussed the matter at length with our attorneys and they assure me there's no such expectation in a public place when someone sitting two feet away might overhear you."

"But surreptitious microphones in a public place—"

When Kelly got on her high horse it wasn't easy to get her to dismount. Claudia broke in before a serious debate about privacy law took them completely off the track. "Why don't you tell us what it was that you overheard, Mr. Stedman, that made you want to talk to us?"

Harold Stedman nodded. He leaned forward, elbows on the table, hands clasped under his bearded chin. Claudia noticed that he wore no ring, and she remembered Erin telling them that his wife had died.

"I believe you said something about one of the confessions being untruthful," Stedman said. "You seemed very sure. Something about the *handwriting. . . .*"

"She's one of the world's foremost handwriting experts," Kelly offered.

Stedman's dark brows lifted, looking like two dark boomerangs above his eyes. He turned an appraising glance on Claudia. She didn't bother with false modesty. Stedman said, "Is that so? Then please tell me what is it about handwriting that would indicate that someone is being untruthful?"

"If the person feels guilty about what they're writing, there are often markers that might show a handwriting analyst where he's lying."

"I see." His full lips pursed again as he seemed to consider what to do with this information. He sat back on his folding chair and smoothed his tie with the flat of his hand. "Interesting."

Claudia wanted to know what was going on behind those eyes, but they seemed impenetrable. "What is it that interests you about it?" she asked.

He leaned forward. "May we speak confidentially?"

"You mean without hidden microphones recording our conversations?" Kelly put in.

Claudia nudged her foot under the table. "Please tell us; I'd like to know."

Harold Stedman hesitated, glancing around as if concerned that someone might be listening in right now. Satisfying himself that no one was within earshot, he said, "I have reason to think that outsiders may have infiltrated our home base—we call it the Ark. If I were to show you some handwritten documents, would you be able to tell me if they were lying about their motives for joining us?"

Now it was Claudia's turn to hesitate, not at all sure that she wanted to involve herself with him. "It might be possible. As I said, it depends on whether the writer feels any guilt about what they're writing. For example, if someone were a sociopath, that would mean by definition that they have no conscience, so their handwriting would probably look more or less normal. It's important to understand that handwriting shows *potential*, but there's no way to predict whether the writer will ever act on that potential. That would depend on a lot of other factors all coming together at the right time. There simply are no guarantees."

"I understand. But from what you've said, it sounds to me as if this could be helpful for my needs. I would be interested in hiring you."

Claudia felt a tingle of surprise. She had not expected an offer of a work assignment to come out of attending the Temple of Brighter Light rally. They couldn't have planned it better if they'd tried. Working for Harold

Stedman might open a way to get some insider information about Rodney Powers.

"Write something," Kelly urged Stedman. "Let Claudia see *your* handwriting. She can tell you about yourself. That way you'll know whether she's any good at it."

Excellent idea. Most of the time, Claudia refused to do on-the-spot analysis and Kelly knew it. But obtaining a sample of Stedman's handwriting would help her gauge whether she could trust *him* to tell the truth. She glanced over at him, waiting to see whether he would refuse, but he was nodding, giving no indication that he was afraid she might see something he wanted to hide.

"Fine, fine. Have you got something to write on?"

Claudia rooted around in her purse and produced a pen and spiral notebook. Opening to a blank page, she pushed it across the table. "Just a sentence or two and a signature will do for now. It doesn't matter what you write about."

Stedman sat very still for about thirty seconds, holding the pen in his left hand, hovering above the notebook as he thought about it. Then he began to write, swiftly covering the small page with small, oddly uneven writing.

As she watched, Claudia began to wonder whether he suffered from some physiological ailment that was affecting the writing rhythm. Handwriting sometimes revealed the location of illnesses in the body, though not specific diagnoses. The jerky quality of the writing trail suggested to her that he might have a neurological problem.

When he handed her the paper she scanned the writing he had produced, curious to see how her personal perceptions of him stacked up against what his handwriting might reveal about his personality. She did not need to read the text of what he had written in order to

form an opinion. The way he had arranged the writing on
the paper, the letter forms he had chosen, and the writing movement were the important keys: Thready writing, indefinite, barely legible letterforms. A tall personal
pronoun *I*, wide loops on the letter *d*. She felt the back
of the paper. No pen pressure to speak of. Combined
with the thready forms, the lack of pressure told her that
the TBL guru was operating at a level of emotional tension that was higher than was good for him.

Claudia wondered how he would react if he knew
that Rodney Powers, who wanted to be a TBL elder, had
bolted with his daughter, leaving his young wife desperate to find their child. In light of the emotional fragil-
ity she saw in Stedman's writing, Erin probably had the
right idea about not informing him about what was going on. She glanced up from the notebook.

He was watching her, his chin resting on his fists
again, waiting with anticipation for what she had to say.
She chose her words with care.

"Your mind moves so fast that you can hardly form
whole thoughts. It's more like you soak up information
rather than think things through logically. It's not easy
for you to trust on an emotional level, but you have a
very well-honed ability to *know* what somebody is going
to say or do, almost before they say or do it. Being able
to tune in to people that way gives you a big advantage."
She considered him, hoping he wasn't tuning in to *her*.
Hidden microphones were one thing; mind reading took
invasion of privacy to another level.

He withheld comment as she continued. "Your handwriting suggests to me that you're currently function-
ing under a tremendous amount of emotional strain.
Maybe that's why you tend to skim the surface of emotion, and don't allow anything to touch you too deeply,
because ..." *Because you're afraid it could send you*

over the edge. Because you're paranoid. "Because you feel as if you have so much on your shoulders, you may wonder if you can take on any more. Yet, at the same time, it's as if there were no barriers between you and the environment. You leave yourself wide open to everything." She stopped again to gauge his reaction.

Harold Stedman looked thoughtful. He nodded. "That's quite astonishing. Are you sure you got all that out of my handwriting?"

"As I see you now, and as you were on the podium, you don't project an image of being stressed to the max. So, where else would I have gotten it? *I* don't have a hidden microphone." She couldn't resist that jab. Looking back at what he had written, Claudia let herself read the words now.

"Now I'm tired and I can tell the creative juices have subsided temporarily, but I'm optimistic about rejuvenation, my own and this earth's. No matter what happens, I have traveled a hundred thousand miles, and no one can take that away from me. Harold Stedman"

Claudia thought about the confessions they had viewed earlier in the evening. What would Brother Harold have written if he had been tasked with that assignment?

"You're quite right about me reacting quickly," he said. "And I'm going to prove it. I would like you to come and spend some time at the Ark. I want you to examine some handwritten statements and tell me what you think about the people who wrote them—whether what they wrote is the truth, whether they're loyal, and so on. I want to know whether they're being honest about what motivated them to join us."

Claudia's mind raced. If Rodney had indeed confided

in James Miller, being on site at the Ark could provide opportunities that they otherwise wouldn't have to question him on the whereabouts of Erin's husband. It was the only lead they had and they needed to move fast. She glanced at Kelly, whose expression told her she was thinking the same thing.

As if he thought she was taking too long to answer, Stedman added, "I know it's a long way from here, so you're welcome to stay over for as long as it takes for you to do these analyses."

"I'd love to come too," Kelly chimed in. "I thought what you were talking about tonight was fascinating."

Stedman considered her for a moment. "Aren't you afraid of being humiliated?"

Kelly leaned into his space and gazed into his eyes. "It's true, I didn't like that part of the program so much. But what you said about the earth being destroyed got me thinking about the future and I want to learn more about how I can get saved. I don't want to die in the end of times."

That seemed to convince him. He beamed at her, nodding with approval. "That can definitely be worked out. You can both come right away, tonight, and we'll get started first thing tomorrow."

"If we're spending a couple of days, we'll have to get some clothes," Claudia said, refusing to be bulldozed into the arrangement by Stedman's need to be in control. "I'll also want to pick up some equipment for the work you want me to do. We can drive out in the morning and be there by noon."

For a moment, Harold Stedman looked nonplussed. "What kind of equipment could a handwriting analyst need?"

"Magnifying glass, measuring tools, things like that. I'll also need to print out a copy of my standard retainer agreement and ask you to sign it. Since we're staying over, I'll be charging my day rate."

When she him told her rate he looked taken aback, but he merely said, "All right, tomorrow then."

Claudia said, "As it happens, I'm scheduled to give a lecture later in the week at UC Riverside. If the work you have for me lasts that long, I can conceivably leave from your location on Thursday evening and return there afterward."

"That's fine," Stedman said. "The university is only about thirty miles from us, which is a lot closer than it would be for you to return here to the Valley."

"Your Ark is in Hemet, isn't it?" Kelly asked.

He shot a quick look at her and Claudia could see Kelly wishing that she hadn't revealed that she already knew the location of their compound.

"We're in the hills above Hemet," Stedman said. "I'll give you directions; it's easy to get lost up there. May I have your notebook back, sister? You know, I've just realized, I don't even know your names."

They introduced themselves and Claudia wondered how quickly he would dig up some intel on them. Considering the electronic eavesdropping, and the paranoia she had noted in his handwriting, she was fairly certain that he would want to check them out before actually bringing them into the Ark. As long as he didn't dig into family background and discover Kelly's connection to Erin, they should be okay.

Stedman spoke as he wrote the directions. "Our property is about a hundred miles east of here."

"Isn't there another big religious compound in that area?" Claudia asked.

"The Scientology people have a place there; you'll recognize it by the blue tiled roofs. It's quite an impressive piece of real estate. I'm afraid you won't find the

Ark nearly as large or elaborate. We're a little more re-
mote and at a slightly higher elevation. You'll take the
San Bernardino Freeway east, past Riverside." He scribbled a few lines on the paper. "Here are some directions
and the phone number at the Ark in case you have any
problems."

They had a quick and easy drive back to Kelly's place.
Most of the commuters had gone home to their dinner and other evening activities, leaving traffic blessedly thinner on the 5. As they drove, Kelly and Claudia
chewed over what they had seen during the evening, and
Harold Stedman's invitation to the Ark.

"How much do you know about cults?" Kelly asked.

"I had a case a couple of years ago. Mayor's wife in
a small town up north near Yreka got involved with a
satanic cult. He tried to go in by himself and get her
out, got beat up pretty badly; broken bones. Then they
framed him for something—I forget exactly what, but
there was handwriting involved—an anonymous note.
He hired me to prove he hadn't written it. That was an
easy one. It's really hard to forge someone's handwriting and he had an interesting way of forming some of
his numbers that the forgers totally got wrong. People
don't think about changing the numbers when they're
forging. Anyway, to answer your question, I did some
Internet research and learned a little bit about cults in
general."

"And you weren't scared to go up against them?"

"Well, yeah, of course I was. But it pissed me off, what
they were doing to him. It wasn't right."

Kelly honked the horn a couple of times, oblivious to
the SUV in front of her. "Claudia Rose to the rescue!
Were you Sir Lancelot in a past life, or what?"

"Yeah, that was me, the knight in shining armor sav-

ing damsels in distress. Which brings me back to our
situation. What do you think our chances are of finding
out where Rodney and Kylie are?"

"We've got to turn every minute of this visit to our
advantage," Kelly said. "The first thing we'll have to do
is track down James and make him tell us where that
damn Rodney Powers has my niece stashed."

Claudia doubted it would be as easy as Kelly made it
sound, but she kept her thoughts to herself.

Back at Kelly's house, Erin gave them a crash course in
TBL culture.

When she'd heard they were invited to the Ark, her
eyes had grown large the way Magdalena's had when she
heard that Harold Stedman had invited them backstage.

"That's fantastic! You'll probably be assigned to a
guest room in the main house, which means you'll be
close to the computer room where James works. It's
right next to Rod's office, downstairs. Everyone eats
meals together, so that should be another chance to
talk to James. You'll have to watch out for Sister Ryder,
though. Don't let her get near you. If you give her an
inch, she'll sniff out that you're not for real."

Kelly asked, "Who's that?"

"Lynn Ryder. She's the head of security."

"Hidden microphones aren't enough? You need a
head of security, too?"

"It's an unusual position for a female to hold in our
church, but Lynn had a lot of experience on the outside
before she joined TBL. She was a top security specialist at a Fortune One-Hundred corporation. That's why
Brother Stedman gave her the job. We have to make
sure that the people who come to the Ark have pure
motives." She had the grace to look sheepish as she said
that.

"So, tell me, Erin," Kelly said. "Are you guys keeping people out, or in?"

"Neither one," Erin answered defensively. "We sometimes have guests—obviously; you've been invited, haven't you? So there's nothing to hide. And we're free to come and go as we please, but . . ."

"But you just don't choose to," Kelly finished for her. "You've got everything you need there, right?"

Claudia jumped in. "Erin, do you have any ideas on how we should approach James?"

Erin sat down on the couch and seemed to ponder the question for a long time, until Claudia began to feel as itchy as Kelly looked.

"Come on, Erin," Kelly urged, sitting down beside her. "You've got to have thought about this already. What the hell were you doing while we were at that meeting tonight?"

"Of course I've been thinking about it, but I didn't know you were going to actually get inside the Ark. Okay, here's what I think: don't both of you rush James at the same time. If you act like you're ganging up on him, he'll be suspicious."

"Well, duh. I think we could have figured that out. What else have you got?"

"Quit pressuring me, Kelly, this is really hard for me. I hate being deceptive, and Brother Stedman—" She stopped, seemed to rethink what she was going to say. "If one of you sits at James's table in the dining hall, that should make him more comfortable. He'll get to know you a little, so his guard will be let down."

"Where's his table?" Claudia asked.

"Each table has an elder or a minister—that's the step before you become an elder—assigned to be the table captain. James's is the table closest to the kitchen at the back of the room. You'll see when you get in the dining hall. It's to the left of the head table where Brother Harold sits with the governing board."

"I'll take James on in the dining hall," Kelly volunteered. "Claudia can go after him in the computer room since I assume she'll be working in the office while I'm getting edjumacated in TBL teachings."

Erin shot her an annoyed look, presumably at her levity. "Please be subtle. And don't take too long, okay? We've only got a few days before Rod will come back and want to turn Kylie over to Jephthah's Daughters."

Chapter 6

Joel Jovanic shook his head, pretending despair. "Are you ever going to be *just* a handwriting analyst?"

"What are you saying?"

"I'll tell you what I'm saying. In the two years I've known you, you've gotten yourself into more dangerous situations than I have in twenty years as a cop." He put on a radio announcer voice: "Got a weird-ass job? Call Claudia Rose, handwriting expert. She's your gal."

Claudia turned from the fridge, a bottle of Heineken in hand. She poked around in the junk drawer for the bottle opener, popped the cap and held it out to him. "I don't go looking for weird-ass jobs, Columbo. They find me."

"I'm not so sure about that."

She took the seat across from him in the breakfast nook. Jovanic was looking pale and thin, as he had ever since a second surgery to take care of an infected wound. He'd been shot twice in the gut a couple of months earlier and was still recovering from the last hospital stay. The surgeries had adequately repaired the damaged organs, but left him with a serious intra-abdominal infection that had given them a big scare. He'd come away from the experience missing his spleen and six inches of intestines, but his surgeon had insisted he was lucky he hadn't lost his life.

It wasn't the way they had planned for Claudia to meet

his mother and sister, who had flown in from northern California to hold a vigil at his bedside, but the women had formed a bond in the hospital waiting room. Claudia admired the strength she saw in his mother, who had lost her husband many years ago to a street thug. Her children had inherited that strength.

Once he was lucid enough to receive instructions, Jovanic's surgeon had warned him that full recovery would take another two to three months—*if* he behaved himself.

He had proved not to be a good patient. He was chomping at the bit to get back to work, but he was at the mercy of his body, which currently was being a stern taskmaster. He still hadn't got his appetite back and the general weakness was driving him crazy. Until the last week or two, even walking across the room made him tired. He'd flat out refused to get on the scale, but Claudia was convinced he'd lost at least twenty pounds.

She was aware that Jovanic knew how much she worried about him, but they didn't talk about it anymore. He just became exasperated when the subject came up, so for the peace of mind of both of them she had decided to let it go.

Claudia got up again and moved behind his chair. She wrapped her arms around his neck and leaned down to press her warm cheek against his cool one. "Are you jealous, Columbo?" she said into his ear, teasing. "I get all the good cases?"

He took a swallow of beer, then bent his head and kissed her bare arm with moist lips. "You know you worry me, babe. You never take these things seriously enough, and then you end up in trouble."

"This *is* serious, Joel. There's a three-year-old at stake."

"I know that, but do you really want to get between

the unhappy couple? You *know* what happens in domestics most of the time: the Good Samaritan who intervenes ends up with the short end of the stick. That's why cops hate taking those calls. I'm telling you, Claudia, the parents won't thank you. They'll end up ganging up on you and you and Kelly'll be the bad guys."

She returned to her seat across from him. "Of course I know there's that possibility, but Kelly's got this crazy wild hair about making up for Erin's past, and I don't want her to go into it on her own. Besides, I'm really worried about little Kylie. Who knows what's happened to her? What if—"

"So you're, what—going undercover in a cult? Come on, honey, is that really a wise thing to do?"

"It's not undercover. I have a legitimate reason for being there. Harold Stedman is hiring me to do a job. If Kelly gets some information about Rodney while we're there, so much the better."

The skeptical look he gave her told her he wasn't buying it. Claudia glanced back at him sidelong. "Okay, detective, would it make you happy if I called you and reported in every hour on the hour?"

"Sarcasm doesn't suit you, babe. Every *four* hours will be fine."

She had to laugh at that. She said, "It's only a two-hour drive if you need me. I can jump right in the car and come home." She measured his drawn face and saw the pain shadowing his eyes. "Honey, if you're not feeling good, I'll . . ."

He waved her off and took aim at the trash can with the Heinie bottle. "I'm fine. Go, do your thing, save the little girl. Just call or send me a text message, let me know you got there." The bottle made a smooth arc across the kitchen and landed neatly atop the Domino's Pizza box he had folded and stuffed into the trash earlier in the evening. "If I don't hear from you by eleven, I'll be sending the Hemet cops out there to check on you. Call if you need me; if anything gets weird. . . ."

Claudia couldn't miss the frustration in his voice. "Holy shit, Joel, these people are fundamentalists. They believe the world's coming to an end through *environmental* disasters. They're not Branch Davidians. It's not Waco. I'd be surprised if they had weapons or anything like that."

"They're a cult. Their weapon is mind control. So humor me and call, okay?"

That night, she heard Jovanic groan under his breath, as he often did when he thought she was asleep. He rolled carefully out of bed so as not to disturb her. She heard him rummaging in the medicine cabinet for his pain meds. She didn't offer help, having learned that once he was able to walk on his own following the surgeries, he had resisted what he called being dependent on her.

After he slid back in beside her, she listened to his labored breathing until the meds kicked in; then his respirations evened out in sleep. Claudia stayed awake for a long time. It wasn't the pang of guilt she felt for leaving Jovanic while he was still not up to par that kept her mind churning. She couldn't get little Kylie out of her head. She wondered whether the child was missing her mother and Tickle, her stuffed bunny; whether she was being properly cared for wherever she and Rodney Powers were tonight.

Claudia had already packed her overnight bag. She had put her travel microscope and lighted hand magnifier into her briefcase, ready to go. She would salve her conscience by getting up early and cooking Jovanic breakfast—get some weight back on him.

Since she would have to leave the Ark to drive out

to Riverside to give her lecture on Thursday evening, they would take her car. She had arranged to pick up Kelly at nine, when traffic would be more reasonable and they could arrive at the TBL headquarters by noon. As she finally drifted off, she promised herself that the trip would not be a futile effort.

July in Hemet put them just a couple miles short of the barbecue pits of hell. Somewhere between San Bernardino and Riverside counties, Claudia jacked up the air-conditioning full blast, hoping the 1985 Jaguar's electrical system wouldn't take a dive as it did on a semi-regular basis. The car was a classic, which, of course, always put into question its reliability.

Kelly pointed the air vent at her face and leaned into the cold stream. "I'm so glad I brought some shorts with me."

"You'd better have brought something besides shorts. They just might expect us to put on a burka. Remember what Magdalena said—you have to wait for the guy to ask you out. Very fifties, don't you think?"

"Oh, my, where *did* I put my petticoat and pearls? Now, if you ask me to practice demure giggling, I'm outta here. Seriously, though, Claud, we're guests. You don't think they'll expect us to—"

"What? Follow the rules? When in Rome . . ."

"Yeah, yeah. I'll be diddling while Rome burns. Oh, wait, I meant *fiddling.*"

"I think Nero already took care of that for you."

Ninety minutes later they took the cutoff at Highway 79 that would lead them into Lamb Canyon, where boulder-strewn hillsides rose on either side of the road. The treacherous downhill winding road took Claudia's full concentration. She felt cheered when the Gilman Springs sign appeared and she was able to exit the treacherous downhill winding road and get onto the rural highway that took them through Hemet.

"You never told me how Erin got to your house from the mountains. I can't see her hitchhiking all that way," said Claudia.

"She drove. Rod left the car they took from the Ark."

"Kelly! Don't you think that's an important piece of information you might have shared? If he left the car, he must have been working with someone else who picked him up. That changes things, don't you think?"

"No, it doesn't. We always thought someone else must be in the mix. The car just confirms it. Anyway, I didn't know until this morning. Erin snuck out of the house early and I followed her. She unlocked the car door and I asked her what she was doing. She about jumped out of her skin . . ." Kelly's voice trailed off. When she spoke again she sounded troubled. "Kylie's car seat was in the back. Why wouldn't Rodney have taken the car seat?"

Claudia contemplated the question, but she could only come up with one answer. "The person who picked him up could already have had a car seat."

"But who else would that have been? Erin insists that Rod doesn't know anyone outside the damn Ark, and the only one he would confide in would be James Miller. He's *got* to know somebody else. Besides, it's a good thing he did leave the car or Erin would have been stuck in that place in the mountains."

"Don't you think you could have told me about this earlier?"

"What the hell's the difference? We're still going to the Ark and find out what's going on. Erin never said she didn't have a car, she just never said anything about it. Why should she?"

Arguing with Kelly was futile when she took a certain

attitude, which was probably why her law practice was successful. But Claudia knew her well enough to recognize the depth of concern she had for her niece, and to know that she was trying to cover it up with the blasé manner. She glanced at the GPS. They were twelve miles from their destination. "We still need to come up with some kind of plan before we get there."

"The plan is, I'm gonna get James alone so I can make him talk."

"Please tell me you're not gonna seduce him."

"*Seduce* him? Ick! He's a brown polyester kinda guy, and you know I don't do brown polyester, ever! Not my type."

Claudia grinned. "Or, more to the point, you're not *his* type. I can't wait to see the handwritings Stedman wants me to analyze, the members he said he was suspicious of. Do you think Stedman's right? Could someone really have infiltrated the TBL?"

"Who knows; he's probably just paranoid. While you're working with him this afternoon, I'll see if I can find out more about this Jephthah's Daughters thing. I'm gonna try and find our buddy Magdalena. If she knows anything, I'll get her to talk, even if James Miller won't give it up."

Highway 79 eventually turned into State Street as they drove through the once-dusty, now-burgeoning municipality of Hemet: old neighborhoods populated with small homes and large yards, larger tract homes with small yards; scads of mobile home parks, brand-new subdivisions boasting their own public parks, schools, and shopping precincts.

"I Googled Hemet last night," Claudia said. "It used to be a retirement community. Now it's mostly young families providing services to the older ones."

Kelly smirked. "I get it: 'newly wed or nearly dead'."

They left the highway for a two-lane road, desert scrub and low trees flanking them on either side as they wound their way into the hills. As the incline got steeper, the trees grew taller and closer together. Mostly mulberry and cottonwood.

"He wasn't kidding when he said they were hidden away," Kelly noted. "We're in bumfuck Idaho already."

"You'd better clean up your language, young lady. They'll send you packing in a New York minute."

"Enough with the clichés, I know how to behave when I have to." She pointed to the dash clock. "We're late; it's twelve-thirty already."

"Well, if you hadn't spent that extra twenty minutes chatting with Erin. . . ."

"C'mon, Claud. I haven't seen my little sister in— Hey, look, is that where we're supposed to turn?"

It was little more than a gash in the trees that grew alongside the road. Having lowered the volume on the GPS, Claudia would have missed the turn if Kelly hadn't spotted it. She said, "I bet it's pitch-black out here at night. I can't say I'm looking forward to driving back out here after my lecture on Thursday night."

"Claudia Rose, have you *no* sense of adventure? You can drop breadcrumbs to help you find your way back."

Kelly's flippant suggestion brought an image of Hansel and Gretel and the wicked old witch. Was that what they were going into? The witch's gingerbread house— sweet and tempting on the outside, but dark and menacing inside? She shook off the vision. She would never choose Jephthah's Daughters for her own child, and she would do everything she legally could to help Erin keep Kylie from such a fate; but from what she'd heard, it didn't sound as if there were anything inherently dangerous in the program.

The road was well-maintained and continued for about a half mile before they came to a sudden hairpin turn. Rounding the curve, she hit the brakes. There were no signs posted to indicate what lay behind it, but a tightly packed eight-foot-tall hedge ran in both directions as far as the eye could see. A small guard shack and a gate prevented them from driving on.

They glanced at each other, assessing the situation. Kelly said, "I guess no one's gonna be breaking in."

"Or out?" Claudia eased the Jag forward and stopped at the gate. A scorching blast of late July hit her in the face as she rolled down the window, rendering the air-conditioning ineffectual.

A muscular man in shirtsleeves and khaki pants, his eyes hidden behind wraparound dark glasses, leaned out of the guardhouse and asked politely how he could help them. Claudia gave their names but his face remained as expressionless as a secret service agent. He asked them to wait a moment and stuck his head back inside the guardhouse.

"Who hid *his* lollipop?" Kelly murmured.

"I guess they save those really big smiles for the rallies."

A moment later the gate opened and the guard waved them through with a nod. Claudia drove up the curving road to an open parking area. Most of a dozen parking spaces were filled with a fleet of maroon-colored bus-sized SUVs, the silver TBL logo on the sides, and a couple of Toyota sedans. Unlike the Jag, which had picked up dust from the country road, the Ark vehicles were clean and polished to a high sheen. "They must carpool to the rallies," Claudia said.

"Happy little outings, everyone singing 'Ninety-nine bottles of beer on the wall' and playing Truth or Dare."

"Or 'Old MacDonald' if they're teetotalers. Hey, did

Erin say anything about alcohol? Are they allowed to drink?"

"What I got from Erin was, they can drink, but aren't supposed to get drunk." Kelly's eyes sparked with devilment. "Does my otherwise calm and dignified best friend want to issue a challenge?"

"No freaking way. Just make sure you don't get James Miller so drunk that he can't tell you anything."

"Oh, Claudia, are you forgetting your most valuable resource? Hello, *it's me!* I promise you, I can get these guys from charming to bulletproof by the time one ice cube melts in their glass. You are talking to the Drinkophilia Master, Grasshopper. I may not be modest, but when it comes to booze and men, I absolutely know how to deal the cards. And even if *they* hold the cards, I got the moves, baby."

Claudia just shook her head and hoped for the best. The truth was, she knew Kelly was a loose cannon. There was simply no predicting how she might behave at the Ark. Claudia grabbed the door handle and prepared to face the hundred-and-four-degree heat. "Okay, Drinkophilia Master," she said over her shoulder. "Let's get this show on the road."

Chapter 7

The Ark's office was located in a massive old Victorian house with an extended veranda and front porch. A balcony perched outside one of the second-floor windows. At the very top was a widow's walk. The wooden siding had been painted a soft dove gray with white trim that reminded Claudia of an old-fashioned nun's habit. Edging the pathway to the front door was a carefully tended rose garden that scented the air as they walked from the parking area. *Picturesque* was the word that came to her mind as they mounted the steps to the porch, where the entry door had a transom and panels of elegantly crafted leaded glass.

Already overheated from the short walk across the parking area, Kelly was fanning herself with the baseball cap she'd been wearing in the car. Claudia knocked and opened the door, looking forward to leaving the heat behind.

She was dismayed to find the temperature in the office only slightly lower than that of an oven. No air-conditioning in this climate? That was something she had never contemplated. She and Kelly exchanged doubtful glances and lifted their eyes to the two ceiling fans rotating lazily overhead. Unless the temperature plunged during the evening hours, it didn't bode at all well for a comfortable night's sleep.

The Victorian exterior had led Claudia to expect

ornate flocked wallpaper, Moroccan leather, and over-stuffed furniture. Instead, the ground floor had been gutted and converted to an attractive open-plan office space. There were four handcrafted wooden desks, two of which were occupied. A youngish woman sat at one, engrossed in paperwork.

Kelly gave Claudia's ribs a sharp nudge and whispered, "You know who that is?"

"Shhh, yes I do." She had recognized the woman from the previous evening at the rally: Karen Harrison, the first person to be publicly humiliated when Harold Stedman shared her confession with the group. She remembered that Karen was the one who had written about her attraction to her brother's wife. Someone must have worked her hard to get her here at the Ark so fast.

Ripe for the picking.

At one of the other desks a woman working at a computer rose and came forward to greet them. "Good afternoon, sisters. I'm happy to see you found us." Her voice had a musical quality, and to Claudia, there was something sweet and guileless in the smile she gave them.

Silver-shot wavy hair surrounded a serene face. She wore a simple green linen shift and hemp sandals. The dress was clean but wrinkled in the lap, as if she'd been sitting for a long time.

Now that they were actually inside the compound, Kelly was unusually subdued and Claudia answered for both of them. "Yes, thank you, the directions helped a lot. I'm sorry we're a little later than we'd planned. Is Mr. Stedman ready to see us?"

"Brother Stedman is at lunch at the moment," the woman said. "Have you eaten?"

Kelly found her voice. "Not yet, but you could twist our rubber arms."

The woman smiled again. "No arm-twisting will be necessary; we'll be more than happy to take care of you. By the way, I'm Rita, Brother Stedman's office assistant."

They put down their overnight bags and introduced themselves. Then Rita said, "Before I send you over to the dining hall, I'll need you both to fill out some forms."

"What kind of forms?" Kelly asked.

"Nothing complicated. We ask all guests to provide their contact information in case of emergency, things like that." Rita went to a file cabinet in a corner and took some papers from the top drawer. "You can sit at these desks and fill them out. It'll just take a minute."

Karen Harrison glanced up as they each took a set of papers and sat down. There was no recognition in her gaze, but she gave them a tentative smile and returned to her task.

Claudia was still skimming the first page when Kelly looked up. "This is a nondisclosure agreement."

"Yes," Rita said. "We are a private community, and we need to make sure it stays that way. I'm sure you understand."

Claudia quickly flipped to read the text at the bottom of the page. They would be signing an agreement not to discuss anything they saw or heard at the Ark. It seemed a little over the top, but she had signed similar confidentiality agreements with clients before.

"Do you have a problem with it, Kelly?" she asked.

Kelly looked none too pleased, but it appeared to be the only way they would get their investigation started. "It's pretty standard," she said, and scribbled her signature.

When they had completed the forms and handed them to Rita, she thanked them and said, "If you wouldn't mind waiting here for just a moment, I'll get someone to take you over to the dining hall."

She disappeared through a doorway, returning a few moments later with a girl of about twelve. The girl was dressed in a shift similar to Rita's own, even the same color. Her tawny hair was drawn away from a delicate oval face and braided into two old-fashioned plaits that were draped over her shoulders, reaching nearly to her waist.

Rita brought the girl over to where Claudia and Kelly waited. "This is Esther. She'll take you to Brother Stedman and see to it that you're properly fed."

Kelly nodded toward Karen Harrison and asked, "Isn't that lady going, too?"

"Sister Harrison has already had her lunch. She'll be going to class in a few minutes."

The woman raised her head from her paperwork. "Yes, I'm scheduled for the one o'clock orientation, *What It Means to Be a Temple of Brighter Light Member.*" Her face glowed with anticipation. "I'm so happy to be here, Sister Rita. You have no idea how wonderful it is to be free at last."

"And we're very happy to have you here, Sister Harrison," Rita said with what sounded like genuine warmth. She turned to Claudia and Kelly. "Why don't you leave your overnight bags here and I'll have them taken to your rooms." She put a hand on the young girl's shoulder. "Go on now, Esther, you'd better get them over to the dining hall."

Esther gave them both a shy smile and beckoned for them to come with her. Walking between Claudia and Kelly, she took them along a dark hallway where it was thankfully a little cooler than the main office, and out through the back door. As they left the building, Esther assumed the role of tour guide, explaining that the area directly behind the office was the Ark's vegetable garden.

Claudia gazed over the large plot of ground, recognizing the leaves of summer squash and beans planted close to the back door. Toward the far end of the garden, cornstalks rose high in the air. There must be at least two or three acres of plantings. Several women in shifts the color of natural flax worked between the rows of plants, hoeing and weeding, their arms deeply tanned in the sleeveless dresses, protected from the brutal sun only by wide-brimmed straw hats. There was a primitive tone to the scene, as if they had time-traveled a hundred years into the past.

One of the gardeners looked up and gave them a cordial wave as they passed by. Her cheeks were flushed from exertion and heat, and she swiped a hand across her forehead before returning to her work.

"Do you grow all your own food here?" Claudia asked, welcoming the respite from the heat as they entered a grove of tall shade trees bordering the gravel path along which Esther led them.

The girl nodded, looking surprised at the question. "Of course."

"Of course," Kelly echoed, raising her eyebrows at Claudia.

"Well, most of it, anyway," Esther amended. "We get our meat from outside. I don't eat flesh, though. I'm a vegetarian." .

"Good for you, Esther," Claudia said. "Have you lived here all your life?"

The girl nodded again. "This is where I was born."

"Have you ever left the Ark? Gone outside?"

Esther's eyes grew large. "Left the Ark? *No!* There's

too much evil outside. The Lord told the elders to build the Ark to protect us. As long as we stay inside the Ark, we'll be safe."

She's learned the party line well, Claudia thought.

Kelly stopped walking. "Shoot." She had been punching a number into her iPhone.

"What's wrong?"

"No cell signal. Must be the hills around here. I wanted to check my voicemail."

Claudia checked her own phone and got the same results, zero reception bars. "We'll have to use a phone in the office."

Esther said, "You have to get permission from Sister Ryder." Just then, a cluster of buildings came into view that had not been visible from the office: a series of long, low-slung structures of weathered stucco, adobe, and concrete that looked as though they had risen from the earth like mushrooms and squatted there for a long time. Claudia remembered that Harold Stedman had mentioned that this group had been in existence for more than fifty years. Might the buildings originally have been Cold War bunkers? She asked Esther what they were used for.

"That one's the bookbindery." The girl pointed at a square concrete building on the far side of a patch of gravel. "That's where they make all the books and pamphlets that we send out. And that smaller one over there is our school. The nursery and the infirmary are behind it. The sewing rooms are over there. The farm is farther back over there beyond the trees. The chapel is even farther. That one is the store, and that one, the biggest one, is the dining hall where we're going right now. There are two seatings. I already had lunch at the first seating."

She swung her arms to encompass an area beyond a

stand of tall trees. A group of about twenty to twenty-five small adobe houses and a wood-frame four-story structure made up a small village. "Over there, that's where we live. Each of the houses has a name. Ours— my family's—is Sinai."

"Sinai?" Kelly echoed. "You mean, like the desert?"

Esther turned puzzled brown eyes toward her. "Like Mount Sinai in the Bible," she said, as if she didn't understand why Kelly didn't know that.

"How many people live at the Ark?" Claudia asked.

Esther thought for a moment. "I think there's around two hundred here."

Claudia was struck by the complexity of the compound. Until now, she had not imagined it would be the size of a small village. "I didn't realize there were so many members," she said.

"There are the satellite branches, too. Those are like smaller Arks in other states."

Claudia was ready with the next question. "What about children? Are there many little ones?"

"Little ones?" Esther stopped on the path, cocking her head to the side as she thought about it. "Hmmm, let's see. Sister Abigail had a baby a couple of weeks ago, and we have some toddlers." She started counting on her fingers as they walked on. "Aaron and Deborah are twins. They're five. Cassia is three; Michael and Paul are around four or five, I don't remember which. Kylie is almost . . ." A shadow flitted across her face and she started walking again. "Well, Kylie doesn't really count. She's gone."

"What happened to Kylie?" Kelly asked quickly.

"She went away with her parents, Brother and Sister Powers. They took her to the mountains for two months to pray and meditate. Then she'll be entering into Jephthah's Daughters."

Claudia asked, "What does that mean, to enter into Jephthah's Daughters?"

"It means you go away and serve the Lord God in a special place."

"For how long?"

Esther looked puzzled. "How long? Forever, I guess. How can you ever stop serving the Lord?"

"Don't the Jephthah's Daughters ever come back to the Ark?"

They had reached the building that housed the dining hall. Esther stopped, her hand on the door, and looked back at Claudia with a frown. "I don't think so. Only girls who are specially favored get to go, and it only happens once in a while. They're not all from here. Some of them live in the satellite Arks. They just come here for their consecration."

"Does that mean you don't know them?"

"Well, we all get to go to the consecration ceremony, so I've *seen* them. But the last time there was a ceremony I was only nine." Esther's lips curved into a reminiscent smile. "She looked like a baby angel, all dressed in white, with pretty flowers in her hair." She laughed. "I remember she didn't want to lie down on the altar—you know how little kids get all fidgety. She was too little to know what was going on, and she kept squirming around."

Icy fingers sent chills up Claudia's spine. Even if it were a symbolic gesture, she could not fathom putting a child on an altar. Kelly must have had the same thought, as she gripped Claudia's arm tight enough to leave imprints from her fingernails.

"Why did she have to lie on an altar?" Claudia asked, making an effort to keep her voice level.

"The governing board elders were saying prayers over her."

"What happened after that?"

"We all went to the dining room and had a party with carrot cake and ice cream. The grown-ups had wine. I tried to sneak some, but I got caught red-handed and had to go to Brother Stedman's office." She grinned like any twelve-year-old might. "He was really pretty nice about it and just told me there would be time for wine when I got older. Anyway, some of the sisters from Jephthah's Daughters took the little girl with them. She started crying because she wanted to stay with her mommy. Her mommy was crying, too, but my mother said it's because she was happy to give her child to God."

Happy to give away her three-year-old?

Aloud, Claudia said, "And now, there's going to be another ceremony?"

Esther nodded. "My mother says Kylie Powers is an extra special child. She told me that when Kylie was born, Brother Stedman said she would be the next chosen one, and now she's turning three, she's the right age."

Kelly finally relaxed her grip on Claudia's arm. "That sounds pretty young to leave your parents."

"I think her daddy will be really sad," Esther said. "He takes care of her all the time."

"What about her mother?"

"She works in the kitchen a lot. Kylie mostly stays with Brother Powers in his office because the kitchen is too dangerous for a little kid."

Esther pushed open the dining hall door and they entered a room with long tables and benches arranged in rows, and a head table at the far end. As in the office, ceiling fans chugged above them, churning the air, but they had little effect on the heat, which was intensified by the activity in the kitchen. A wide pass-through at one end of the room was all that separated the diners from three kitchen helpers in long aprons who were busy at massive cooking pots.

Dozens of eyes turned to look as Claudia and her companions entered. At the head table, Harold Stedman, who was already standing, beamed at them and spread his arms wide in welcome. Even without a microphone, his deep voice boomed along the dining hall. "Welcome to the Ark! Bring them over here, Esther. Brothers and sisters, I'm delighted to introduce you to our guests."

Esther delivered them to his table and scurried away. Although several other diners sat at his table, an empty place had already been set on either side of him. Stedman brushed off their apologies for being tardy as Kelly and Claudia slipped into their seats. He addressed the congregation. "Sister Kelly and Sister Claudia are going to be visiting with us for a few days. They're eager to learn the way to salvation, so I know you'll all welcome them and help them understand our ways and our beliefs."

In dutiful unison, the group chanted, "Welcome, sisters," and Claudia felt as if she were attending a twelve-step meeting. *What would they do if I said, Hi, my name is Claudia, and I'm here to spy on you?* Then everyone returned to their meal and she might as well have thrown a rock into a pool: the ripples vanished, leaving the surface undisturbed.

Moments later, Esther returned with a large tray on which two plates were heaped with steamed broccoli, cauliflower and rice, grilled chicken, and a slab of buttered cornbread. They might get overheated, but they would not starve during their stay at the Ark.

Stedman said, "We eat plain, but nutritious. We rise early, work hard, and retire early. Especially in the summer when it's so warm, we try to get most of our work done in the cooler hours."

Kelly dabbed her forehead with her napkin. "I guess you don't use air-conditioning."

Stedman smiled. "That would run counter to our beliefs, don't you think, Sister Kelly? Admittedly, we do use electricity, but we want to contribute as little as possible to the coming cataclysm. There are swamp coolers in some of the buildings."

Kelly shifted her body closer to him, her chin tilted toward his face with an earnestness that made Claudia cringe.

"Brother Stedman, I can't tell you how much I'm looking forward to learning about the Temple of Brighter Light. It feels like I've been wandering in the desert, spiritually starving for ever and ever. But since hearing your sermon at the rally last night, I believe that it's possible I've found God's manna at last."

Claudia silently telegraphed a message: *You're overdoing it.*

Stedman returned her gaze with a long, searching one of his own. "That's just fine, Sister Brennan. I've already asked Brother Norquist to spend the afternoon with you and introduce you to our teachings." He nodded in the direction of a frail-looking man seated at the end of the table, nodding over his plate. Claudia guessed he must be ninety if he was a day. "Brother Norquist is one of the founding members of the Temple of Brighter Light, so he's the best equipped of all to answer your questions."

Kelly's face fell, but she quickly recovered. "That sounds great, but I'd love to just wander around the grounds for a while and chat with some of the members."

"When I told him how interested you were to learn, brother got very excited. We wouldn't want to deprive him, would we, sister?"

"I guess not, but . . ."

Stedman turned to Claudia. "You and I will go over to the office, Sister Rose. I'll show you what I'm looking for in regard to what we discussed last night, and then

you can get to work. We've got you set up in our purchasing agent's room. Brother Powers is away from the
Ark for an extended period, and I know he wouldn't be
averse to your using his office while he's gone."

Claudia's interest quickened, hearing that she would
be assigned to Rodney Powers' office. The more they
knew about Jephthah's Daughters, the easier it should
be to discover something about Rodney's plans to have
his daughter inducted. She said, "Esther was telling us
about a family named Powers. She said they'd gone away
to the mountains. Is that who you're talking about?"

"Yes, the family has been away for a while. In fact,
they're due back in a few days."

"Esther told us their little girl is going into a special
program."

"That's right. Kylie has been enrolled since her birth.
It's a great privilege to be chosen."

"How does one get chosen for the program?" Kelly
managed to sound casual as she asked.

Stedman's eyes lit up with the fire of messianic zeal.
"The Lord God spoke to me in a vision. When Kylie
Powers was born, the Lord showed me a golden halo
around her perfect little head. It was immediately clear
to me that she was destined for something great. Her
parents were serving in missionary work at one of our
satellite offices at the time, but after that vision, I knew I
had to send for them to return to the Ark right away, so
that Kylie could be in the proper environment from the
very beginning."

Everyone they had met so far looked and sounded
eminently normal, the surroundings were beautifully
maintained, but Claudia found Harold Stedman's tale
of visions deeply disturbing. It wasn't that she didn't believe in miracles, just not this one.

                    *   *   *

The sound of a gong interrupted the question Claudia was about to form: What exactly might a three-year-old be trained for? Everyone rose together as an elderly woman wearing a purple shift slid onto the bench of an old upright piano and played a few opening bars. The room became filled with voices raised in a hymn Claudia didn't recognize. They finished with another prayer and the dining hall emptied within a few minutes.

Claudia and Harold Stedman returned to the office, leaving Kelly to charm Brother Norquist. "What is it that makes you think you've been infiltrated, Mr. Stedman?" Claudia asked, hoping Kelly could get some helpful information from the old man.

Stedman walked a little faster, his sandals kicking up dust on the gravel. "The government is always digging around. They've sent health inspectors here, openly harassing us. There's nothing for them to find, but I know they continue to look."

"You think the *government* has someone inside?"

"Who else?"

Claudia suppressed a smile. *Just because you're paranoid it doesn't mean they're not out to get you.* She didn't pretend to have much faith in government, but she couldn't imagine why they would send someone undercover in the Temple of Brighter Light. Unless, perhaps, they had reason to believe the group had a cache of weapons or something of that magnitude. It wouldn't be the first time a fringe group had been investigated, especially since 9-11.

Stedman seemed disinclined to talk further and they walked on in silence. The vegetable garden was empty now, and Claudia felt glad for the women who had been working there. If there was any justice at the Ark, they were home, relaxing in a cool bath.

*   *   *

Rita the office assistant was there to meet them. Harold Stedman spoke kindly to her. "Rita, Sister Claudia and I will be in Brother Powers's office. We're not to be disturbed, please." He took Claudia along a short hall and into Rodney Powers's office, which was only slightly larger than an elevator car; scarcely enough room to walk around the desk that filled it. As he shut the door behind them Claudia felt the walls close in. She had a hard time picturing a two-year-old playing in here while her father tried to work.

A four-drawer metal filing cabinet rose behind the desk, and a head-high shelf that held a set of oversized three-ring binders made it feel even more cramped. On the wall to the left of the desk was a large framed photograph of sand and surf, with a poem Claudia had seen before: "Footprints in the Sand." To the right was a wall calendar. The date of Kylie's third birthday had been circled in red.

"I've got everything ready for you," Stedman said. "I've always been fascinated by the written word. Earlier in my life I spent many a day in museums, studying ancient texts. I've even collected some antique writings. Perhaps while you're here, I'll show you a couple of items that might be of interest to you."

"I'm certainly interested in ancient writings."

Stedman looked pleased at her response. "We'll see what can be arranged. But for now, to the business at hand." He maneuvered behind the desk and opened a drawer, took out a thick manila envelope, and unsealed it. "We ask our applicants to write an essay about why they want to join the Temple of Brighter Light. What I would like you to do is review a few of these essays and tell me whether you believe they're telling the truth or not. I'll have more for you later."

Claudia took the sheaf of papers he handed her. "I'll

do what I can, Mr. Stedman, but I want to make sure you understand something: if the person didn't experience guilt over what he or she wrote, it might not show up in their handwriting as a lie."

"I do understand." The piercing blue eyes met her gaze. "But if you find anything, anything at all, you will let me know, won't you?"

"Of course."

"I have reason to believe there is some murmuring going on—dissent among some of the members, which is bad for the entire body. There are certain ones whose loyalty concerns me and I need to know whether I can trust them."

"Murmuring? I suppose you mean someone making negative comments about TBL teachings."

"We must be a unified body, and that means rooting out those who disrupt the peace of the organization."

"What will happen to them if you find out that you're right?"

"They'll be excommunicated."

"Meaning?"

Stedman slapped the envelope against his hand and his expression grew stern. "The first step is for the judicial commission to offer loving counsel. If they are found to be unrepentant evildoers who, by their actions or behavior, discredit the good that the Temple is doing, they will be cast out. No longer will we welcome them in our midst, nor will we say a greeting to them. If we see them on the street, we will cross to the other side. If they attempt to approach one of us, we will turn away."

"But if they've given up everything to live at the Ark, or to be a TBL member . . ."

"It *is* sad, sister, but the Bible tells us that the wages of sin is death. Betrayal of the Lord God is deserving of spiritual death."

Laying the envelope on the desk, he edged his way around Claudia, apologizing as he brushed against her, and opened the door. "I'll be working upstairs in my office all this afternoon. Sister Rita can show you where I am if you need me for anything. I'd like you to return the handwriting samples to me before dinner this afternoon, whether you are finished with the work or not. If you aren't finished, you can get them back from me tomorrow morning."

After he left, closing the door behind him, Claudia contemplated what he'd said about excommunicating recalcitrant members. She imagined that for someone who had been thoroughly indoctrinated in TBL teachings, it might be a living hell to be cast out of the Ark. She already had an inkling that members were cut off from their former friends and family upon joining, which made their only support system the one within the confines of the Temple of Brighter Light. It seemed to her a cruel punishment.

She turned to the handwriting samples with even more mixed feelings than before. It had become clear to her that her reports could potentially assist in causing harm to their authors. Claudia was accustomed to testifying in trials, both civil and criminal. Sometimes she worked for the defendant, sometimes for the person suing them. In every case she recognized the burden imposed upon her. It was the nature of trial testimony that someone invariably got hurt. But somehow, this was different. She faced the task before her with the responsibility weighing heavier than usual.

Then it came to her that since she had the stunning good fortune to be working right in Rodney Powers's office, there would be no better time to check out his files and look for clues to his whereabouts.

Chapter 8

Seating herself behind Rodney's desk in the stifling office, Claudia got out her notepad and pen and prepared to make notes. Normally, she would have waited to read the contents of the handwriting sample until after she had first formed an opinion about the writer. This time, however, since her task was to look for signs of lying, she would need to know what had been written. This part of her job came under the heading of forensic statement analysis rather than handwriting analysis, and would ensure that she didn't overlook anything important.

She tipped the batch of papers out of the envelope. Ever-conscientious, she felt pressured to begin the work she was being paid for. But she also wanted to concentrate on the main task she had set herself: learn anything she could about Kylie Powers's whereabouts.

At this point, she had no way of knowing whether her presence and Kelly's would advance that aim. Nor did she know whether she would uncover evidence that Harold Stedman was looking for against his members, but at the very least, it gave her a legitimate reason for being at the Ark.

Using the manila envelope to fan herself, Claudia began her examination of the first handwriting sample. The handwriting was crammed full of strokes that should have been rounded but had been turned into angular forms; upper and lower loops squeezed tight, indicating an abnormally high state of tension. She looked for a name or other identifying information, but found none. Someone had redacted the personal information with a heavy felt pen. Handwriting could not conclusively reveal gender, but she made an educated guess that the author of the sample was probably male.

The essay rambled on for two pages about how, after twenty-five years, the writer no longer felt fulfilled by the dental career he had chosen. He was ready to sell his practice, turn over all his material goods to the Temple, and devote the rest of his life in service to the Lord. The degree of tension in the handwriting disturbed Claudia. From what was written, there was no obvious reason to believe he had been anything less than truthful in his statement, but her experience told her he was withholding something.

She made some notes, then set the sample aside and turned to the next one. Written in a simplified, super-efficient hand, there were no superfluous strokes to slow it down. The clarity and speed of the writing were hallmarks of a fast thinker who could be impatient with routine details, but who was an excellent problem solver when it came to complicated issues. Again, she could find no identifying information, and this sample contained no strong indicators either way for the writer's gender. The person had written in a selfless way about the writing talents he or she might contribute to the Ark's publications. No overt evidence of lies there.

The small office felt confined, airless. Claudia yawned and stretched her arms above her head, beginning to feel oxygen deprived. She reached for the next sample.

Written in block printing with bold, dark lines, the writing showed rapid rightward movement, revealing stamina and energy, a desire to get things moving. There was a masculine quality in the confident, strong strokes and the pressure was strong enough to leave slight indentations in the paper.

Rodney Powers's handwriting had been block printed, she remembered, but from her recollection, the handwriting in the note Erin had showed them had a different type of rhythm and flow from this one. Too bad Erin had snatched the note back so fast. She would have to remember to ask Kelly whether she'd been able to retrieve it.

As she read through the essay, Claudia noticed a gap in the text that she thought might be significant: "My main reason for becoming part of the Temple of Brighter Light is the desire for greater spiritual guidance. I am deeply impressed by what I've learned . . ." The slightly wider space between "the" and "desire" indicated that the writer had taken a microsecond of extra thought—time to stop and think about what he or she was going to write, rather than letting it flow smoothly and naturally, which sometimes indicated a lie. Also, the personal pronoun *I* was slanted slightly to the left, while the balance of the writing slanted to the right. It was by no means conclusive, but Claudia made a note and set the sample to one side to look at again later.

The next essay was written in a school-model style. Her educated guess was that the writer was more than likely female, someone who had grown up with many rules to follow; someone who needed to be told what to do and when to do it. Adults who stuck with copybook school-model writing virtually always identified themselves as having attended a religious school.

What stood out in this sample was the way the spatial arrangement departed from the school model. The words and lines were jammed together, filling the paper from top to bottom and left to right. Symbolically, the writer had left no "breathing space" that would allow room for her to consider new ideas or to step back and look at an alternative perspective on an issue. She had written about leaving her abusive husband, and how she sought refuge in the Temple of Brighter Light. What about truthfulness? The degree of subjectivity that Claudia saw in the writing left her confident that this woman would create her own truth and would find it difficult to see anything outside of her carefully constructed image.

The next sample she took from the pile was another printed one, but the style of printing was different from the earlier one she had examined. Here, the writer had used upper- and lowercase letters with a jumpy rhythm that indicated nervous energy. *Jitterbug,* Claudia thought. Comparing writing rhythm to dance rhythms sometimes helped her form a mental image of the writer's demeanor.

This was someone who would be easily bored by long periods of forced inaction. The handwriting slanted strongly uphill on the page, an indication that the writer was probably fighting depression. If the baseline slant had been less extreme the interpretation would have been somewhat different. It might have indicated an optimistic outlook. It was the *extreme* degree of the uphill movement that gave the clue that the writer was working too hard to raise his mood, trying to convince himself that if he could just keep on going one more day, things would *have* to get better, his problems would surely be solved.

As she read through it, looking for signs of lying, Claudia realized that the sample was unlike the others in content. This was not an essay about why the writer wanted to join the Temple of Brighter Light. The subject dealt with the writer's desire to grow into a leadership position in the group, to become part of the board of governors. He wrote passionately of a wish to see the

earth cleansed of wickedness and returned to its natural
state, and of his faith in the leadership of TBL to bring its
congregants to a new earth after the old one was plowed
under. He wrote about the chosen ones being removed
to a place of protection until the earth was renewed.

Engrossed in what she was reading, Claudia glanced
up, startled when the door opened. She looked at the
woman framed in the threshold, noting, even in her surprise, that unlike any of the other women she'd seen
at the compound, who had all been dressed in simple
shifts, this one wore workmanlike khaki cargo pants and
a sleeveless white shirt that stood out against the deeply
tanned skin. Her curly black hair was shorter than the
other women's, too. She appeared to be mid-thirties and
looked like she worked out. Altogether, she was an interesting contrast in masculine/feminine.

Claudia took in all this in an instant as the woman's
gaze swept Rodney Powers's desk. Before she could stop
her, the woman snatched up one of the samples. "What
are you doing with these papers?" she demanded.

Claudia stood. "I don't believe we've met."

The woman continued to glare at her with furious
eyes. "Who *are* you?"

"My name is Claudia Rose."

"What are you doing here?"

"I'm here at the invitation of Harold Stedman." Claudia picked up the remaining samples from the desk and
slid them back into the envelope. She closed the flap and
held it firmly in her hand, a message that the woman was
not going to have access to any more of the essays.

"These are private and personal papers." The woman's voice was stiff with tension. "Now, I want to know
who you are and what you're doing with these documents. Why are you in this office?"

Claudia reached across the desk and took the hand-

writing sample from her hand. Glancing at it she noted
that it was the first sample she had examined. The one
where she'd noticed a possible problem.

"Is this your essay?" she asked, not really expecting
an answer. She was surprised when she got one.

"I'm sure you already know it is. Now I want to know
why you're reading it."

"I'm sorry; I'm not at liberty to discuss what I'm doing here. If you want to know anything about what I'm
doing, you'll need to ask Harold Stedman."

The woman bristled. "All visitors have to be cleared
by me. That includes Brother Stedman's visitors."

"And you are—?" Claudia asked, but she had remembered Erin's warning.

"I'm the chief of security here, that's who. Let me see
some identification, please."

Claudia fished her driver's license from her purse
and handed it over. What was the name Erin had mentioned? *Lynn Ryder.*

Ryder glanced at the driver's license and stepped
back into the hallway. "Okay, Ms. Rose, I'll need you to
come with me."

With a shrug, Claudia followed her to a flight of stairs
and up to the second-floor landing.

Harold Stedman looked up from his desk as they appeared
at his open door. "Ah, Sister Ryder." His shirtsleeves
were rolled up, shirt collar open, his only concession to
the heat. "You've met Sister Rose, I see."

"What's going on, Harold?" Even though she addressed Stedman by his first name, Lynn Ryder's tone was
respectful, less combative than it had been with Claudia.
"You didn't tell me you were expecting a visitor."

Harold Stedman's expression remained placid. "As it
happens, *two* visitors. It must have slipped my mind. I've

invited Sister Rose here to help me with a project. She's a handwriting expert and she's brought along her friend, a spiritual seeker—Sister Brennan. They attended our rally last night in Burbank. I made a decision to invite them here today."

"A *handwriting* expert?" The unspoken question of why he needed a handwriting expert bounced around the space between them like a live grenade as Claudia watched the exchange with interest.

Stedman gave the security chief one of his long looks, speculation in the deep-set eyes. "It's a personal matter, Sister Ryder."

"Personal? But—"

"Personal. Something you don't need to be concerned about."

"Everything at the Ark concerns me, Brother Stedman. That's what you've always told me. My job is to—"

He spread his hands. "I'm making an exception in this case. Sister Rose will be working in Brother Powers's office while she's here."

"But Rod—"

"Won't be back for a few days yet. He won't have any objection to her using the space while he's away. Besides, when he and Sister Powers return, they'll be busy preparing for little Kylie's consecration. He won't be needing his office for some time yet and we'll be through with it long before then. As you know, Brother Treadwell is handling his work assignment for the time being." Stedman gave Lynn Ryder a pointed look. "Was there anything else, sister?"

From the corner of her eye, Claudia could see the angry set of Lynn's chin. She gave a sharp shake of her head and spun on her heel, leaving Claudia to follow her.

*   *   *

At the head of the stairs, Ryder handed back Claudia's driver's license and preceded her to the ground floor. "So, you've got clearance," she said in a flat voice when they reached the bottom.

"I expect he's got his reasons for keeping you out of the loop," said Claudia. Was the Ryder woman so agitated because she had lied in her essay, and now she was afraid she might be found out? It was unfortunate and understandable that she might take Stedman's refusal to keep her apprised of the details of Claudia's assignment as a personal affront.

But Lynn Ryder's next words gave the lie to that assumption. "Brother Stedman is our spiritual leader." Her attitude was a little prim, considering her hard demeanor. "He knows what he's doing."

"Oh yeah, I forgot, the Lord speaks to him in visions."

"You sound skeptical, Sister Rose. Do you not believe that the Lord speaks directly to his servants on earth?"

"It's what *you* believe, isn't it?"

"Yes," Lynn said. "Of course it is. That's why I'm here."

"How long have you been at the Ark?" Claudia asked, remembering what Erin had said about her former work in the security field.

"About two and a half years."

"You've really worked your way up. Mr. Stedman must have a lot of trust in you."

Lynn swung around to face her. "Look, with the understanding that I'm not going to be in on your little project here, whatever it is, can you just tell me what a handwriting expert does—in general terms?"

"Of course." That was an easy one. Claudia had answered this question a thousand times over her career. "There are two sides of my practice. One side involves authenticating questioned writing in cases of forgery.

The other has to do with assessing personality characteristics from handwriting. Sometimes I work with human resource departments when they're hiring new
applicants, sometimes within the court system, such as
in custody cases. Sometimes for people who are in a relationship and want to know how to get along with the
other person better. Things like that."

Lynn Ryder fell silent and Claudia knew she was
wondering why her essay was among the handwritings
that Stedman had given her to analyze. Lynn had not directly challenged him on that, so Stedman was unaware
that she knew Claudia had seen it.

They continued along the hall to Rodney's office.
Claudia slipped back around the desk, putting a physical
barrier between herself and the other woman. "By the
way, it's a couple of days off, but just to let you know, I'll
be going to Riverside Thursday evening. I'm scheduled
to lecture at the university. I'll be returning here afterward. Will there be any problem getting back inside the
gate after ten?"

Lynn shook her head. "No, there's someone in the
guardhouse twenty-four seven. I'll let them know to expect you. Is your lecture on handwriting?"

"Yes, I teach handwriting authentication there in the
fall. They like me to give an introductory lecture during
the summer to get new students interested. It was coin-
cidental that I was scheduled there this week while I'm
visiting here."

"Sounds interesting." The security chief's eyes shifted
to the essay that she had admitted was hers, still in Claudia's hand, but she didn't mention it again. "Let's talk
more about it later."

She closed the door behind her and Claudia looked
at her handwriting. The masculine-type block printing
was logical in light of what Lynn Ryder did at the Ark.

The job of security chief in a male-dominated culture like The Temple of Brighter Light would traditionally be a man's job. She must have an amazing résumé to have been tasked with that responsibility.

Claudia was more convinced than ever that the woman had not been completely honest when she wrote her essay to join the Temple of Brighter Light. Glancing through the sample again, she looked for the sentence that contained the point of hesitation. As a paid consultant at the Ark, Claudia knew that her duty was to report it to Harold Stedman. But realizing that if she did, it might lead to Lynn's excommunication, she wanted to be extra careful before sharing that information.

The red flag in Lynn's handwriting was real, but that did not mean she was necessarily hiding anything that would be detrimental to the Ark. It could be that she was resisting making the kind of confession that had caused Karen Harrison to be persuaded to the podium at the rally the evening before. Surely Lynn deserved some privacy.

It was an ethical dilemma that Claudia would eventually have to face, but for the moment, finding Kylie Powers took precedence. And there was the possibility that somehow, her knowledge of that hesitation in Lynn's handwriting might prove to be an ace in the hole.

With the door closed again and no windows to open nor a fan to stir the sauna-like air, the temptation to get up and take a walk outside was strong. But the time had come to tackle the file cabinet. She dabbed her forehead with a Kleenex, feeling a strong repugnance for prying into someone else's private files. But it was exactly the kind of opportunity she and Kelly had come here for and she could not afford to be squeamish now about opening drawers that were not hers.

She thought about Harold Stedman making the little girl lie on an altar. Even if it were only a ceremonial altar, the idea filled Claudia with outrage. She summoned a mental image of Kylie in the photo Erin had showed them. The memory of the sweet baby face with its plaintive eyes and button nose bolstered her resolve. Keeping that image planted firmly in her mind, she swiveled the chair around and reached for the bottom drawer.

Manila files were categorized and placed in a series of green folders and neatly labeled with the names of various vendors. She recognized some familiar company names. As the Ark's purchasing agent for goods and products not grown or made by members themselves, Rodney would have more contact with the outside world than perhaps anyone else in the compound. Might one of them be the person who was hiding him and Kylie?

Swiftly riffling through the files, she came across an unlabeled folder at the back of the drawer.

A sheaf of papers, covered with handwriting she knew she had seen before.

Holy shit.

This was the same nervous printing, the same extreme uphill baseline. What she read confirmed that the content had a similar theme to the handwriting she had been examining before Lynn's interruption: the destruction of the earth and all the malefactors who had contributed to its demise; the desire of the writer to serve as a leader in the Temple of Brighter Light. The date scribbled at the top was two years earlier. The essay was in Rodney Powers's office. The implication seemed clear: more than likely it was his handwriting.

Claudia puzzled it out. Stedman had given her Rodney Powers's handwriting to examine. Did that mean he believed Rodney's loyalty was suspect? Did he already know that Rodney had virtually kidnapped little Kylie from her mother? Or had he thrown it in as a ringer to test her skills?

Something about the handwriting troubled her. If only she had been able to keep the note Erin had taken back she could have compared the two. This sample didn't jibe with her memory of it, and that conflicted with a basic tenet of handwriting authentication: If major differences existed between handwritings that were supposedly authored by the same hand, there must be a reason for those differences. Reasons could include mental state, medication, aging, and many other factors.

Kidnapping your child and making the decision to leave your religion could affect your mental state.

Still, it would have been helpful if she had Erin's note to look at. She replaced the file and closed the bottom drawer. She was reaching for the next one when there was a light knock and the door opened.

The second visitor of the afternoon was Rita, who said she would show Claudia to the room where she would be staying.

"It's just upstairs," Rita said. "You'll be on the same floor as Brother Stedman."

As they climbed the stairs together, Claudia managed to hide the relief she felt that she had not been caught prying in the file cabinet. She had pretended to be looking for something in her purse under the desk. Thank heavens there hadn't been time for her to open the second drawer. She would have been caught in the act, and what credible excuse could she have given for snooping in Rodney Powers's files?

Rita was still speaking. "Only the brothers on the governing board have their quarters in the house, but all except Brother Stedman are on the third floor."

"Does that include their whole family?"

"Oh, none of them are married. They've devoted their lives to TBL. We're their family."

"That's true devotion," Claudia replied, following Rita past Stedman's office to a room at the end of the hall.

It had been pointed out to her that there were few locks in the compound, so she carried the envelope containing the handwriting samples with her. Harold Stedman had said she was to return them to him, rather than keeping them overnight. Maybe there was a good reason for his apparent paranoia. Confidentiality had already been breached the moment Lynn saw her own handwriting among the samples.

The room to which Rita took Claudia was small and spare, but pleasant enough with a twin bed and night table, a student desk and wooden chair, a matching chest of drawers. The quilt that covered the bed looked handmade, as did the lacy pillow on top. A set of small watercolors of nature scenes made an attractive grouping on the wall.

"Nothing fancy, just clean and comfortable." Rita went to the window and pushed it open a crack. "I know it's quite warm up here now, but if you leave the window open, the room will get a breeze and be nice and cool for you tonight. The bathroom is across the hall. You won't have to share it with anyone. Brother Stedman has his own, of course."

"Thank you, Rita. Where's Kelly's room?"

Rita looked uncomfortable. "Sister Brennan will be staying in Ararat."

"Ararat?"

"When Esther took you to the dining hall, you probably saw a tall building in the distance? Four stories?

That's Ararat. That's where the accommodations are for single workers." When Claudia frowned, Rita added, "She'll be comfortable there, I promise you."

"Why isn't she staying here?"

"We don't have another room available." Rita's eyes slid away, giving Claudia the impression that she was being less than truthful.

"Could you tell me where to find her right now? I'd like to speak with her."

"I'm sorry, Sister Rose, but I don't know where she is at the moment. I expect you'll be able to find her if you walk around a bit. Pretty warm weather to be outside, though."

"*Somebody* must know where she is." Claudia started to reach for her cell phone, then remembered that neither she nor Kelly had been able to get service in the hills.

"Brother Norquist might have taken her just about anywhere. They could be in a meeting room, talking, or he might have taken her to a classroom so she could hear one of the lessons. He might be giving her a tour of the facilities. There's really no telling." Rita headed for the door and added more briskly, "Dinner is at five o'clock."

"Thanks, I'll see you then."

Rita excused herself and left Claudia to unpack the few items of clothing she'd brought along for her stay. She set her laptop on the desk, thinking she would check her e-mail, but there was no Ethernet cable or phone line in the room. No point in looking for a wireless connection. She wouldn't be able to go online while she was at the Ark.

Double damn.

Almost pathetically grateful for the electrical outlet she found behind the desk, she booted up the laptop.

Even though she wouldn't be giving her lecture for a couple of days, she copied the PowerPoint presentation over to a thumb drive. The university would use its own AV system so she wouldn't need to bring the computer with her.

Seating herself at the desk, she went through the handwriting samples once again, refreshing her memory, then opening a new word processing file on the computer. She quickly typed up her notes on the samples, powered down the laptop, and replaced the samples in the manila envelope, ready to return them to Harold Stedman.

She wondered how Kelly was doing and why there seemed to be some effort to keep them separated. Or was she just imagining things? Paranoia could be contagious.

Chapter 9

"It all sounds pretty harmless," Jovanic conceded when she phoned him late in the afternoon from the Ark's office. "But I don't like it that I can't easily reach you."

"It's the hills around here, there's no reception." Claudia lowered her voice. "It's not like they're blocking calls . . . at least, I don't think so." She tucked away that question for later consideration.

Her request to use a landline had created a minor disturbance, even after she'd explained to Rita that her mobile phone had no reception here. She might as well have asked for an introduction to Jesus Christ himself.

It seemed that the office phone was kept in a locked drawer in Rita's desk and Rita insisted that she had to get permission from Lynn Ryder before she could allow access. They were trying to avoid abuse of the privilege, she explained. As if that were a good enough answer.

Now Claudia regretted that she hadn't just taken her car and driven away from the Ark, where she could speak freely, knowing her call would not be monitored. Here, she had no such certain knowledge, and she counted on Jovanic to understand that when she avoided talking about her covert reason for being at the Ark, it was an attempt at circumspection.

She studied his voice the way a good doctor listens to her patient. "How are you doing?"

"Fine. I got some curls in this afternoon, a few crunches. Felt pretty good, getting back to the gym."

Of course he would start working out the moment she was out of sight. It would do no good to ask whether he'd gotten clearance from the surgeon. "You're supposed to take it slowly," she reminded him. "You don't want any more setbacks."

"Yes, Mom."

"Don't do that. You know I hate it."

"As much as I hate you hovering?"

"Okay, fine. Lift as many weights as you like. Do sit-ups till you throw up. You won't hear a word from me."

This time, Jovanic laughed out loud. "Baby, that's why I love you."

At dinner, Claudia and Kelly found seats at separate tables. They had scoped out the one where Erin told them James Miller presided as table captain, and Kelly made sure to wangle her way to a seat there. From across the room, Claudia could see from the way she tilted her body toward Miller that she had already begun working on him.

She took her own place with a family group that included Magdalena, the young woman who had taken charge of them at the previous evening's rally, along with her younger sister, Rachel, and their parents. There was also a lovely African American woman of indeterminate age who said her name was Vera, and a white-haired couple who appeared to be in their eighties.

The elderly woman stretched across the table and shook Claudia's hand with the grip of a much younger person. She had a face with a thousand wrinkles, an osteoporosis-bent spine, and an oxygen cannula in her nose, but Claudia could see from the wicked glint in her eye that she was a firecracker.

"Oka Diehl," the woman said by way of introduction. She pointed at her husband. "That's George. He's been trying to keep me in line for sixty-three years, but it don't work."

"I'll bet it doesn't," Claudia agreed with a grin.

George Diehl's boyish smile made him look like a schoolboy in an old man's body. "She's never quite learned what it means to be a submissive wife," he said. "So I've just learned to put up with her antics."

The bantering was interrupted for a lengthy blessing over the food, which was given by one of the governing board at the head table, but picked up again as dinner was served. As they began to eat, the conversation waned and Claudia seized the opportunity to ask her table mates how long they had been associated with the Temple of Brighter Light.

Magdalena's mother sat quietly, waiting for her husband, the table captain, to speak. He had introduced himself to Claudia as Brother Samuel Kingston. "My wife and I were both raised in the church," he answered her question with pride. "We're third-generation TBL."

"And what a little brat he was, too," put in Oka Diehl. "Always getting into hot water; gave his poor mother fits, young Sammy did." Her husband tried to shush her but his efforts were ineffective.

"That's enough, Sister Diehl," Samuel Kingston said kindly. "We don't want to scare Sister Rose away, do we?"

"Well, you're all grown up now, Sammy. Can't spank you anymore. But there were always other boys to take your place."

"Sister Rose came to the rally the other night," Magdalena said, deflecting the attention from her father. "I took care of her and her friend, Sister Brennan." This was said with a self-satisfied air, from which Claudia inferred that she was taking credit for Kelly's and her presence at the Ark. Maybe brownie points of some sort were awarded for the number of converts members recruited.

"We were quite impressed with the presentation," Claudia said, improvising as she went along. "Mr. Stedman's talk about the end of time really made us sit up and think. We've been looking for answers and we feel as if *something* led us to the Rally."

Samuel Kingston said, "First John 5:14, sister. *'No matter what we ask, if it is according to God's will, we will receive an answer.'* Since you were permitted to come to the Ark so quickly, Brother Stedman must have been convinced of your sincere desire to learn. I promise you, if you apply yourselves and study with us, you can be assured of being saved when the cataclysm arrives. You've arrived here just in time."

"It's that close?" Claudia gave him wide-eyed innocence.

"It's right upon us, sister. It's a blessing that you and your friend came to the rally when you did."

George Diehl added, "You'll start out with a class on how the Temple got its start, and what you can do to support its aims."

"Oh, I thought we would be studying the Bible."

"Well, of course you will, my dear, but that comes later. First, you need to know who we are and what we believe in. Remember, the Temple of Brighter Light is God's chosen representative on earth. Understanding about the organization is an important part of learning how to avoid being destroyed with all the other nonbelievers. Our name is the Temple of Brighter Light because the light keeps getting brighter as we get closer to the cataclysm, and we are given new truths all the time."

Claudia nodded as if in agreement, but her insides were churning, every inch of her being resisting what she was being told. Her inclination was to argue that they were being blinded by the light that they claimed imparted knowledge; that it was just a man-made organization—and why didn't they start thinking for themselves? But to do so would be counterproductive to her goal of finding Kylie Powers. She pushed aside the mostly uneaten plate of macaroni-and-cheese, which already felt like a deadweight in her stomach, and turned to Magdalena's younger sister. "How old are you, Rachel?"

"I'm eleven, but I'll be twelve next month."

Claudia smiled at her enthusiasm. "Twelve? You're almost grown up. What's it like for a girl your age to live at the Ark?"

Rachel looked puzzled. "I don't know what you mean."

"Some things are different here from the outside. You don't have television or video games . . ."

"Oh! My friend Rosalie Garcia told me about those things. Her family just moved here last month. She tells me all about what it's like outside the Ark."

Claudia noticed Rachel's parents exchange an unhappy glance. Her mother said, "I'm sure she tells you how much better her life is here, where we're safe and taken care of."

Rachel wrinkled her nose. "It sounds like more fun out there. She showed me a magazine called *Teen People*. The girls were wearing really pretty outfits." She looked down at her own plain shift with distaste. "Not like these old rags. *Their* clothes *rock!*"

"Rachel!" Her father's outraged expression said it all. "You can be sure I'll be speaking to Brother Garcia about his daughter today. I just hope you took the opportunity to be a good example to Rosalie and not follow her bad one."

The girl looked as though she would like to say something more, but she wisely kept her thoughts to herself. At the other end of the table Oka Diehl added her two cents. "Leave her be, Sammy. If you try to squash her spirit, she'll just push against you harder."

The way Samuel Kingston looked at her over the top of his glasses made him resemble an old-fashioned schoolmarm. "Thank you for your advice, Sister Diehl, but I believe I know how to raise my daughters according to the truths we've learned here at the Ark."

Oka tsked in disapproval, but reserved further criticism. Claudia watched it all with interest. She addressed Rachel again, hoping to avoid another controversial topic. "So, what do you do here at the Ark that's fun?"

The girl nearly bounced out of her chair. "We're going to have a big party on Saturday. There's going to be music and dancing, and—"

"Calm down, now, Rache." Her father turned to Claudia with an apology in his gaze. "There's going to be a very special and very private ceremony, and then there's a celebration afterward. But I'm afraid it's something we discuss only among ourselves. Once you're inducted, you'll learn all about it."

"Actually, I've heard something about it already. I must admit, I'm curious about the place where the little girl will be going afterward, where it's located."

"I'm sorry, we can't disclose that."

"Putting babies in a nunnery," Oka Diehl muttered. "Makes no sense to me."

"That's enough, Oka." This time, her husband's rebuke had a sharp edge and carried the undertone of a threat. She scowled at her plate, but George Diehl had sounded serious to Claudia and it appeared that his wife knew when it was better to stop.

Vera said, "Is everyone ready for Bible study tonight?" Around her head she had wound a band of yellow cloth that matched her shift. It gave her an air of individuality in this society of followers.

Sister Kingston said, "I studied ahead last night. I've already got my text underlined with the answers to the questions Brother Stedman sent out. It was a very important section on the cataclysm and what we need to do to survive it."

"What's the text?" Claudia asked.

Samuel Kingston named a book that he told her was published by the TBL in the Ark's own bindery. "The governing board writes our texts based on the direct communications received by Brother Stedman from the Lord," he said. "They explain the Bible and help us to understand what we're required to do to be saved."

"It sounds like your members have great faith in the governing board."

"Yes, indeed, they give us spiritual food and light at the right time for it." He got up from his seat. "If you've finished your dinner, it's time for us to get ready for tonight's Bible study. We'll see you later at church."

This seemed to be the signal for everyone to rise and disperse.

Looking around for Kelly, Claudia saw her talking with Harold Stedman and went over to join them.

"Ah, Sister Rose," Stedman greeted her. "Sister Brennan and I were just about to head over to the church for Bible study. You can join us."

"Thank you, but I'm going to beg off. I have a slight headache, so if you don't mind, I'll go back to my room and lie down for a while."

"You okay, Claud?" asked Kelly.

"I'll be fine, but the heat has done me in. You're going to church?"

"Well, yeah. That's what I came here for, isn't it? To

learn." Kelly had softened her usual smart-ass attitude for Stedman's benefit. It felt a little weird to see her act meek and chastened.

Stedman said, "As you wish, Sister Rose. You can leave those papers for me on my desk. See you tomorrow at breakfast. Let's go, Sister Brennan."

With no phone, no television, no e-mail, the evening dragged. Claudia had cleared out the trunk of her car just before the trip to the Ark, leaving nothing in case they were spied on. Even an old magazine to reread would have been better than this. There was a Bible on the nightstand and she flipped through it, finding long-forgotten passages: Matthew 19:14, where Jesus said, *"Let the little children come to me, and do not hinder them, for the kingdom of heaven belongs to such as these."*

Did Harold Stedman see himself as a latter-day Jesus Christ, calling the children to him? The Temple of Brighter Light members seemed content to accept what he said without question. Or was the truth simply that when they did not comply they were excommunicated, as he had suggested?

She got up and went to the window. Below, the grounds were quiet and still. She knew that the church building where the congregation had gathered for Bible study was at least a half mile away in the far reaches of the compound. As far as she knew, she was alone in the Victorian, a house where there were no locks on the doors. For a fleeting moment she regretted staying behind. Even Kelly, whose view of religion approached Marxism, had gone to the church.

Out of sheer boredom Claudia went to bed early. She slept fitfully, awaking during the night—half the times, kicking off the sheet when the air felt hot and cloying; the other half, dragging it back over her when it was too cool. Even when she managed to sleep, her mind continued to work overtime on the puzzle of how to get information about Rodney Powers and where he might have taken his little daughter. When she awoke at dawn, she felt more tired than when she had gone to bed.

After breakfast she managed to connect with Kelly for a couple of minutes. Kelly immediately began grousing that she'd received a work assignment. "They've got me peeling potatoes! It's supposed to make me show *humility.* I'm a goddamned attorney, not the freaking kitchen help."

Claudia couldn't help being glad that her own assignment would keep her in the office. "Sucks to be you, doesn't it?" she said unsympathetically.

"How the hell am I supposed to find out anything, stuck in the kitchen all morning? They're sending me to a class this afternoon."

"You don't know, Kel, maybe you'll end up working right next to someone who drops some perfect pearls of knowledge on you."

"They'd better hand me the keys to the friggin' kingdom," said Kelly, shooting a false smile at a group of members who walked past.

"I've been racking my brains to find ways to wrench Rodney into the conversation without directly mentioning him," said Claudia.

"Oh yeah? How's that working out for you?"

"All I've learned is that they're planning this big bash in Kylie's honor on Saturday. They won't say anything about where she's going. How are you doing with James Miller?"

"He's hot for me, but it's gonna take some work to get his guard down."

"As long you don't get his pants down, too."

Kelly tried to suppress a giggle. "Claudia! You've shocked me to my depths."

"I'm not too worried; your depths are pretty shallow."

The kitchen supervisor hurried over then and escorted Kelly away to begin her morning duties. Claudia watched her go, not sure whether to be amused or annoyed at the way Kelly's time was being monopolized. She went off to her own assignment, cheered by the fact that Harold Stedman had not attempted to set a schedule for her.

At dinner, Kelly looked worn out, with dark circles bruising the fair skin below her eyes. She was unusually silent and subdued. Peeling potatoes and the classes she was attending had taken their toll. She had to be worrying about her niece, too.

That makes two of us.

The day ended without any significant progress, and Claudia climbed into bed feeling frustrated and discouraged.

Wednesday started as a rerun of Tuesday.

At lunch, Kelly sat at one end of the room, Claudia the other. In an effort to meet as many members as possible, they had once again switched to tables where they had not sat before.

Dan Treadwell was the table captain where Claudia found herself a seat. His name sounded familiar, but she was unable to place it. She would have remembered this large man if she had seen him before. The puffy red cheeks and spider veins that created a map on his nose made her wonder whether overexposure to the sun or alcohol was the culprit. Members were supposed to be moderate in their use of alcohol, but who knew? As preoccupied as he was with his food, Treadwell did not look like someone who would be drawn to outdoor exercise.

His wife, Deborah, was fully engaged with attempting to keep their three young sons in line. Throughout the meal, the preteen boys teased and tormented each other without letup until Claudia was ready to knock their heads together. She could see that the other diners at their table, a young couple, were unhappy with their behavior, too, but they said nothing to complain. Dan Treadwell's failure to help his wife with her ineffectual efforts to control their children was as irritating as it was puzzling.

"What's your job here at the Ark, Dan?" Claudia asked, more to distract herself from his sons than a burning desire to know. He glanced up from the chicken drumstick he was gnawing on and swiped his napkin across his mouth.

"Accountant," he mumbled around a mouthful. "And at the moment, acting purchasing agent, too."

When he said that, the penny dropped and she knew where she had heard his name before. "Oh, Mr. Stedman mentioned you're taking over for Rodney Powers. I've been using his office while he's out of town."

Treadwell's owlish eyes grew even larger behind the thick lenses of his glasses. "So, that *was* you. I heard someone was in there, doing *something* for Brother Stedman."

"Yes, that's me." Claudia could see that he was dying to ask something more, perhaps what she was doing in Rodney's office. But he was either too polite or he knew better than to ask, and she wasn't about to enlighten him. "I understand Mr. Powers and his family are spending some time in the mountains," she prompted.

"Mm, yes, we have a cabin near Big Bear that they're using."

She waited, but when Treadwell seemed disinclined to say anything further, Claudia turned to the young couple, whom she guessed from the way they continually touched each other to be newlyweds. "A cabin in the mountains; sounds like a great getaway. When do *you* get to go to Big Bear?"

The woman shook her head. "The cabin is kept for special times. The Powerses are there for prayer and meditation with their daughter. She's going to be—"

Her husband broke in. "Laurie, sweetheart, I don't think—" He gave Claudia that apologetic glance that she had become familiar with when she asked certain questions at the Ark. "Sister Rose isn't . . ." He trailed off awkwardly.

"I know," said Claudia, exasperated. "It's not something you discuss with outsiders."

She grabbed Kelly on the way out of the dining hall. "Conversations with people here are damned annoying! Every time someone's on the verge of saying something that might be important, they get cut off. Have you had any more luck?"

"James is *coming* around, if you'll forgive the pun."

"Kelly—"

"Don't nag me, Claudia. I'll do whatever it takes. We've still got tomorrow at least."

"Not 'at least.' We're leaving here on Friday. I've had enough of this place. If it weren't for my lecture at the university tomorrow night—"

"James asked if I would be going with you. How did he know about your lecture? Did you tell him?"

"No, I haven't even met him face-to-face yet. Rita must have told him. She seems to be in the office all the time; I bet she hears everything that goes on."

"A place like this, there's probably no secrets. Everyone knows everything." Kelly pulled a tissue from her pocket and dabbed her forehead. "Kylie's birthday is Saturday. Obviously, Rodney will have to bring her back here before then. If we haven't found him before that, we should hang around. We can watch for him, grab her, and run."

"So, now you want *us* to kidnap her? I hate to remind you, but that's a felony. You would be disbarred."

Kelly's face fell. "I know. But we've got to stop him."

"What we have to do is find out where he is and take Erin there. It's up to her after that."

Stedman had Rita deliver a new envelope with four more handwritings for Claudia to analyze. Finding nothing of consequence in the samples, she typed up her notes and returned the envelope.

By midmorning, in need of a break, she took a walk, deciding to look for Oka Diehl again. Since the elderly woman's remark the day before, expressing disapproval of sending babies to a nunnery, Claudia had been hoping to get her alone, positive that Oka would be willing to talk.

But Oka was not in evidence, and when Claudia asked a woman she met on the path where she might be found, she got the answer that Sister Diehl suffered from emphysema and would be at the infirmary for her breathing treatment.

The rest of the day seemed interminable. In the afternoon, she stretched out on the narrow bed, half-dozing. Images of little Kylie on a ceremonial altar, frightened, unaware that she was facing separation from everyone she knew and loved, kept jolting Claudia back to full consciousness and renewed her commitment to finding the child.

Chapter 10

By the time Thursday rolled around, the days had acquired a rhythm of their own. Harold Stedman provided another batch of handwriting samples and Claudia spent most of the morning examining them and writing up her notes. Her findings after the first samples she had examined were unremarkable.

She had begun to feel some real concern over Kelly, whose attitude this morning seemed far less driven to find Kylie than it had been. When they met briefly after breakfast, Kelly had chattered on with enthusiasm about how interesting the classes were, and how much she was learning about the TBL teachings. She added almost as an afterthought that James was softening up, so maybe there would be progress at last.

Claudia was developing a restless desire to leave the Ark. She continued to replay in her mind every conversation she'd had, every handwriting sample she had examined, looking for some clue to Rodney's whereabouts—anything that might help them reach their objective.

It was such a small community that she was afraid if she continued to ask the same questions of too many members, it would get around and arouse suspicion. Her dissatisfaction with their failure to make any real progress was keen. But ultimately, fed up with feeling thwarted at every turn and with little expectation of get-

ting a helpful answer, Claudia decided to seek out Oka
Diehl again.

Thunderclouds had formed over the foothills, leaving
the air sticky with humidity. As Claudia opened the
back door of the Victorian, the damp hit her like a wall.
Within seconds, her hair was clinging to her neck, as wet
as if she had just stepped out of the shower.

Taking the footpath, she kept an eye out for someone
who might tell her where the Diehls lived. After reaching the cluster of outbuildings without encountering
anyone, she entered the first open door she came to and
found herself in an old-time general store filled with the
aroma of fresh-baked goods.

Her granny Arlene had taken her into such a store
as a child. There was even the same potbellied cast iron
stove in one corner. Not for the first time, it felt like she
had stepped back in time. Nostalgia assaulted her as she
made her way through shelves of paper goods and sun-
dries, coming to an old wooden counter, behind which a
man with flowing white hair sat reading a magazine.

He stood at her approach and laid the magazine on
the counter. A surreptitious glance at the magazine gave
Claudia the title: *Increasing Light.* The TBL magazine.

"Good morning, sister," the man said in a friendly
manner. "I do believe you're one of our visitors. I've
seen you in the dining hall, but we haven't gotten close
enough to speak. I'm Brother Treadwell."

At her look of confusion, his face split into a grin.
"Don't worry, you're not crazy. I think you must have
met my son, Dan Jr."

"Oh, yes. I sat at his table. So you've got three genera-
tions of Treadwells here?"

"We do. Did young Dan's kids drive you nuts?"

"Well, they were a little—shall we say, obstreperous?"

"They're spoiled brats is what they are. I don't know why he doesn't discipline them. He certainly didn't get away with that kind of nonsense when he was their age." He rubbed his hands together briskly. "Now, enough of that. What can I get for you today, missy?"

"I was hoping to stop in to see Mrs. Diehl. I'd heard she wasn't feeling well, but I don't know where she lives. I thought maybe you could tell me."

Treadwell's face became grave. "Yes, Sister Diehl isn't at all well. But I believe she's at home. You'll find her in Emmanuel. It's number six in the second row of adobes just past the dining hall. She's got a lot of cactus out front. Look for the garden gnomes, you can't miss it."

"Thank you. I'd like to take her a small gift. Do you have any idea what she might like?"

He pointed to a plate of cookies covered by a glass dome, the origin of the wonderful aroma she had noticed upon entering. "She's got a real sweet tooth, Oka does. Take her a couple of ginger biscuits, she'll be your friend forever."

"That sounds good. I'll take a half dozen." Claudia took her change purse from her pocket and asked how much she owed him.

Dan Treadwell Sr. shook his head. "We don't exchange money here. Our needs are all cared for at the Ark, spiritual and material. But if you feel so moved, you're welcome to make a contribution in the box at the church. You'll find it right by the back door."

"I'll do that," Claudia said with a smile as he carefully set out the cookies in a small box. "I've never been in a store where I wasn't allowed to pay."

"That's all right. You give Sister Diehl my well wishes, now."

*   *   *

Treadwell Sr. hadn't been joking about the Diehl house. Foot-high gnomes, and bunnies, frogs, puppies and kittens galore had turned their garden into a ceramic barnyard. A variety of potted succulents surrounded the place.

Oka Diehl herself came to the door, pushing a walker with a portable oxygen tank attached. The nasal cannula prongs were in her nose, the tubing hooked around her ears.

"What took you so long?" she wheezed, already turning and shuffling back into the room.

Claudia followed her inside, wondering whether the old woman had mixed her up with someone else. She need not have been concerned. Oka sank into a well-worn recliner and waved at her to take a seat on the couch. "Figured you'd get here eventually." She had to pause for breath every couple of words. "Sit on the couch. What's that you've got there?"

Claudia offered her the box. "Ginger biscuits. I heard you like them."

"Yes, I do. Well, thanks a bunch. Put them on the coffee table. I'll have them after lunch."

Claudia did as she was bid. "I'm a little confused. How did you know—"

"You were asking about the Powers child. You wanted to know about where she's going."

"Just idle curiosity. I'd heard about the party and—"

"Hah! I think not."

Claudia found herself grinning at the woman with the bright, intelligent eyes. She looked like one of the gnomes in her garden. "You're very perceptive, Mrs. Diehl."

"Call me Oka." She coughed appallingly for several seconds, holding a handkerchief over her mouth, spitting into it.

"Can I get you anything?" Claudia asked. "A glass of water? Medicine?"

"No, no, don't fuss. I'm a dying old woman, nothing to get in an uproar over. I'll just keel over one of these days."

"That's a pretty philosophical way to look at it."

"Young lady, I've been waiting for more than sixty years for the end of the world to come, and now I can see that *my* end is probably going to come first." She sighed. "It's all right. I'm tired; I'm ready to go. I'll just have to see them all on the other side when they get there. But that isn't what you came here for. You want to know about the temple."

"The temple?"

"That's where the Jephthah's Daughters stay. Why do you want to know about it?"

Claudia hesitated, wondering whether she should answer truthfully. She decided on a partial truth. "I'm concerned for the well-being of the children there."

Oka peered at her through narrowed eyes. "There's more to it, I can see, but never mind. They don't think I know, but I hear things. George used to be on the governing board and they still come to him for advice, even after he retired and stepped aside." She paused. "There's something going on and I don't like it. I don't like it at all."

Their eyes met and Claudia saw an intensity in Oka Diehl's that startled her. "What is it that's upset you, Oka?"

"The preparations they're making this time are for something different. Harold keeps going on about this child being the Chosen One, and I'm worried. I think he's got some crazy bee in his bonnet." She was breathing heavily, sucking the oxygen greedily through her nose.

Claudia was beginning to wonder whether she should call someone to help the old woman. "What do you think he's going to do?"

"I don't know, but I'll tell you this: George usually has to sign off on purchase orders for supplies. He has me review them. Still got good eyes, though everything else is going to the dogs. I used to be a copy editor for our publications back in the day. Always got to read the magazines before—"

Seeming to realize that she was beginning to wander, Oka pulled herself back on track. "The last supply order won't take us past another week. Why haven't they ordered more food? That's what I want to know. What are they planning?"

Claudia leaned forward. "Tell me about Jephthah's Daughters, Oka. Have you ever seen one of the girls after she's left here?"

She closed her eyes, reminiscing. "One of my best friends sent her daughter. Oh, that was long ago. Lessee, must be a good fifty years ago. We had word of Wendy now and again; but no, they don't come back. When they go, they go for life."

Claudia thought it sounded like a prison sentence, but it probably wasn't politic to say so.

Oka added, "They didn't always do it on the third birthday, though. Harold started that a while back."

"How often does it happen that a girl goes there? Is it an annual event?"

"No, no, dear. Just once in a while. Don't always have families willing to give up their daughters. Sent one off a couple of years ago. Don't know where she came from, though. Musta been one of the satellite branches, as she wasn't born here. Cute little thing just appeared here one day and we had a consecration ceremony. Then she was gone again." Her breathing was beginning to get ragged.

"I think you need to rest." Claudia pushed herself to her feet. "Just tell me one last thing. Where is the temple located?"

But Oka started coughing again. She flapped her hands, trying to get air. Claudia ran to the kitchen and found a glass on the draining board, poured her some water. When she returned to the living room, Oka's skin had a bluish tinge. The water helped a little, but it was an enormous relief when George Diehl opened the door and took over.

Claudia spent the remainder of Thursday afternoon thinking about her visit with Oka Diehl, wondering what it all meant and hoping the old woman was doing better. She hadn't really learned anything new, but her fear that something was wrong had been confirmed and left her with a deep sense of unease.

As the afternoon progressed she began to gather her things for her drive to the university campus in Riverside. She hadn't spoken to Jovanic in two days, and she missed him. By the time she opened the door of the ovenlike Jaguar and climbed in, a feeling of isolation had begun to set in and she could scarcely wait to drive through the Ark's gates and onto the highway.

Once she hit the 91 westbound she phoned him.

"How's the investigation going?" he wanted to know as soon as he had determined that she was okay.

"I've been working on my paying assignment every day—remember, that's the ostensible reason why I'm here. But I've been asking a lot of questions."

"You mean you haven't solved the case yet?" He was laughing at her, but in a nice way.

She laughed, too. "Not yet, honey. Give me another five minutes." Then she got sober. "Most of the TBL members I've met so far have been really *nice*. Even

Lynn Ryder was okay after she got over her snit. Can't blame her for being territorial, I guess."

"You should know better, babe. A lot of folks who *look* nice—"

"You have a point. Stedman *is* spying on his members."

Then she told him about Oka Diehl and her disparaging comment about Jephthah's Daughters, and their short-lived visit that afternoon. "I had a feeling she had something to say, and if she hadn't started coughing like that, I would have gotten more from her. I just know it."

"Now, don't you go bullying little old ladies."

Claudia chuckled. "Believe me, this is one little old lady who can hold her own."

The university had advertised Claudia's lecture in the local newspapers as well as the catalog that was mailed to all the students. When she arrived at the Extension building, close to a hundred people already occupied the many rows of chairs in the lecture hall—a full house.

Thanks to the many CSI/Forensic Files–type shows having made every viewer an "expert," fascination with all things forensic had exploded. She knew that only a handful of those who attended this evening's event would sign up for her fall session, a forensic document examination class, but Claudia was pleased that the introductory offering had generated so much interest.

The large theater-style projection screen had already been dropped into place; the projector was set up and ready to display her presentation. She handed the thumb drive containing her presentation to the AV tech waiting at the side of the room. He loaded the file onto his computer and gave Claudia a microphone battery pack, which she stuck in her jacket pocket, then clipped the lavalier mike to her lapel.

"Excuse me, Professor Rose, excuse me."

Claudia turned to the young woman, evidently a student, who was tapping her shoulder. About five foot four and chunky. Her pasty complexion suggested an unhealthy diet. Wire-frame glasses perched on a pug nose gave her a studious look, even with the purple streak that bisected a swath of coal black hair half hiding her face. The epitome of Goth.

"I'm afraid I can't take credit for being a professor," Claudia said. "I'm just a part-time instructor."

A strong cigarette smell clung to the young woman's black T-shirt and jeans, hung unpleasantly on her breath, mingled with coffee. "Oh. Well, I just wanted to tell you, I'm totally looking forward to hearing your lecture. I was massively excited when I heard about it. I've been interested in handwriting analysis since high school." She ducked her head as if she were shy, and a hank of stringy black hair fell over her right eye.

Claudia smiled at the girl, trying to get her to look up. "Are you enrolled in the Forensics program?"

Goth Girl nodded, still not quite meeting her eyes. She looked early twenties, but sometimes students tended to hero-worship lecturers. "I'm going for my private investigator's license. I think handwriting examination would be cool."

Having worked with several private investigator clients over a long period of time, Claudia knew they generally tended to be less conventional than most people—after all, they often had to lie and con during their investigations. But that purple hair would need to be toned down a notch if she wanted to succeed in the field. It would make her far too memorable.

"You're right," Claudia said. "Handwriting analysis is very cool. You should sign up for my fall class. I get a lot of work from PIs." She started to move around the girl. "Excuse me, but I have to get started."

"Wait!" Goth Girl grabbed her sleeve. "Uh, I wanted to ask—uh." She jerked her head around to look behind her, then let go of Claudia's jacket. "C'n I have one of your business cards? In case I have any questions later."

"Of course." Claudia took a card from her pocket and gave it to her.

Goth Girl thanked her and trotted away. She dropped into a seat on the aisle, halfway to the back of the lecture hall. Claudia watched her go, thinking that something was a little off about the meeting. She saw the girl lean over and speak briefly to the man in the next seat before facing front, waiting for the program to begin.

There was no time to examine what, if anything, might be behind the exchange. Shrugging off the feeling, Claudia took her place at the podium and got her notes from her briefcase on the shelf under the lectern.

Lecturing felt comfortable and familiar after the strangeness of the Ark. Claudia easily slipped into the zone and spoke for an hour. She covered the basics of what it meant to be a forensic handwriting examiner; showed slides to illustrate the different types of forgeries, different types of forgers; some cases she'd worked on that had been featured in the news. Afterward, there were many questions from the audience, which meant they had enjoyed the presentation. At the end of the evening when she packed up her things, Claudia was confident that her fall class would be filled.

At ten minutes past nine she was back in the Jag, on the way to the Ark. Traffic was light on the Riverside freeway and then the 60 eastbound. Within thirty minutes Claudia was taking the Hemet off-ramp. She navigated the dark, winding roads, wondering whether Kelly had been successful in getting James Miller to talk about Rodney yet.

She had no doubt that if James had any information about Rodney, Kelly would wangle it out of him. She had seen Kelly perform in court. Under her cross-examination, witnesses seemed unable to stop themselves from blabbing the most incriminating information.

There was something eerie about driving into the woods at night. Claudia found herself leaning forward over the steering wheel, as if doing so would allow her to better see the road. When a rabbit bounded in front of her headlights, she gasped and slammed on the brakes, narrowly missing the frightened animal.

At last she rounded the final curve. This time the guard waved her straight through the gate and she parked in the same parking space as before. The dashboard clock said nine fifty. Early enough to seek out the building where Rita had said Kelly was staying—*Ararat*. The name of the mountain where Noah's ark had landed. All Claudia would have to do was follow the path past the dining hall.

When she stepped from the Freon-cooled air in the car, the temperature was still in the eighties. A good twenty degrees since she'd left the Ark, but walking across the parking lot felt like slogging through maple syrup.

Claudia turned the knob on the front door and walked into silence, deafening in contrast with the chirping of crickets and croaking of frogs in the bushes outside.

A small lamp had been left on in the entry, lighting her way to the stairs. She tiptoed up to her room, noticing a strip of light under the closed door of Harold Stedman's office. She had not been told whether his sleeping quarters were attached to his office, but he appeared to be working late.

She waited until she was inside her room with the door closed before turning on the bedside light. With the windows open wide, the place had cooled appreciably. She kicked off her shoes and exchanged the Donna Karan summer suit for chocolate-colored Capri pants and a sleeveless T-shirt; pumps for running shoes.

She had already started back to the door when something stopped her. Like a cat whose whiskers are in tune with the finest changes in the environment, Claudia stood still, reading the room.

Moving on automatic, without consciously knowing why, she went to the desk and opened the laptop. Almost immediately she spotted a curly black hair about two inches long wedged between the H and J keys. Her own hair was long and auburn. Claudia's mind flicked through the various TBL members she'd met. Her memory told her that Lynn Ryder was the only one who had short black hair.

Lynn Ryder had known that Claudia would be away from the compound for several hours. The only plausible explanation for the hair being in the laptop was that Lynn had been in her room, trying to gain access to her computer.

A flash of anger burned her face and neck. Despite knowing that there had been hidden microphones at the rally, she had not expected to be spied on in her own bedroom. She thought about what was on the computer that might tip anyone off to their real mission here, besides the notes she'd typed up.

Nothing, she decided with relief. She had password protected it anyway. Unless her skills as head of security included hacking, it was unlikely that Lynn Ryder had gotten into her files.

Claudia slipped quietly out of her room and back downstairs, keeping to the edges of the risers to avoid any steps that might squeak. The hallway was dark, and she had to feel her way along by staying close to the wall. The back door opened without a sound and she stood on the porch for a moment, getting her bearings before setting out.

Her rubber-soled running shoes kept her footsteps silent on the dirt as she sped along the path next to the vegetable patch. Too bad she hadn't the foresight to bring the Maglite she kept in the Jag. But the moon and stars sparkled in the near-desert terrain, not hidden behind a haze of smog as in Greater Los Angeles, but making the sky brighter than in the city. Until she reached the avenue of tall trees where the air was far cooler, her route remained well lit.

Outside, the crickets were raucous; there must have been thousands of them. A coyote howled in the distance, probably calling its mate. Somewhere closer, the hoot of an owl startled her. Loping along at a near run, she soon closed in on a lumpy dark shadow that she knew was the dining hall. She passed it by, then the other buildings Esther had pointed out on their first day at the Ark.

In another five minutes she'd reached the four story building where Rita had said single members of TBL were housed. A plaque on its front wall read *Ararat*. She had reached the right place.

No lights showed in the windows. With a seven a.m. breakfast call, and no TV to distract them, she assumed the residents probably retired to bed early.

Inside the dimly lit lobby, a wooden board fixed to the wall reminded Claudia of her college dorm. There was a list of room numbers beside sliding slots that held the name of the occupant. She scanned the names and found only one room listed as Guest: 339.

Not wanting to risk the noise of the elevator, she took the stairs and walked along a narrow hall, silently counting down the numbers until she came to 339.

Her soft tap on the door went unanswered. Kelly

wouldn't be asleep at this hour, even if she had to get up early. She was a night owl who stayed up past midnight most nights. Hoping she had the right place, Claudia turned the knob and quietly entered the darkened room.

A dim table lamp at the end of the couch threw just enough light to illuminate the man sprawled across it. Even at the awkward angle, Claudia recognized James Miller.

Chapter 11

Kelly was on her knees, straddling Miller, who looked helpless beneath her. Her shirt was pulled up, her full breasts pressed close to his face. Her right hand was buried in his Jockeys—*Of course he would wear Jockeys and not the bikini-brief type*—his trousers pushed down almost to his knees.

What happened to "no brown polyester seduction"?

Claudia stepped inside and closed the door behind her with a snap.

James's body jerked like a marionette. Kelly twisted her head to see what he was looking at. Seeing Claudia, she pulled her hand out of his pants and climbed off. "What the hell are you doing here?"

James was on his feet before Claudia could blink, tripping in his haste to raise his trousers, tuck in his shirt, and get his belt buckled. He rushed across the room, trying to salvage any shred of dignity he might have left.

"Wait, James." Kelly was still glaring at Claudia as she spoke to him. "We're not done!"

He mumbled something incoherent and clutched at the door handle, fumbling it in his haste to get it open. His face was pale and pinched with anxiety, or maybe it was guilt. Claudia was positive he wouldn't want Stedman knowing what he had been doing in Kelly's room. She called after him, embarrassed by her own intrusion. "Please don't go, James. *I'll* go."

But he wasn't listening. Intent on escaping, he ignored them both and finally got the door open. He tore off down the hallway; a moment later Claudia could hear him clattering down the stairs.

Kelly shut the door and leaned over, hitching her bra and T-shirt into place. "Well, that was bright," she said acidly. "What are you doing here?"

Claudia colored up. "I, uh, came to see if you'd gotten anything out of James."

"Holy shit, Claudia; if you'd given me another five minutes I would have gotten every last detail. Now I'll never get anything out of him. He'll avoid me like the swine flu."

"Well, you weren't supposed to get the information that way."

"Hey, sistah, this is not the time to turn all prissy-righteous on me. If a hand job is the fastest way—"

Claudia held up her hands in protest. "I just thought sexually assaulting the man was a little over the top."

"You know what they say: The lion shall lie down with the lamb, but the lamb won't get much sleep."

"That poor guy; he didn't stand a chance." Claudia reached over and tucked in the tag sticking from the neck of Kelly's T-shirt. "Seriously, do you think he knows anything?"

"Of course he does. He knows exactly where Rodney and Kylie are, and he wants to tell, too."

"What do you mean? Did he actually say something?"

Kelly smirked. "Lawyer's instinct. Never fails."

"Oh, great. We have to rely on your psychic abilities to save the day."

"Hell, Claudia, that boy was ripe for the pickin' before you busted in."

"You were pretty ripe yourself," Claudia retorted.

But she felt bad because she knew it was true. She might have just ruined their best prospect for getting the information they needed. "I have to wonder how you managed to get such a decent, God-fearing guy like James into the sack so fast."

"Are you kidding me? They're the horniest guys ever—the more decent they are, the more horny. I finagled my way into sitting at his table; worked on him all through lunch." Kelly patted her lips in a fake yawn. "That had to be the longest meal of my life. You were damned lucky, getting a ticket out of here. How was your lecture?"

"Fine, good crowd. I talked to Joel. He said he'd check out whether the Ark has ever been visited by Children's Services."

"Good idea, though I can't say I've seen anything that remotely resembles child abuse. The kids I've seen at lunch have been well behaved." Kelly interrupted herself. "Well, unless you call it abuse to make the little guys play statues the whole time everyone's eating."

The two of them went over and sat on the couch Kelly and James had occupied. With its budget crimson velvet fabric, it might have been borrowed from a low-rent motel.

"So, lunch was boring?" Claudia prompted. "Did you get to ask anything about Rodney and Kylie?"

Kelly shook her head. "There was just no way to wrench it into the conversation without being über-obvious. That's why I got James to come up here tonight. He was actually pretty interesting to talk to, believe it or not, once he was away from all the holiness." Kelly folded her hands as if in prayer and adopted a saintly expression. "As far as I'm concerned, the well-hung mind is the sexiest part of a man."

Claudia rolled her eyes. "Save the bullshit for someone who brought their high boots and just tell me what happened."

"First, we had to wade through this entire ritual. A blessing that went on and on until the food was cold. Then someone read a text about the end-of-time days. Then we all had to discuss it. Everyone looked so freakin' happy at the idea of all life on earth being wiped out. There's something wrong with that."

Kelly waited for Claudia's nod of agreement, then continued. "Then we had to discuss in mind-numbing detail about the workday, for Chrissake. I was so bored I wanted to scream. And mind you, that was after spending the afternoon stuck in a hot-as-hell room the size of a closet being spoon-fed TBL propaganda by Methuselah. He just had to explain what horrible sinners we are."

Claudia couldn't help being amused by that vision. "You mean that sweet little old Brother Norquist?"

"It's actually not funny. I'd swear he was trying to hypnotize me. The sucky thing is, it almost worked. Between the heat in that room and his voice droning on and on like crinkly paper, I had to fight like hell not to go under. Indoctrination City, Claudia. I had to pinch my upper lip to stay awake."

This was disturbing news. "What do you think he wanted you to do?"

"He didn't come right out and say it, but the message I got was, I should first pay for some courses in how to be a good convert; then if I fit the mold, I would have a *strong* desire to turn over the rest of my worldly goods to the TBL and give my life over to the Lord so I could be saved. Only I think the Lord he was talking about is Harold Stedman." Kelly shuddered. "It was a downright unpleasant experience. But I can understand how Erin got drawn into it, as young and vulnerable as she was when they got their hooks into her. They come along and take her off the street—for which I *am* grateful, make no mistake. But they become a substitute parent; pretty soon she owes everything to them. I bet it's really tough for her to go against Stedman on this thing with Kylie. Shit. We've only got a couple more days to find her. Have you found out anything?"

Claudia brought her up to date on the handwritings she had analyzed that afternoon, and her encounter with Lynn Ryder.

"She sounds like a real charmer. I don't like this no-locks-on-the-doors business. I intend to push that chair up against the front door as soon as you leave." Kelly glowered at her. "No telling who might barge in."

Claudia ignored the shot. "What I want to know is why Ryder was trying to get into my laptop. What did she think she would find? She's taking this security chief bullshit a little too far." The memory of her privacy being breached angered her anew. Then her conscience pricked her: *I'm doing the same thing.*

But we're trying to protect a child.

"Maybe she was looking to find out why Stedman had you analyze her handwriting," Kelly suggested.

"Well, she wouldn't have found it in my damn laptop." Claudia pulled her hair into a ponytail to get some air on her neck, then fanned herself with her hand. "The most interesting thing I've found out so far: I think one of the handwritings Stedman gave me was Rodney's. It matched a sample I found in a personal file in his office."

Kelly stared at her. *"Rodney's?* He suspects Rodney of disloyalty? Maybe Stedman already knows about him taking Kylie. But that's not logical, is it?"

"I don't know, Kel. I'm still trying to figure it all out."

"After my session with Methuselah, nothing would

surprise me. These people are totally paranoid about the world outside those gates. They believe God wants them to keep separate from the rest of the great unwashed—which would include us, Grasshopper. Of course, the only way to salvation is to become one of them, yada-yada. You heard the rest of it the other night at the rally. They really believe the end of the world is upon us and they're the only ones who are going to survive." Kelly stopped for breath, looking troubled. "The creepy thing is, I got the impression that, for them, survival might actually mean death."

"Say that again?"

"I know, twisted, huh? Remember that cult in San Diego a few years back? The members all killed themselves because they believed a spaceship was coming to pick them up and save them after they 'crossed over'?"

"I remember. Weren't they called Hale-Bopp, or something?"

"That was the name of the comet the spaceship was hiding behind. The group was called Heaven's Gate."

"They killed themselves and expected that they were going to be resurrected and taken to the UFO behind the Hale-Bopp comet. Did I get it right?"

"You got it."

"And the TBL people believe something like that?"

"That's definitely the vibe I got."

Claudia puffed a breath through pursed lips. "Oh, man. That's worse than we imagined. Okay, tomorrow, *I'll* go to work on Brother Miller."

Chapter 12

Claudia hurried back along the path to the Victorian. She'd traveled the route enough times now that it was becoming familiar and the walk went quickly. Closing in on the clutch of buildings that included the dining hall, she came to a sudden halt, her eyes scanning the darkness for an indefinable something that had registered at the edge of her vision.

Then the crickets stopped chirping and the night went silent.

Instinctively, she stepped close to the nearest building, blending into the shadows cast by bright desert starlight on gray stucco walls. Unsure of what she was hiding from, she obeyed whatever primitive instinct was telling her to crouch low against the wall and stay close to the ground.

An instant later five robed figures appeared across the lawn, materializing as if from nowhere. Their faces were concealed by hoods, making it impossible to identify them in the darkness. Three of the figures hurried off in the direction of Ararat. The others went toward the Victorian.

Claudia held her body motionless, hardly daring to breathe as she followed them with her eyes. Realizing that her low vantage point might be skewing her perspective, she guessed that two of the figures were probably close to six feet tall, probably male. The others, several inches shorter, might have been either gender.

Who were these people, and where were they going, dressed as they were? Or perhaps the question should be *Where were they coming from?* Either way, judging from the furtive way they moved, Claudia was certain they would not welcome exposure.

She waited until they had vanished from sight and the crickets were stirring again before she straightened and fled to the Victorian.

The house loomed, its peaked roofs forming a shadow pyramid against the sky. The hooded figures she had seen in the darkness had unnerved her and Claudia ran the last twenty feet, dashing to the back door as if it were a safe haven.

In her absence, someone had turned off the night-light in the reception area. Concentrating on keeping quiet, she edged her way through the gloom and started up the staircase, cursing to herself when she stepped on a tread that creaked.

The strip of light still showed under Harold Stedman's door and she tiptoed along the landing. Passing his office, she released a sigh. But her relief was short-lived. The door opened, revealing Stedman, who looked as though he might have just left a meeting. *Had a monk's hooded robe covered his short-sleeve Oxford shirt and trousers a few minutes earlier?*

In his hand was an envelope similar to the one Claudia had returned to him after dinner earlier that evening. "Good evening, Sister Rose, I thought for sure you must already be asleep by now. I saw a while ago that your car was in the yard out front."

She thought she detected a mild hint of reproof in his voice. "After I got back from Riverside I went for a walk."

"You shouldn't be out so late alone." He gave her

a paternal smile. "Don't be fooled, sister. We're in the wilds up here. The woods are full of nocturnal animals, predatory animals. You should be more careful. I would be beside myself if you were attacked while you were here, in our care."

"What sort of animals might there be, Mr. Stedman?"

"Coyotes for one. When they're hungry and hunting in a pack, they're extremely dangerous. Especially in this weather, they're out there looking for food and water. We have a terrible time keeping them away from the small animals on the farm. You'd be surprised. They've run off with chickens, cats, even goats."

Claudia knew he wasn't talking about coyotes. The light from his desk lamp bled into the hallway, making his eyes dark and menacing in the shadows. He was issuing a warning; she was sure of it.

What is he afraid of me seeing? Hooded figures walking around the grounds, or something else?

She didn't plan to ask. "Thank you, Mr. Stedman. I appreciate the heads-up. Good night."

"Oh, before you go, sister . . ."

Claudia turned back and he stepped into the hallway. As he got closer she could feel waves of body heat radiating off him, invading her space. She caught a whiff of some subtle unidentifiable odor. Not cologne or aftershave. *What is it?*

"I know it's late," Stedman said. "But we haven't had a moment to talk since you got here. How is your work coming along? Have you discovered anything that would be of interest to me?"

He spoke without particular inflection, but Claudia could feel his hunger for answers. She said, "I've come across a couple of handwritings that have raised some questions. But you have to remember, Mr. Stedman, these are not absolutes that I'm able to give you; they're just markers, possibilities. You'll have to also take a careful look at any other data you might have to confirm what my findings suggest."

"Yes, yes, I fully understand that. Now, tell me what you've found so far."

"As you know, there are no names on the samples, so I can't identify them that way, but I do have some concerns about the one who mentions having been a dentist. It's not so much that there was evidence that he was directly lying, but I believe he wasn't telling everything. He was holding something back."

Stedman's expression didn't change, but she saw a flicker of interest in his eyes. Then he nodded as if her information settled something for him. "Lying by omission, is that what you mean?"

"Possibly. I'm sorry I can't be more definite, but this is not an exact science."

"All right. Anything else I should know?"

"There was a woman who I believe might have been less than truthful in what she wrote about. She mentioned an abusive husband."

"Is that everything?"

"For now, yes."

"Thank you very much, Sister Rose. I'm looking forward to reading your complete report when you're finished." He indicated the envelope in his hand. "I'll also have a few more handwritings for you to analyze tomorrow. I'm planning to be away from the Ark for a few hours in the morning, so Sister Ryder will deliver them to you after breakfast."

Claudia hesitated. She wanted to ask him whether he had sent Lynn Ryder to snoop in her room while she was away, but that was a nonstarter. She was sure he would never tell the truth about it if he had. "Will there be any other samples after that?" she asked.

"I think this will be all for now. There could be more later."

"Then, after I've examined the new samples, I'll get all my findings together and write up my report. We'll leave tomorrow afternoon. Would you like me to take those samples with me now?"

"No, I don't want them out of my hands overnight."

"All right then, I'll say good night."

He bowed his head in acknowledgment and Claudia turned away again. She knew his eyes were on her as she walked to her room. It wasn't until she reached her room that the light in the long hallway dimmed, there was a distant click, and she knew that Stedman had finally closed his door.

She quickly changed into her nightclothes and took her toiletries bag to the bathroom across the hall to prepare for bed. His sudden appearance disturbed her. Had he been waiting for her, listening for her footsteps on the stairs?

As she was brushing her teeth, she realized that she hadn't mentioned her observations about Lynn Ryder's handwriting. Why had she held back? Maybe meeting Ryder face-to-face put a different light on it. Having not met the other writers allowed her to maintain some distance.

Following Kelly's lead, she propped the desk chair under the doorknob. It might not stop someone entering, but it would at least be an early warning system.

Even though the temperature had dropped, the guest room was still too warm for sleep. She could have used a cold beer, but doubted anything of the sort would be at the Ark, even if she had known where to find it.

Earlier, on the way to the university, she'd stopped at a 7-Eleven and picked up a bottle of water, which was in her briefcase, still half full.

Claudia opened the briefcase and reached for the bottle. Tepid water wasn't exactly a substitute for Dos Equis, but it sure as hell beat being parched. Too tired to do any work, she decided to arrange her lecture notes. She got out the folder with her notes and laid it on the desk. Inside among the papers she found a torn piece of lined notebook paper that had not been there earlier.

It was a note addressed to her:

Ms. Rose,
   Don't believe all you're told. It's not the way it seems.
   There's proof of the evildoing.
   You have to find it—for my child's sake, and the others.

The note was unsigned, but what stunned her even more than the words was the handwriting, which Claudia recognized at once.

The writing was a match for the samples she had discovered at the back of Rodney Powers's file cabinet.

Even though she didn't have the other writing to compare with it side by side, there was no question in her mind. This handwriting shared the same features as the file cabinet writing. The same uphill baselines; the same jumpy, nervous rhythm.

Claudia's mind went back to the note Erin had showed her and Kelly—the one written by her husband. She was reasonably certain that the handwriting had substantial differences from the handwriting she had viewed in Rodney's office and thus was different from this one, too. Her memory of Erin's note was that the writing had been block printed with heavy pressure, unlike the one she held in her hand. In this one, the ink trail had light pressure and stayed very much on the surface of the paper. The pen tip made no impression at all. She knew that it was virtually impossible for two such different pressure patterns to be adopted by the same writer.

And then there was the matter of the different printing styles. One was block printing, the other, manuscript printing in upper- and lowercase; another reflection of two quite different personality types. Unless she was dealing with a multiple personality, which was possible but rare enough to make the possibility unlikely, Claudia would have to look elsewhere for answers.

Had she made an error in assuming that the writing in the file cabinet and the sample that Stedman had given her were Rodney Powers's? It seemed unlikely, considering the content of the note.

She read it again, asking herself what the note might mean: *the evildoing.*

The "my child" had to be Kylie. What the hell was going on here? This was a far more serious accusation than sending a child off to what amounted to a convent.

What were the chances of someone trying to trick Claudia into believing the note was from Rodney? *Who? Lynn Ryder? For what purpose?*

Then it struck Claudia that the more troubling question was, how had the note found its way into her briefcase? Had Ryder come to her room while Claudia was out barging in on James Miller's assignation with Kelly? No, that didn't work. Why put it in the briefcase, rather than leaving it out in the open for her to find?

The answer arrived in a flash of memory. *Goth Girl with the purple hair.* She had been a decoy, distracting Claudia while the note writer—whoever it was—had slipped the paper into her briefcase. She remembered that the briefcase had been on a shelf under the lectern while she spoke with the AV guy. Her back had been turned to it for at least four or five minutes. She'd quickly stuffed her papers back into the folder after her lecture without paying much attention. She might not have found this note at all if she hadn't decided to organize her papers tonight.

Goth Girl had detained her with a question, then abruptly let her go. Maybe she had received a signal from a cohort that he or she had succeeded in placing the note in the briefcase. Claudia tried to recall the man seated next to the girl, but she hadn't gotten a strong impression of his appearance. Distracted by preparations for opening the class, she had not paid enough attention and was unable to visualize anything about the man.

Goth Girl had leaned over to speak to him. *Was he the one who had left the note? Could it have been Rodney?* The possibility both excited and angered her. So close, yet still elusive.

She pulled the quilt off the bed and draped it over the back of the desk chair, wondering what she ought to do about the note. It referred to proof of something evil going on at the Ark. Her stomach clenched. *All the more reason to find Kylie.*

Before getting into bed, she slipped the note back into her briefcase, snapped it shut and spun the combination lock, which she rarely had reason to use, then stood it on the floor right beside her. Switching off the lamp, she thought, *It's going to be a very long night.*

Chapter 13

The crowded breakfast room was filled with the noise of TBLers chattering. Having slept as little as she'd expected, and fitfully when she did, Claudia rose grumpy and out of sorts. Before parting at Kelly's room the previous evening, they had agreed that Claudia would make her move on James Miller after breakfast.

The conundrum she faced about the odd note and its writer had not miraculously solved itself overnight, nor did anything fall into place when she rethought it again this morning. The note was still locked safely in her briefcase.

She was itching to tell Kelly about it, but there had been no opportunity to speak privately.

A familiar face came out of the crowd. "Sister Rose, come and sit with us!"

"Esther!" Claudia was pleased to see their young guide.

A welcoming smile lit the girl's face, but the woman walking with her gave her a sharp poke in the ribs and spoke into her ear. Esther's smile faded. Wordlessly, she ducked her head and hurried off toward the kitchen.

What was that about?

"Welcome to the Ark, Sister Rose. I'm Martha Elkins, Esther's mother." The woman faced Claudia with a cool glance that was at odd with her words. She looked young to have a daughter Esther's age—no more than thirty, Claudia guessed. Her skin was smooth, unflawed. Glossy brown hair, pulled back from her face.

"You have a lovely daughter, Mrs. Elkins. She was a great tour guide when we arrived."

"Well, today she's got work to do, so she won't be available to take you around."

Claudia blinked in surprise. The woman's taciturn manner didn't fit with the smiles that had greeted her up until now. She pulled out a chair, wondering what was behind Martha Elkins's sour expression. "Do you mind if I sit here?" Claudia asked.

"Suit yourself, there's a place if you want it." Then Esther's mother relented. "I'll save your seat for you. Go on up and get what you want." She indicated a buffet line where the members were dishing up plates of sausage, eggs, and pancakes. Claudia took her place in line, looking for lighter fare. Like Kelly, she was a night owl who found it hard to face a big breakfast so early in the morning.

She spotted Kelly, already seated across the room, chatting with a young man Claudia had seen around. Kelly always went for younger men, and they were usually happy to oblige.

Claudia carried her plate of fruit and yogurt back to the table where Martha Elkins had saved her seat as she'd promised. The elder in charge of the table turned out to be Esther's father. He looked substantially older than his wife, but a good match with his unsmiling demeanor. Esther must have gotten her sunny nature elsewhere.

Brother Elkins acknowledged Claudia with a nod and welcomed her to the table. Asking everyone to bow their heads, he launched into a blessing so lengthy that Claudia was glad she had selected cold foods. When they had echoed his Amen, Elkins picked on a boy at the end of the table, assigning him to read a Bible verse and a

TBL-authored article about the importance of abstaining from sins of the flesh.

Poor kid.

The boy cleared his throat several times through the reading, his face flaming with embarrassment. He stumbled through phrases like "anal sex" and "self-abuse," which the article stated were ungodly practices strictly forbidden to TBL members, including married couples. Apparently the governing board of TBL had appointed themselves the Bedroom Police.

Claudia noticed that the others at the table ate fast, with their heads down, shoveling food into their mouths as if eating their last meal. She wasn't sure whether it was more due to the subject matter or that Brother Elkins began encouraging them to finish their meal and get ready to go to their work assignments.

Seeing that there would not be much time for her to ask questions, Claudia jumped into the first lull in the conversation. "Esther was telling us yesterday about a little girl who's been chosen for a special program. It sounded really interesting."

The woman seated next to her perked up. "That would be Erin and Rod Powers's child, little Kylie." She had a round face that didn't suit the Buster Brown haircut many of the women at the Ark seemed to favor. She'd introduced herself simply as Mary.

"Esther needs to keep her lip buttoned," said Martha Elkins. "She's turning into a little gossip."

"It wasn't like that," Claudia said quickly, not wanting Esther to get in trouble. "My friend and I were asking her about young children at the Ark, that's all. We hadn't seen many here, and we were just curious."

Mary said, "Kylie's a beautiful child. Very special."

A woman across the table nodded. "It's a shame she and Sister Powers didn't bond better."

Claudia looked at her in surprise. "Didn't bond? What do you mean?"

"I think Erin wanted a baby too badly; she needed too much from her. Sister Powers—Erin—didn't have a good family of her own to raise her properly, you see." The woman leaned forward as if she could hardly wait to spill what she knew. "That's why having the baby was so important to her. The sad thing of it is, when Kylie was born, she wasn't the kind of baby that wanted to be picked up and cuddled all the time. Not all babies do, you know. At least, Kylie didn't want to be held by her mother. Different story with Rod, though. He was always—"

"Now who's gossiping?" Martha Elkins interrupted sharply. "Erin's a fine mother."

"Of course she is, Sister Elkins," the woman said in a mild tone. "I'm not saying she isn't, but you do have to admit that the child is closer to her father."

Brother Elkins rose and frowned down at them all. "Brothers and sisters, it's time we got to work. If you have time to sit around, talking idly about our brethren who aren't present, then perhaps you need some extra duties added to your load."

Everyone stood up and began hurrying to disperse.

"Are you taken care of, sister?" Brother Elkins said to Claudia, who was scanning the room for James Miller. "Do you know where you're meant to go?"

"Yes, thank you. Mr. Stedman has something for me to do." She spotted James walking toward the door, chatting with another man. She excused herself and left Brother Elkins staring after her.

By the time she caught up with him, Miller was alone and moving fast along the path in the direction of the Victorian.

Claudia sped after him. "Mr. Miller, James. Could I speak with you, please?"

He turned back, the beginnings of a smile on his lips. She saw in his eyes, and the way he blanched, the instant he recognized her from the evening before in Kelly's room. His shoulders tensed and he started to hurry away. "I don't have time to talk. I have to get to the office. I have a project—"

"Wait, please, James, I promise not to take long. It's really important."

"I don't know you. I have nothing to say to you that won't get me into trouble."

He wore a long-sleeve white dress shirt and tie, a crew-neck T-shirt peeking out from the neck. It must have been uncomfortably warm and gave him the look of a nerd. The navy blue serge trousers and brown dress shoes didn't help, either. The only thing missing was a plastic pocket protector.

His panicked look made her feel sorry for him, but for Kylie's sake, Claudia hardened her heart. She said matter-of-factly, "Maybe you'd rather say it to Brother Stedman."

James stopped short at that and gave her deer-in-headlights fear. "What is it you want from me?"

"Do you think we could we find someplace private where we can talk for a moment? Please?"

His eyes darted left and right, seeking a way of escape. Not finding one, his shoulders sagged. His voice held defeat as he told her to follow him.

He left the dirt path, Claudia trailing, and headed through the trees about fifty feet to a small glade. They were only a hundred feet from the dining hall, but were well hidden here from curious eyes and ears.

James turned to her and held out his hands in entreaty. "If you report me, I'll be excommunicated. Look,

I know I've committed a grievous sin, but at least if you give me a chance to confess it myself, it won't be—"

"James, stop! You don't have to worry; I'm not going to say anything to Stedman or anyone else. I really don't care who you have sex with."

"We didn't—it wasn't—we just—"

"Yes, I could see what you didn't do. Anyway, I don't care. It's your business and Kelly's, not mine. I'm not the sex police."

A tall hedge stretched in both directions as far as Claudia could see, and appeared to run along the borders of the property. The branches had woven around and through the dull metal of a chain link fence. No one would be able to enter or leave the Ark that way.

James backed up against the hedge as if he needed the protection of something solid behind him. He gripped his arms across his chest and stared at her. "Well—what is it you want with me?"

"I'd like you to tell me what you know about Rodney Powers's whereabouts." She felt like a detective, asking him like that. He had no obligation to answer, of course, but if he refused to cooperate, there was still the threat of blowing the whistle on him for hooking up with a nonmember. For hooking up at all.

James's face drained of color. "Rodney's—wait a minute—you know about Rod? How do you know—?"

She answered his question with another. "Do you know where he is?"

"I don't, uh . . . I, uh . . ."

Claudia spoke gently, as if he were a frightened animal who might startle away if she moved too fast. "I know you don't want to lie, James. What would Brother Stedman have to say about that?"

He licked his lips nervously, unfolded his arms and stuck his hands in his pockets. "Why do you want to know about Rod? Who are you two really? And what are you *doing* here?"

"We're looking for Rod. That's what we're doing here. You're the person he's closest to, so you're the most likely person to know where he is."

"Did Sister Ryder put you up to this?"

"Lynn Ryder? Why would you think that?"

"She knows everything that's going on around here."

"Electronic monitoring," Claudia said, half to herself. "They're watching and listening to everything?"

"Anything she knows, *they* know."

"Who do you mean, 'they'?"

James caught himself. "I don't mean anything. I don't know what I'm saying. I haven't had enough sleep, I . . ."

"I know you're under a lot of stress. You're helping Rod and I expect the elders wouldn't approve if they knew you were taking sides between a husband and wife. That must be difficult for you. I know you want to do the right thing, James. Look, little Kylie needs her mother. *Please* tell me where he's taken her."

James drew a sharp breath, and in that moment Claudia caught a glimpse of the inner turmoil that was tearing him apart. She willed him to take the relief valve she was offering him in sharing his secret.

But he shook his head slowly. "They're in a safe place. There's nothing to worry about."

"It's not right to take a child away from her mother, James. Think how it is for Kylie right now, in a strange place with nothing familiar to her; not having her mother to care for her. Do you really believe it's the right thing to send a child of her age into Jephthah's Daughters? She's about to turn three. Only three years old!" As she spoke, Claudia was reminded once again of the words in the note she'd received: *It's not the way it seems.*

James looked down at his shoes. He began picking at a scab on his arm, concentrating on it as if it offered him a way out of the conversation. Finally, he mumbled, "I have to go back. I have to go to work." But he made no move to leave.

"James, do those children ever come back from the program? What happens to them there?"

His head jerked up. *"What are you up to?* Are you from the governmnet?"

"No, we have personal reasons for needing to know."

"What personal reasons? What's going on? I asked you before, I'll ask you again: Did Sister Ryder put you up to this?"

"No, of course not. I'm sorry I can't tell you more right now, but if you help me, you'll understand later."

"Kelly." He choked on her name. "She was using me, wasn't she? She was just using me to find out . . ."

"I'm sorry, James. I know she didn't intend to hurt you."

His eyes narrowed. "I should have guessed that someone like her wouldn't be interested in someone like me."

Exasperation made Claudia snap at him. "Good God, James—*interested in you?* What did you expect from a woman you've known for little bits of a couple of days?"

Color flooded his face. "Maybe you've guessed, I don't have a whole lot of experience with women."

"That's your choice, isn't it? Yet, you stay here and follow the TBL rules."

"The rules are important; they keep us clean. What I did with Kelly was filthy, evil. I have to go to the governing board and confess. I deserve whatever they decide to do to me."

"James, how old are you? Thirty-eight? Forty? Have you ever had sex? How long are you going to let these men tell you what to do?"

"They're teaching us the Lord's will."

From where Claudia stood, she could see that his entire body was trembling so hard he was almost vibrating. He darted a look at her, but glanced away quickly again. "You shouldn't meddle here, sister. You don't know what you're doing."

"That sounds almost like a threat. Is that what you meant it to be?"

"No. I don't know. You should leave right away. It's not wise to engage in independent thinking."

"Maybe a little independent thinking is exactly what's needed right now, James."

"The elders know what's best for us."

It's not the way it seems.

"Is that why you're helping Rodney hide Kylie until the time comes for her to be symbolically sacrificed? Even though her mother has changed her mind, and doesn't want her to go?"

Abruptly, James turned and stumbled a few feet away to a clump of bushes, where he fell to his knees and vomited. He stayed there, hunched over, retching until he had emptied his stomach. Then he retched some more until there was nothing to bring up.

Claudia found some crumpled Kleenex in her pocket. She went over and passed it to him over his shoulder. Bile rose in her own throat as the strong odor of regurgitated sausage forced her to back away. "Think about it, James," she pleaded. "Think about little Kylie. If you don't help, you'll become a part of whatever's going to happen to her. We're talking about a baby, here." Her voice was unsteady with emotion.

James wiped his mouth with the back of a trembling hand. "I can't—I can't . . ." Tears began streaming down his face. "Don't ask me . . ." He faltered, sobbing. "I'm being torn into a thousand pieces."

With a low moan, he bolted off, running in a ragged zigzag back the way they had come.

Chapter 14

Claudia was back at Rodney Powers's desk by eight. She still hadn't talked to Kelly, and she badly wanted to tell her about the note in her briefcase and her encounter with James Miller. Later, she would have to find an excuse to leave the Ark and call Jovanic. But for now, while it was still blessedly cool in the little office, she would finish up her work for Harold Stedman.

Maybe James's conscience would get the better of him and he would decide to tell her whatever it was that he knew before she and Kelly left the Ark in a few hours.

What if he confessed to the governing board? That would not help them in their quest to find Kylie before the ceremony. Claudia felt deeply frustrated, as if the information had been within her grasp when James broke down.

Lynn Ryder stopped by to bring her the new envelope from Stedman. Keeping in mind what James had said about the security chief knowing everything, Claudia kept her conversation bland. She would have preferred to ask what the hell Ryder had been doing in her room, going through her things. But there was no point in tipping her hand.

"Will you be working in here all day, Sister Rose?" Ryder asked.

"I don't know right now. It depends on how much

work Mr. Stedman has for me. Why? Do I need to account for my whereabouts?"

Ryder gave her a strange look. "No, of course not. Brother Stedman suggested that if you finished early, you might want to attend a class."

"I don't think so. I'll have plenty to keep me busy for a while, and after that, I'll probably make a trip into town. And by the way, we'll be leaving for home tomorrow morning."

"Well, okay then. If you change your mind about the class, just let Rita know."

Claudia forced a smile. "I won't. Thanks anyway."

When Lynn Ryder left, Claudia found a letter opener in the desk drawer and used it to open the envelope. She tipped the new set of handwriting samples out onto the desk and shuffled through them, getting an overview of each sample before beginning the actual task of analysis.

The third one made her jaw drop. Block-printed writing that matched the note Erin had showed them at Kelly's condo, she was certain of it. Her memory of the block-printed writing with the scrawled signature, "Rod," was quite clear.

So, if *this* was Rodney's handwriting, then who had left the note in her briefcase, which was not the same writer?

It's not the way it seems.

Claudia shoved the samples into the envelope and pushed her chair back from the desk. She strode out of the purchasing agent's office in search of Rita the office assistant and found her at one of the desks in the main office, underlining text in a TBL magazine.

Rita looked up with a smile. "Good morning, sister. I missed you at breakfast. Did you enjoy it?"

"Yes, thank you, breakfast was fine. Rita, I need you to tell me where I can find Kelly. Now, please."

Rita's face closed up. She returned her gaze to the computer monitor. "Sister Kelly is in class this morning; I'm afraid she can't be disturbed."

"She never said anything about going to a class."

"It was arranged after breakfast. She said she wanted to learn more about how the Temple of Brighter Light got started, so it was arranged for her to have a private session."

"Didn't she already take that class with Mr. Norquist?"

"I don't think so, sister. Anyway, she'll be busy for the next few hours. They'll break for lunch."

Claudia put iron into her tone, not caring how demanding she might sound. "I need to see her now."

Rita was shaking her head. "Once the doors are closed, they can't be opened until the lunch break at noon."

"I need you to tell me where to find her. It's critical that I speak to her."

"I'm telling you, Sister Claudia, the doors are locked and—"

"What do you mean? You told me there are no locks here."

"Did I?" Rita looked flustered. "Oh, I didn't mean it literally. Of course there are some locks. The classrooms . . ."

"The classrooms are locked but there are no locks on private sleeping rooms? What's wrong with that picture?" Claudia leaned her hands on the desk, getting into Rita's face. "Tell me where I can find Kelly, Rita. *Where* is the classroom?"

Rita sighed, a gusty breath that sounded like irritation. Maybe she just didn't know what to do with someone who thought independently. "I'm not sure it will do any good, sister, but come with me. If you're sure it's that serious, I'll take you over there."

*   *   *

Rita had been telling the truth. The door to the class-room was locked, and no one was answering Claudia's knock. Leaving her at the door, Rita hurried away. Claudia knocked harder, all her pent-up feelings channeled into the heel of her hand as it slammed against the door. *Bang. Bang. Bang.* The door rattled against her hand.

"What in the good Lord's name is going on here?"

She heard the voice, foghorn deep, come from inside. Then the turn of a key and the door opened on a man she hadn't seen before: a dark-skinned giant of a man. Six five, three-fifty, Claudia guessed, looking up at the narrowed eyes, annoyed features. He wore a shirt and tie similar to James's; a name badge on the pocket read "Jermaine Johnson."

"Why are you making that racket?" he demanded. "Didn't anybody tell you—"

"I'm sorry to interrupt your class, but I have to see Kelly Brennan right now. It's an emergency." She tried to look behind him, but his bulk effectively blocked her view.

The man tried to stare her down, but Claudia stared right back at him, refusing to be intimidated by his size or his antagonistic glare. When he understood that she wasn't going away he told her to wait and shut the door in her face with some force. She heard the turn of the key in the lock.

After several minutes, Claudia was preparing to start banging again when the door opened once more, and Kelly stood there, alone. Something about her eyes—

"Kelly, are you okay? We have to go. I've got to talk to you. A bunch of stuff has happened . . . come on."

Kelly just stared back at her with that odd, empty look. "You shouldn't be interrupting, Claudia. I have to go back inside. I'm in class."

"Kelly! Snap out of it!" Claudia grabbed her friend's shoulders and shook her, but that was about as effective as shaking a dishrag.

Kelly twitched out of her grasp. "Don't bother me while I'm in class."

Before she could react, Kelly slipped back inside and closed the door.

Chapter 15

Claudia stood there staring, the closed door challenging her. *Okay, what now?* Kelly in what appeared to be a hypnotic trance, James throwing up breakfast because of something he knew, an anonymous note telling her to look for proof of something. *Proof of what?* The pounding in her head felt like her fists banging on the door. She hurried back to the Victorian and found Rita back at the computer.

"Did you find your friend?" Rita asked.

"Yes." *And she's either hypnotized or drugged, or both.* "I have to go into town. I need to get some medicine."

Rita looked at her with concern. "Oh dear, what's wrong, Sister Claudia? I'm sure we've got whatever you need here."

"It's a prescription," Claudia lied. "I won't be long." Without waiting for a reply, she ran up to her room, grabbed her briefcase, and headed for the Jag.

Claudia hooked her Bluetooth headset over her ear. As soon as she had cleared the hills and had a sufficient number of reception bars on her cell phone, she called Jovanic and told him everything.

He listened until she was through but he didn't comment on what she'd said. Instead, he surprised her.

"After we talked last night I called a buddy of mine, a

federal agent," Jovanic said. "You're gonna have to get out of there right away."

"Why? What's going on?"

"I asked if he'd heard of the Temple of Brighter Light or Harold Stedman." Long silence while Claudia waited, her nerves beginning to twang. "What I'm going to tell you has got to stay right here. If anything gets back, they'll be glad to hand this guy his ass on a stick. This information is absolutely confidential. You can't repeat it to *anyone*, including Kelly."

"Honey, in her present condition I wouldn't tell her what's for lunch."

"Claudia, I'm dead serious. Give me your word to keep it to yourself."

Her mind was racing, already trying to guess what she might hear. The migraine continued to hammer and she pulled off to the side of the road, leaving the engine running with the AC pointed at her face. "Of course you've got my word, Joel. Now, would you tell me!"

"My buddy did some digging around. The church and Stedman both have been on the bureau's radar for quite some time."

"For what reason?"

"He couldn't tell me that."

"So they're under FBI watch, but we don't know why?"

"That's about it. You know the Feds, it could be any-thing—Homegrown terrorists. Money laundering. Kid-napping. You choose."

Claudia massaged her neck, willing the pounding be-hind her right eye to stop. "Okay, so the Feds are 'look-ing at them.' What about the note I got? It claims there's proof of *something* going on at the Ark. Do you think that might be what the Feds are investigating?"

"Could be. But it could also be intended as a decoy to throw you off track."

"If Rodney didn't put the note in my briefcase, who else would have done it? Stedman *invited* me to the Ark. And if Rodney did do it, why would he want to throw me off track? And what about the difference in the handwriting on the note in my briefcase and the one Erin showed us?"

"We need to get that note you found to the Feds. They can check it for prints."

"Joel, how long has this investigation been going on?"

"A couple of years. It's about to come to a head, which means it's absolutely vital that it doesn't get fucked up now."

"That's it? This is what you wanted me to keep confidential? This cult is being investigated but we don't know why? That's pretty weak."

Jovanic was silent and Claudia prepared for what she deduced was going to be the real news.

"There *is* something more. But . . ."

"I've already told you, you've got my word. If you don't trust that, then don't tell me."

"You know I trust you completely. It's just a twitchy situation." He sounded annoyed. "When my buddy started putting out feelers, it set off an alert. He was contacted by the case agent in charge of the investigation, who wanted to know exactly who was asking about Stedman and the group, and exactly why they wanted to know. So when my buddy told him I was LAPD, but was asking unofficially, the case agent called me directly. I had to explain to him what you and Kelly were doing at the TBL compound." Jovanic went silent, and Claudia's intuition started pinging again, but she never guessed what he told her next.

"The Feds have an operative at the Ark, in deep cover."

"What?"

"The only reason he clued me in was because my guy vouched for me. Undercover operations are extremely sensitive. They can't risk a *whisper* of it getting out—not only to safeguard the operation, but as you can imagine, for the safety of the operative." Jovanic gave a short laugh. "You know those federal agents are so tough, they never break a sweat. But when this guy heard what you were doing, he freaked; said your presence could put his operation in jeopardy. You and Kelly have to get out immediately and leave it to the professionals."

Claudia took a swig of water from the bottle she'd brought with her and swallowed a couple of extra-strength aspirin. "But Joel, what about the 'proof' my note mentioned?"

"That's something you'll have to leave to the Feds, babe."

"Maybe the person who left me the note will make contact again and tell me what I'm supposed to know there's proof of." She watched a small lizard run into the road, hesitate, then turn back, scurrying onto the dirt berm. "The whole thing is so hard to fathom: there's the first set of samples with the handwritings that match—the one Stedman gave me with the jumpy printing, plus the one I found at the back of Rod's file cabinet. But neither of those matched the writing Erin showed us. Then there's the note in my briefcase that apparently I'm supposed to *assume* came from Rod because of what it says about 'my child,' but that also doesn't match the one Erin showed us, nor either of the other two. Then there's the sample in the other envelope that *does* match Erin's note. Jeez, no wonder I have a headache."

"Bring the note home with you; we'll have to turn it over to the case agent."

A spurt of professional jealousy. "So he can give it

to *their* handwriting experts. Do they have samples to compare it to?"

"That's not our problem. I just want you out of there before things get ugly. The investigation is on the verge of breaking wide open. I don't want you involved when that happens."

"I know, honey. You never want me involved, and it just seems to happen anyway. I guess graphology can be as dangerous as police work, huh?" It was easy to joke about it from a distance.

"Don't try to distract me, Grapho Lady. How soon can you get your stuff packed up and get out of there?"

Claudia felt a tightening in her gut. "I don't know what to do about Kelly. God only knows what they've done to her. I don't think it was just hypnosis. I think she was drugged; her pupils were enormous. How am I going to get her out of there?"

"Do you want me to come and—"

"No, Joel. Thanks, but I'll think of something." Claudia mentally calculated the time she would need. "According to Rita, she'll be released from the class for the noon meal. I'll go pack our stuff and get ready. We'll leave as soon as I can get her in the car. Too bad Stedman has insisted on taking back all the handwriting samples. I still have the set I got from Lynn Ryder today. They're in my briefcase."

"Just leave them at the Ark," Jovanic said impatiently. "Leave it to the undercover agent on site. The guy in charge can alert him. You have to get out of there."

Claudia said goodbye, making a promise to call him when she and Kelly were on the way home. She made a U-turn and drove back to the Ark with misgivings that grew stronger with every mile.

Chapter 16

Avoiding the front steps to the Victorian, Claudia took the side path that led to the back of the house.

The women were out working in the fields. One of them looked up and waved—Karen Harrison. The newest recruit had received a tough work assignment.

Maybe it's a test of her commitment, Claudia thought as she left the path and made her way across rows of string beans and eggplant, careful to avoid stepping in the plants. Karen Harrison had returned her attention to the tomatoes she was inspecting and carefully placing in a tray. She did not look up when Claudia called her name.

"Karen," Claudia spoke louder. "Could I speak with you?"

The woman looked up then. "I'm Sister Harrison now," she said. Her eyes had the same unfocused quality she'd seen in Kelly's.

"Were you in a class with Ke—Sister Brennan this morning?"

Karen tipped her head to the side. "Sister Brennan? I think so. Oh, yes, she was the disruptive one." She went back to searching the tomato vines for the fruit she wanted.

"What do you mean, disruptive?" Claudia asked, though she wasn't surprised. The Kelly she knew would find it hard to just sit quietly and listen to the TBL teachings without debating anything she disagreed with.

Karen glanced up again, looking anxious. "Kept arguing with Brother Johnson. He had to escort her out."

"Do you know where he took her?"

"Reeducation room."

What the hell is the reeducation room? Was that where Kelly had been drugged? Drugging a guest for being "disruptive" had to be against some law. The FBI might be interested in that bit of information.

"Do you know where the reeducation room is?" Claudia asked her.

Karen shrugged, shook her head.

The Ararat building seemed deserted. Claudia checked her watch: eleven twenty-five. The occupants would still be at their work assignments. If she moved fast, there should be enough time to get Kelly's belongings packed up before she was released for lunch. She hurried to the four-story building and took the elevator to the third floor. As there was no lock on the apartment doors, she went straight inside number 339.

The room had a Murphy bed that could be stored in the wall opposite the couch. Kelly had left the bed down, as if she'd gone out that morning in a rush.

There was a kitchenette with a bar fridge that had an electric hot plate on top and a small wooden table with two chairs. With all meals served in the dining hall, there wasn't much point in giving space to food storage and preparation. One more means of controlling the members, it seemed—keep them where they could be seen most of the time.

On one wall of the living room was a set of framed colored prints that Claudia had been too preoccupied to notice the night before when she had burst in on Kelly and James. She studied them now. The first was a skyscape: dark, towering storm clouds, forked lightning slamming into the earth. The second could have been taken from Hieronymus Bosch's *Last Judgment:* a scene of destruction—floods, fires, the earth torn open by a monstrous earthquake. Human figures tortured by repulsive black-winged creatures with pitchforks.

The third print, a family scene, was the polar opposite of the others and portrayed a multigeneration family in soft pastels. The children played catch with a golden retriever while parents and grandparents looked on from a background of lush, brilliantly colored plants. A soft gold halo gave the scene an otherworldly glow. Everyone in the picture wore a happy smile. *Rockwellesque. Or should that be Rockwellian? Orwellian was more like it.*

Claudia sank down on the couch, taking a moment to center her thoughts. It was clear to her that the paintings were grouped in that sequence to convey a message. The earth and everyone on it is going to be destroyed except Temple of Brighter Light members who get to go someplace else and live happily ever after. As long as they do what the governing board tells them to, of course. No independent thinking here.

The message conveyed by the pictures disturbed her. She got up and turned her back on them, starting on the task she had come to Kelly's room to complete.

Kelly's suitcase was in the closet. She unzipped it and opened it on the floor. The shorts and T-shirt from the evening before were strewn across the unmade bed. Claudia scooped them up, along with lingerie and a nightgown, and tossed them into the suitcase, then started pulling garments off hangers. Kelly wasn't one to travel light. She'd brought enough outfits to last a week, and shoes to match.

Claudia checked her watch again. Eleven fifty. She emptied the medicine cabinet, stuffing hair spray, toothpaste, and mouthwash into the toiletries bag; added the makeup from the vanity.

Should she wait here in case Kelly came to her room before going to the dining hall? Knowing her friend, she would want to freshen up before the midday meal. Or should she go to the classroom and try to nab her as she walked out the door? *Ten minutes, I'll give it ten minutes.*

She tossed the toiletries bag into the suitcase and zipped it up. Once she got hold of Kelly, they would have to return to her room and get her bag. Claudia still needed to pack her own things.

Too impatient to wait. Downstairs and out the front door. She would return later for the suitcase.

Twenty feet from the dining hall entrance, she recognized the back of Kelly's blond head through the crowd. She was at the front of the line and had disappeared inside before Claudia could reach her.

Excusing herself, Claudia pressed her way past the queue of TBLers waiting to get into the dining hall. As she entered the room she saw Lynn Ryder headed her way. Ignoring the security chief, she forged ahead.

"Kelly!"

Kelly either failed to hear, or ignored Claudia's attempts to get her attention, and seated herself next to Harold Stedman, who had returned from his early morning absence. The other governing board members were filtering in and taking their places at the head table. Claudia noted that two of them were quite tall. She tried to picture them in dark, hooded robes, and decided they might well have been among those mysterious figures that had alarmed her the previous evening.

"Sister Rose." Lynn Ryder's voice over her shoulder.

Claudia turned, not bothering to pretend to be polite. "What do you want?"

Ryder faltered; her eyes narrowed. "I just wondered when we could have that chat about handwriting."

"I don't know. This isn't a good time." Claudia left her standing there and moved toward the head table. Handwriting was the last thing she wanted to think about right now.

Stedman indicated the empty chair at his other side. "Good afternoon, Sister Rose, please join us."

Claudia stayed where she was on her side of the table. "I need to take Kelly and leave right now. We have an emergency."

Kelly was huddled over her plate, protecting her food like a jailed felon. She glanced up for a moment, then returned to the meal before her, attacking it as if she were starving.

"An emergency?" Stedman repeated. "Is there anything we can do to help?"

Claudia had already decided to give him a near truth. "My boyfriend has been ill. He's taken a turn for the worse and needs me at home right away."

Stedman's face wore a sympathetic expression. "I'm very sorry to hear that, sister. We'll certainly pray for his recovery, and if there's anything we can do—"

Claudia shook her head and thanked him. "Kelly, we need to go."

Kelly glanced up again. "Can't you see I'm eating?"

Even in that brief moment, Claudia could see that the vacant look hadn't left her. If she ever got her out of here, Kelly would need a month in therapy to work this through. "We need to go *now*. We can stop at a drive-thru on the way home."

"I'm hungry now."

Claudia glared at Stedman. "What's going on? Why is she behaving this way? What did they do to her in that class?"

Harold Stedman looked back at her, eyebrows arched in surprise. "I'm not sure what you mean. Sister Brennan requested to learn more about the end-of-times and the new order, so room was made for her in that class." He touched Kelly's hand and she stopped eating to look at him. "No one has done anything to her. Have they, sister?"

Her cloudy blue eyes met his and locked on them. She shook her head and spoke, still looking at Stedman. "No one has done anything to me. I'm fine. For heaven's sake, sit down, Claudia; have some lunch, it's really good."

Stedman's round face held nothing more than compassion. "Sister Rose, if you want to leave and go take care of your boyfriend, why don't you go ahead. Sister Brennan will stay here with us. We'll bring her to our next rally on Wednesday when we return to the Valley."

"She has to be in court on Monday," Claudia said, pulling the excuse out of the air. She felt an impulse to grab Kelly and drag her away from Stedman's influence, but she was beginning to doubt her ability to get Kelly to leave with her at all. She considered the possibility that Kelly might be faking her behavior for some reason, but those dilated eyes were too real. The wide, dark pupils had all but blotted out the blue irises.

"I'll wait." Claudia moved around the table and took the seat Stedman had offered her, feeling like Alice joining the Mad Hatter's tea party. Someone slid a plate in front of her: enchiladas covered in red sauce, a mound of rice, refried beans, corn cake. Heavy food for the middle of the day. She picked at it, not hungry, not wanting to get sleepy on all the starchy carbs and lose her edge when Kelly finally decided she was ready to go.

For the first ten minutes the meal progressed with little conversation. Claudia couldn't help glancing around the dining hall, wondering which member might be the FBI operative. Had she met him yet? Did Stedman guess there was a mole in his organization? Was that why he had hired her—to help him smoke out the mole?

She thought back on what she had said to him about the problematic handwriting samples—the ones whose truthfulness she had questioned. She had told him that the man who claimed to be a dentist had been withholding information. Was the information he was withholding that he was really an FBI operative?

Oh God, please don't let it be him.

A young man brought Harold Stedman a portable microphone. Stedman rose and called for the members' attention. Instantly, there was the clatter of forks being laid on plates. All eyes turned in his direction.

Stedman's voice as he spoke into the microphone was somber. "Brothers and sisters, I regret to inform you that I must make an unfortunate announcement. You may have noticed that Brother John Talbot is not with us today." He took a pair of reading glasses from his pocket and donned them, then picked up a letter-sized envelope on the table beside his plate. Removing a sheet of paper and unfolding it, he began to read.

"'The judicial commission of the governing board has met and counseled John Talbot for behavior that will not be tolerated by the Temple of Brighter Light. After several such meetings, this person was deemed unrepentant and therefore he has been excommunicated.'"

An audible gasp went through the room. Claudia heard someone break out in sobs. She caught sight of James Miller at the head of his table. He looked stricken.

Stedman continued reading.

"'This individual has been put outside the gates of the Ark and will not be readmitted for any reason. His

name no longer means anything to us. Members are not
to speak to him or aid him in any way. He is no longer
one of us. Anyone who gives this person assistance will
be considered just like him and the same punishment
will be meted out.

"'Curiosity about this person's misdeeds is inappropriate and you are not to discuss this matter among
yourselves. From this day forward, your former brother
ceases to exist.'" His gaze roamed the room, resting on
one shocked face after another before continuing to
read the announcement.

"'Brothers and sisters, as you know, the governing
board is the Lord God's spokesman here on earth. We
accept the information given by the board without question. To question the righteousness of the board is to
question the Lord himself.'"

Stedman refolded the letter and replaced it in the envelope. He cast an unsmiling look at his congregation as
if daring the members to argue with the edict he had just
read, and resumed his seat.

Claudia thought of the ghostly figures she had seen
the evening before and wondered again whether they
made up the judicial commission Stedman spoke of,
meeting like some secret society to decide the fate of
John Talbot.

And she wondered what Talbot might have done
to deserve such a punishment. He had probably sat at
one of the tables in this dining hall just yesterday. Had
she seen him from a distance as she'd walked through
the Ark's grounds the day before? The announcement
drifted like a pall of ashes over the members. Their faces
were as downcast and sorrowful as any she had seen at
a funeral.

"What will happen to this man now?" she asked Harold Stedman, guessing that this excommunication busi-

ness might have been the reason for his early morning absence. *Had he driven John Talbot into town?* Surely he wouldn't have literally put him outside the Ark's gate with no transportation. There were miles of deserted highway between here and Hemet or any other town. Even starting out walking early in the morning, the heat could be dangerous.

Could John Talbot be the federal undercover operative, and he'd been found out?

Stedman had no hold over Claudia. She wasn't obliged to follow his instructions to let the matter drop. "Did you give him some money at least?" she quizzed. "Does he have family outside the Ark? How is he supposed to care for himself when his entire emotional support system is probably right here in this room?"

Stedman cocked his head to one side. "How is your work coming along, sister? I'm eager to hear the results of your analysis."

Claudia wanted to shout at him that this was all bullshit, but Jovanic's warning hummed in her brain. She'd had enough. She turned to Kelly and snapped, "I'll pick you up at your room after lunch."

Without waiting for a response, she got up and stalked the length of the dining hall. As she passed James's table, she noted his pallor. Felt his eyes following her all the way to the door.

Chapter 17

By the time she reached her room, Claudia had worked herself into a lather. Grabbing her overnight bag, she began stuffing clothes into it, not bothering to fold the pants into neat, flat squares or roll the T-shirts to fit into the corners. Shoes went in on top, other bits and pieces following willy-nilly. She cleared out the bathroom and zipped the laptop into its case.

After a last fleeting glance to make sure she had forgotten nothing, she carried everything down to the car, thankful not to meet Rita along the way, and loaded the trunk.

With every step her mind buzzed: *If John Talbot, the excommunicated member, was the undercover FBI operative, would the operation be scrubbed? Was he the one who had written about being a dentist? The one who Claudia had told Harold Stedman was problematic?* The thought nauseated her. What would she tell Jovanic? That she had inadvertently helped ruin several years' worth of careful investigation by outing the operative? Her stomach churned with anxiety, making her wish for a Rolaids.

The sun beat on her bare head and neck as she made her way back to Ararat, trying to formulate a plan for getting Kelly out of the Ark if she continued to resist. One-oh-seven in the shade, the radio weatherman had predicted on her drive back the previous evening. She wouldn't be surprised if the temperature exceeded even that outrageous number. On top of that, the humidity was unusually high for Hemet, and the air was as sticky as cotton candy.

Her brain felt mushy as she made her second ascent of the day to Kelly's second-floor apartment. How could anyone live in this heat? Every step felt like a mountain. Just putting thoughts together was a major effort.

Recalling Kelly's dilated pupils, she wondered how the drug had been delivered. *In food?* Claudia considered the possibility that her own sluggishness might be the result of something that had been introduced into the food on her plate. There was no way she could be sure. Luckily, she had eaten very little.

She tapped on the door of number 339, hoping that by now, Kelly would have somehow recovered and be ready to go. The door opened and she got a shock.

Not Kelly.

"Magdalena! What are you doing here? Where's Kelly?"

The girl who had shepherded them around at the rally regarded Claudia with equal surprise. She held a dust rag and wore a long white apron over her shift. A babushka type scarf covered her hair. "I'm cleaning Sister Brennan's apartment," Magdalena said. "Sister Goldberg sent me. It's my job, housecleaning. She's my supervisor."

That explained the sweat on her forehead and her flushed face. But it didn't explain her nervousness.

"Where is Kelly?" Claudia asked again.

"Um, she's not here, sister."

"You mean she hasn't come back from lunch?" Claudia looked past Magdalena, noting that the Murphy bed had been returned to its storage place in the wall cabinet and the living room was spotless. The bags she had packed earlier were no longer standing where she had left them. "Where is she?" she repeated, hardening her tone.

"Sister Goldberg told me she got ill at lunch. She was taken to the infirmary."

"What are you talking about? I was with her in the dining hall a half hour ago. She wasn't ill then."

Magdalena's face registered alarm and Claudia realized her voice had risen to a near-yell. Whatever had happened to Kelly was not Magdalena's fault. Claudia lowered her voice and made an effort to control her rising fear.

"Where's the infirmary, Magda? Either tell me, or take me there."

Martha Elkins stood behind the counter in the Ark's medical office with her arms crossed, her severe expression mocking the cheerful flowered scrubs she wore. Claudia could feel the force of her disapproval, and wondered where it stemmed from.

"Something she ate, I expect," Martha said when she asked what was wrong with Kelly. "Brother Jarrett is with her right now. You'll have to wait and see if he's going to allow her to have visitors. He's the doctor."

On the way over to the infirmary, Claudia had promised herself that she would remain calm, in control. She knew she wouldn't get anywhere if she allowed herself to go ballistic. But now she felt her temper boiling up again. "Everyone ate the same thing, didn't they? Did anyone else get sick?"

Martha's face was set in uncompromising lines, as if she were preparing to do battle. "I haven't heard of anyone yet, but that could always change. Anyway, it might have been just one batch that was affected. Or maybe she has the flu."

"She didn't look like she had the flu when I saw her. In fact, she was eating more than I've ever seen her eat. What she looked like was drugged."

Martha Elkins frowned. "Drugged? You're saying she's a druggie? We don't allow addicts here. If she's a druggie, Brother Stedman will insist on her leaving as soon as she's able."

Was the woman being deliberately obtuse? "She's not a goddamned drug addict!"

"Sister, mind your language! And if you won't lower your voice, you'll have to step outside."

"Kelly is not an addict," Claudia said through gritted teeth. "It's obvious someone slipped her something. I want to talk to the instructor of that class she was in this morning."

"You think someone at the Ark drugged your friend? That's outrageous! As if—"

A man in a white lab coat rounded the corner and stood beside her at the counter. In his sixties, thin-faced with frameless glasses. He handed the clipboard he was holding to Martha Elkins. "What's all the racket about? Don't you realize we have sick people here, sisters? They need their peace and quiet." His gaze rested on Claudia. "I believe you are Sister Rose, Sister Brennan's friend. I'm Dr. Jarrett."

"Yes, I'm Claudia Rose. Would you tell me what's going on here?"

"Your friend doesn't have a fever at the moment, but she's been complaining of stomach pains. She's lying down and I've given her a sedative. She needs to rest."

"I'd like to see her, please."

"You can see her if you stay only a minute or two, before the medicine takes effect."

Claudia quickly agreed to the terms and the doctor nodded at Martha Elkins. The nurse told her to follow, and led her through a door marked Private and along a hallway bounded by closed doors on either side.

Opening one of the doors to a small private room, Martha stood aside. Claudia walked into the room and felt her heart skip a beat. Lying in a hospital bed with her eyes closed, the lashes dark against waxy cheeks, Kelly looked like a corpse. She wore a hospital gown, her arms arranged on top of the sheet at her sides. In the corner, an electric floor fan hummed, blowing tepid air at the bed.

Martha stood in the doorway until Claudia turned and glared at her. "Would you mind leaving? Close the door behind you, please."

She felt a tug on her hand. She looked down and found that Kelly's eyes were half open. She said something in a weak voice too faint to make out. Leaning down, Claudia put her ear close to Kelly's lips.

"What happened?" Kelly whispered.

"They drugged you." Claudia kept her voice low. She doubted there would be electronic surveillance in the infirmary, but under the circumstances it seemed preferable to err on the side of caution. "What happened in that class you went to?"

Kelly shook her head. "Don't remember anything, except . . . was talking to that woman . . . security woman, then . . . nothing. I was walking into the cafeteria." She sounded bewildered. "Lost the whole morning. Like going on a bender; waking up not knowing where I'd been or what I'd done, but I didn't have any booze. Claudia, what happened to me?"

"Honestly, I don't know, Kel, but I'd already packed your things and was ready to take you home. Why didn't you just come with me when I asked you to?"

"I don't know. My head felt like it was stuffed with

old socks. I didn't—" She broke off, tears trickling down her face.

Claudia reached for a tissue from the box on the table beside the bed and handed it to her. "Don't worry about it; it's gonna be okay. What were you talking about with Lynn Ryder?"

Kelly squeezed her eyes shut, her brow furrowing as she strained to recapture the conversation. She shook her head. "It's all blank. I remember . . . she came into the classroom and asked for me, then . . ."

The door opened. "Time's up. Doctor wants her to get some sleep. You can come back later." Martha Elkins was smug with the satisfaction of giving the orders.

"I'll just be a moment longer. *Please.*"

The woman clicked her tongue in disapproval. She walked away, leaving the door open. Claudia turned back to Kelly. "Can you travel? I've got all our things packed. If I can just get you to the car—"

"Lemme sleep a while. Maybe later." Kelly's words slurred, eyelids drooping.

"Kelly?"

Her eyes fluttered open. "Stick around, Claud, don't leave me." The words trailed off.

Claudia sighed. "I'll come back in a couple of hours to check on you." But her promise was lost on Kelly, who was already asleep.

Claudia decided to complete her assignment by working on the final set of handwriting samples until Kelly regained consciousness. There was the possibility that something in these handwritings would give her additional insight into what was going on at the Ark; something that could be helpful to the Feds.

She retrieved the laptop from the Jag's trunk and set

up in Rodney's office once again. Claudia removed the handwriting samples from the envelope Lynn Ryder had handed her that morning and flipped through them. Trying to decide where to start, she found it impossible to concentrate on the task.

She wondered what part the security chief might have played in Kelly's amnesia. Kelly had said she was talking with Lynn Ryder when she'd suddenly blanked out.

Why drug Kelly?

Claudia searched for an answer, but none came. Perhaps it was standard TBL practice to soften up prospective members: drug and hypnotize, plant a suggestion to hand over their bank accounts and join up. It wasn't such a far-fetched concept. Would Lynn Ryder have participated in that aspect of indoctrination?

Too bad Stedman had insisted on making Claudia return the first set of handwriting samples so fast. She would like to have taken another look at Lynn's.

But since the sample wasn't available to her, she decided to go looking for Rita.

Chapter 18

She found Rita in the kitchen behind the reception area, pouring sun tea from a big glass jar. The curtains were drawn against the afternoon sun, leaving the room in shadows, but still sweltering. Rita's eyes were tired and her green linen shift hung limply on her slender frame. She set the jar on the counter and held the glass to her forehead. The ice cubes were already melting. "I'll be glad when summer is over and the weather cools down," she said as Claudia came into the kitchen. "How about some tea, sister?"

Claudia shook her head. "No, thanks, Rita. I was wondering if you could you tell me where I might find Lynn Ryder."

Rita's brows lifted in question. "I'm sorry, but Sister Ryder isn't here at the moment. She's gone to visit her aunt and uncle. Is there something I can help you with?"

"You mean she's away from the Ark?" Claudia felt a little kick of surprise. She had already become accustomed to thinking of the compound as an entirely self-contained community for its members. Of course some of them must have relatives elsewhere.

"Her aunt and uncle live in San Jacinto next to Hemet. Sister Ryder was so pleased when she was accepted to live at the Ark because it meant she could be close to them. Her uncle's been ailing for the last few years. He's in a wheelchair and they're getting on in years. It's too hard for her aunt to take him around, so Sister Ryder takes them to doctor appointments and does the grocery shopping for them. We try to help out, too. Some of us go with her from time to time to help clean up their house and yard, fix what needs fixing." Rita smiled. "We haven't yet been able to convince them to join us, but we're working on it."

"It's good of you to help them out when they're not members."

"We're happy to do it for Sister Ryder. She's a very capable woman, but she can't do everything by herself. She'll be back in a little while. She's usually only gone for three or four hours at a time. She takes her duties here very seriously."

Claudia wondered again whether those duties might include drugging visitors.

Back at Rodney's desk, the heat brought out a fine glaze of sweat on her forehead and Claudia was soon regretting that she hadn't accepted Rita's offer of iced tea. She sifted through the samples in the envelope, setting aside the one that most interested her—the one her memory told her was similar to the note Erin had showed them from Rodney.

She had a strong feeling that the two would be a match, but until she could put them side by side and make a direct comparison, the sample that she now set aside could be viewed only as block-printed writing. That put it in the same general category as the Rodney/Erin note, which had also been block printed. But there were also many other important elements—the margins, the spatial arrangement, the individual letter forms, and dozens of additional characteristics that she would have to take into consideration before deciding they were of common authorship.

Even though her gut insisted that she was right, Claudia refused to rely solely on her memory and jump to a conclusion that might be incorrect and lead her in a wrong direction. Until she was able to make that comparison, she would look for something else of interest in this batch of writings from Harold Stedman.

It would have been helpful if Stedman had at least let her know the gender of each writer and their ages. It could impact her conclusions if, for example, the writer were actually a young male who wrote like an older female. Or if it were a young woman whose writing was similar to an adult male's.

One of the samples she selected from the envelope was a copybook style, but it contained personality traits that were more traditionally masculine than feminine. She took her magnifying glass from her briefcase and pored over the sample for anything that might escape the naked eye—tiny hooks or extra loops within oval letters, filled-in dots of ink; found nothing of consequence.

The slant of the upper loops was mixed, leaning left and right and straight up and down; the baseline wavering as it crossed the page from one side to the other evidence that at the time of executing the writing, the writer had been plagued with vacillating emotions, moodiness. The personal pronoun capital *I* was stunted in size and width. Add to that the bloated upper loops, which suggested sensitivity to the point of defensiveness the writer had a tendency to blow small slights out of proportion—and you had a picture of a highly emotional person with an immature ego.

After she had reached her initial conclusions, Claudia began to read the text of the essay, which delved into the writer's views about the foreshortened future of the earth and desire to work with TBL's leadership to recruit as many members as possible.

Huh. Not so different in content from the essay she had found in Rodney's file cabinet. Considering the TBL's old-school attitude toward women, she became certain from what was written in the sample that the writer had to be as she suspected—male.

The other samples in the envelope were all over the map. One was an application for membership from someone who referred to her husband's death and her desire to be with him again in the new earth. She wrote that until she could join him, she would devote the rest of her life to the TBL. She wished to be accepted into service at the Ark and was willing to take on any job, regardless of how menial it might be.

The handwriting contained many loops and sloped sharply downhill; the pressure lacked energy, one indicator for depression. A paternalistic religious cult might easily attract a depressed person, Claudia speculated. One who lacked the physical or emotional stamina to bother making major decisions and would rather hand over the responsibility to someone else. One who felt secure only when operating within a strict framework of rules and regulations that were handed down to them by a person in a position of authority.

The next sample she examined contained angular formations in the lower loops where they did not belong. The writer harbored hidden anger directed toward women, which could pop out in overtly hostile behavior at unexpected times. The text of the sample suggested another female writer. Claudia concluded that she would be a difficult person to deal with, but aside from that, there were no red flags in the writing that would indicate that she was lying. In fact, this writer would be apt to share whatever was on her mind in no uncertain terms. How well would she fit into life at the Ark?

Maybe not so well since Stedman had included the sample for analysis.

The heat made it impossible to keep her attention on the samples for very long. Beginning to feel as if she were suffocating in the pocket-sized office, Claudia slid the papers back into the envelope, then got up and stretched. Perspiration glued her shirt to her back and caused the waistband of her pants to chafe. She would have given a hundred bucks to lie down and take a nap. Instead, she decided to take Rita up on her earlier offer of sun tea.

Rita poured the amber liquid into a tall glass. "Do you want any sweetener? I don't put any into the jar."

"No, this is fine, thanks." Claudia accepted the glass and drank a long mouthful. "In fact, it's delicious." She leaned back against the counter, hoping that Rita might relax with her and open up to a casual chat. "Everyone I've met at the Ark seems really happy."

Rita smiled. "We are, mostly. Of course, like any large group of people living in a small community we have our little conflicts and things that go on, but they're always resolved."

"You mean like the person who was excommunicated today?"

Alarm shadowed Rita's face. "Oh, that's something we can't discuss. When someone leaves the fold after knowing the truth about what's going to happen to the earth, they have only themselves to thank. We have to cut them out completely, like a deadly cancer."

"But he didn't leave voluntarily."

"No, and the judicial commission doesn't take such a serious matter lightly. They counsel the sinner several times before taking this final step. When a member is cast out, it means he simply isn't repentant; not interested in mending his ways."

You mean toeing the company line.

"It seems like a cruel way to treat someone who's given up everything to be part of the group."

Rita's posture stiffened and her chin went up as if she felt personally criticized by Claudia's observation. "The elders know what they're doing in these matters. Brother Stedman has been our shepherd for more than thirty years now. He's never, ever led us astray. When he brings us new light, we know it's from the Lord God. We listen to him."

Claudia reached out and lightly touched her arm. "I can see I've upset you. I'm sorry; I didn't mean to."

"We can't tolerate unrepentant sinners, Sister Rose. You know that old saying about one rotten apple . . ."

"I understand, spoils the barrel. Okay, let's talk about something else I wanted to ask you about. I heard some talk at breakfast about a birthday celebration. It sounded like some really special preparations were being made."

"That would be Kylie Powers's consecration."

"Consecration? Oh, I must have misunderstood. I thought it was her birthday."

"It *is* her birthday, she's turning three. And she's about to enter a special school. That's what the celebration is for." Rita's face softened. "Our Kylie is the most beautiful child I have ever seen, bar none. Amazingly bright, too, with the looks and disposition of a cherub. We're going to miss that sweet little face around here, but it's such a tremendous privilege to enter this program, it's worth the sacrifice."

The word *sacrifice* made Claudia inwardly shiver. "It

must have been difficult for her parents to make such a choice."

"Oh, no, not really. Brother and Sister Powers—Kylie's parents—were ecstatic when Brother Stedman told them that their daughter was the Chosen One—overcome with joy."

"Chosen One? You mean chosen for Jephthah's Daughters?"

Rita blinked in surprise. "Oh, you know about that?"

"Just a little, but I'm interested to hear more."

"The one time a girl can be accepted is on her third birthday, so it only happens once in a while. There have been other little girls over the years whose parents have given them to Jephthah's Daughters, but none of them were the Chosen One, as Kylie is."

"Chosen for what?"

"That will be revealed when the time is right." She sounded sure of herself.

"Don't take this as a criticism, Rita, but I think it would be hard on these little girls to be separated from their parents at such a young age. Are they ever allowed to come back to visit their families?"

"It's a lifetime commitment. Once they go away to the program, that's where they live the rest of their lives. They're trained as priestesses."

"And they never return? Their parents don't see them again? That's a huge step to take. You say they become priestesses. What do they actually do?"

"I suppose you could say they're our version of a nun. They do good works for the TBL within the walls of the temple. And they train the next generation of priestesses, of course."

Rita was beginning to sound a touch impatient and Claudia wondered how far she could push the questions.

She gave it another try. "I wonder what would happen if the parents changed their minds and didn't want their daughter to go after all?"

Under other circumstances, Rita's aghast expression would have been almost comical. "That would *never* happen. Can you imagine? The Lord God chooses your child for a special honor and you say 'No, I don't think I'm interested'? Kylie's acceptance into Jephthah's Daughters is vital for the salvation of all of us who are members of the Temple of Brighter Light. Not just here at the Ark, all the satellites, too."

"What does that mean?"

"I really can't say anything more." She gave Claudia an apologetic smile. "It's not something we're supposed to discuss with outsiders."

After refilling her glass, Claudia decided to return to Rodney's office and get things wrapped up. She rounded the corner from the reception area and collided head-on with James Miller. They both gasped as sun tea splashed the front of his white dress shirt. Claudia jumped back. "Oh crap, I'm so sorry!"

"You again!"

"You'll need to soak your shirt in cold water right away so the stain doesn't set."

"Leave it." Miller held the sopping shirt away from his skin. He started to move on, but thinking of how he'd puked his breakfast that morning, and now he was soaked through with tea, Claudia stopped him. "I guess it's not your day, thanks to me."

"Don't worry about it, I'm fine."

She was already trying to think of a way to get him to talk to her; decided to go for broke. "James, when we spoke this morning, I didn't tell you this, but someone put a note in my briefcase last night while I wasn't looking. There was a young woman at my lecture in Riverside, and I think she had something to do with it. Would you happen to know anything about that?"

"Why would I?"

"I've heard that you and Rodney Powers are like brothers. You're the only one who—"

James began motioning frantically with his hands for her to stop. He put a finger to his lips, warning her not to speak. When he beckoned her to come with him, Claudia followed without question. He led her outside, moving with enough speed that she had to make an effort to keep up.

As he had that morning, James Miller took her away from the path, into the trees, which grew thick and provided plenty of cover. He pushed aside branches, clearing the way for Claudia. The dry brush scratched at her bare legs as she plowed along behind him.

When they came to a clearing, she could see that this was another area of the perimeter fence where they'd met after breakfast, closer to the Victorian where the main offices and her guest room were located.

"We can't be gone long." James turned to face her. His hands were moving nervously, clenching and unclenching, and he spoke quickly. "I don't want anyone to miss me. They'll be back soon."

"Where is everyone? I haven't seen a soul except Rita since I left the infirmary."

"The infirmary?" He looked puzzled.

"Kelly's there. I believe she's been hypnotized and drugged."

He looked a bit green when she said that. "There's a service going on, so a lot of the members are in church right now. We need to hurry."

"Okay, but why are we out here? Because of surveillance?"

He nodded. "I helped set it up in the house. It may be in other places, too, that I don't know about. Brother Stedman just wants to make sure there's no murmuring going on among the brothers." He said it apologetically, as if he knew how ridiculous and paranoid it sounded. He didn't know that Stedman had also retained Claudia to check up on some members.

She saw from the warring emotions on his face that he was still struggling with the demons of his conscience. She reached her hands out. "James, I don't care about any of that right now. Please tell me you've brought me here because you've decided to help me find Rodney."

He covered his face with his hands, then dropped them and gave her a look of appeal that she had to believe was sincere. "You don't understand how hard this is. I truly and deeply *believe* that what the elders teach us is the truth from above. I *believe* in the coming cataclysm, and that there are certain steps we have to undertake to be saved. I honestly don't want to disobey the directions of Brother Stedman or the rest of the governing board. Rod feels the same way, but . . ." He sucked in a deep breath; let it out on a regretful sigh. "He's become weak in his faith. He can't bring himself to hand over his child for sacrifice, even though it's an enormous privilege and an honor. And it's the right thing to do, too. But God help me, he *is* more than a real brother to me. I've talked and talked to him, but I couldn't talk him out of what he planned, so finally, I had to do what I could to help him."

The heat was oppressive, but Claudia felt herself go cold all over. "James, what are you saying? You're talking as if they were going to *literally* sacrifice Kylie. That's not what you're telling me, is it?"

When he didn't say anything, she took a step toward him. She grabbed his arms and shook him. "Answer me!

Tell me that's not what you're saying! What the hell is this *Jephthah's Daughters,* anyway?"

James struggled out of her grasp. "Jephthah's Daughters is a school where special young women are raised in service of the Lord. They sacrifice themselves to a life of prayer and service in solitude."

"Where is it? Here, at the Ark?"

"No. It's in a temple in the Colorado Rockies. It's a very small community where they pray for the earth and for those of us who have left the world."

"What do you mean, 'left the world'?"

"Left the evil world *out there.*" James waved his arm, indicating some nebulous location beyond the walls of the Temple of Brighter Light and their Ark. He checked his watch. "I've got to get back to my office."

"Wait—was that Rod last night at my lecture?"

"I don't know. It might have been. I sent word that you were looking for him and that you would be there."

"But how did you know—?"

"I overheard you telling Sister Ryder that you were going to lecture at the university. I wasn't eavesdropping; I was at my desk, working. The sound carries through the wall."

Impatiently, Claudia shrugged that off. "James, if I tell you what the note says, can you help me understand what it means?"

He started shaking his head. "I really need to go. I don't know anything about a note."

She had it memorized. As he turned away, she began reciting the contents to him:

"It says: *Don't believe all you're told. It's not the way it seems.*"

James stopped, half turned.

"There's proof of the evildoing."

Claudia heard his indrawn breath, but she continued

relentlessly: "*You have to find it—for my child's sake, and the others.*"

She moved around him, directly into his path. His eyes were squeezed shut, his respirations shallow.

Please don't let him lose his lunch, too.

"He's gone," he said, almost to himself. "There's no turning back for him now."

"What do you mean, he's gone?"

"He's lost to us. Proof of *evildoing?* How could he—"

"What *proof* is he talking about? What evildoing do you think he means?"

"He's lost his mind." James inhaled a deep breath, gave a long, sad sigh. "It's more than my life is worth to go on trying to shield him. I can't help him anymore."

Chapter 19

Claudia held her breath, hardly daring to hope that he might be ready to give her the information that she and Kelly had come to the Ark to find: Rodney Powers's whereabouts.

James started talking. "The girl you mentioned from last night—what did she look like? I just need to be sure. . . ."

"Black hair, purple streak; a little on the chunky side. . . ."

"She's my niece, Tabitha. Rod and his daughter are staying at her place. When Rod called me for help, Tabby was the only one I could think of to turn to." He met Claudia's eyes, then quickly looked away as if ashamed. "We don't associate with anyone else outside of TBL. Tabby was excommunicated a couple of years ago when she turned nineteen; she'd started causing disruptions among the other young people, creating dissension. She always was a rebellious, disobedient girl; refused to do what her parents told her. My sister and her husband tried and tried to counsel her; brought her before the governing board time and again. Finally, the judicial commission stepped in and had no choice but to expel her from the Ark. It was obvious she'd become a danger to the congregation." James scrubbed his hands over his face and sighed again. "Neither Rod nor I should be having anything to do with her at all. We could be expelled ourselves, but I—"

Something he had said earlier suddenly boomer-anged and struck Claudia with enough force to take her breath away. "Wait a minute, James, hold on. A few min-utes ago, I thought you said that Rodney doesn't want to hand over his child to Jephthah's Daughters. Did I hear that correctly?"

He nodded miserably.

"But . . . aren't you helping him hide her until the cer-emony on her third birthday?"

James gave her a strange look. "Well, I helped him with Tabby, but . . ."

"James, where can I get some of Erin's handwriting?" The words had come out of her mouth before she had consciously formed the question, but her instincts told her she was on the right track.

"Her handwriting?"

Of course, he had no idea why Harold Stedman had brought Claudia to the Ark, or why that would have anything to do with her question. "I don't care what it is," she said urgently. "It can be anything she's written. Can you put your hands on anything?"

"She gave me a letter she wrote before they left for the mountains," James said. "She asked me to read it to all the members after they'd left. I still have it."

"I need to see it."

"Why?"

"That's something I can't explain right now. Please just take my word for it. It's really important."

He was watching her with a mixture of curiosity, anxiety, and more than a little suspicion. Claudia met his eyes and put all the sincerity into her voice that she could muster. "You've got to trust me, James."

She could see him wavering, but in the end he agreed. "All right, I'll get it to you."

"I need Tabby's address, too."

"I can't do that, but I'll contact her and ask her to have Rod call you."

They left the clearing separately. Claudia waited ten minutes before she followed James' trail out of the woods. She checked in at the infirmary and was told that Kelly was still sleeping. "How much longer do you think it'll be before she's able to leave here?" she asked Martha Elkins.

Elkins shrugged, gave her the offhand almost-sneer. "Couldn't tell you."

"What's with your attitude, Martha? What is it you have against me?"

Elkins didn't pretend not to understand, and her answer spewed venom. "You outsiders are all alike. You come here looking for something to use against us. You'll leave the Ark and do whatever damage you can when you get away from here. Meanwhile, we just want to live our lives in peace and prepare for the end-of-time days, but instead, we're forced to waste our energy fighting people like you."

Claudia felt as if she'd been bitch-slapped. She was tempted to strike back at the other woman, but she bit her tongue. "I don't know why you would think that, Mrs. Elkins. We're here because Harold Stedman asked us to come. Neither Kelly nor I have any desire to hurt you or anyone else at the Ark."

Martha made a little puffing noise with her lips that said she didn't believe a word of it. She turned away with a jerk of her shoulder and picked up a file from the basket on her desk. Giving up, Claudia said she would return in another hour.

Her next stop was Ararat. She would pick up Kelly's luggage and take it to the car. The closer they were to being ready to go when Kelly awoke, the better. And if it happened that Kelly was not ready the next time Claudia showed up at the infirmary, she would take stronger measures—though she hadn't figured out yet what those might be.

Magdalena had finished her work, and the room Kelly had stayed in was as clean and empty as a hotel room waiting for a new guest. Claudia managed to get the laptop bag and bulky suitcase down to the lobby and outside, bumping it awkwardly along the long dirt path to the parking lot. After heaving them into the trunk of the Jag next to her own bag, she returned to Rodney Powers's office and booted up the laptop and portable printer.

Preparing her final report for Harold Stedman, she peppered it with disclaimers and strongly urged the use of additional tools to make a determination about integrity. She carefully avoided negative comments about the veracity of any of the writers. If one of these writers was the FBI operative, and if the FBI operation was as close to completion as Jovanic had suggested, it probably wouldn't make any difference what she said, but she wasn't about to make any statements that might come back to haunt her.

Forty minutes later she was printing out the report on her portable printer. She slipped it into the envelope with the handwriting samples and packed up her equipment once again. She had everything ready to load into the Jag and was preparing to go to the parking lot when Rita popped her head around the office door.

"Sister Rose, could I see you for a moment?"

The tension in her face made Claudia immediately rise from the desk and follow her into the hallway. Rita pressed something into her hand, a small envelope. "I've brought you this from James," she said in a whisper. "It's Erin's letter, like you asked for." Without saying anything further, she turned and hurried away.

Claudia went directly upstairs and shut herself in the second-floor bathroom, hoping there was no surveillance on her in there. She leaned against the sink and removed the card from its envelope, suddenly reluctant to look at the handwriting, not wanting confirmation of what she had come to suspect.

The note was hand printed and as she had expected, it matched the one Erin had showed them earlier in the week—the one she claimed to have been written by her husband. It was a letter to the congregation, thanking them for everything they had done for the Powers family. It was signed "with agapé love from Rod and Erin."

But what did it actually prove? Maybe *Rodney* had written both notes. Claudia reminded herself that even though they didn't match the handwriting she had found in his files, without someone to authenticate those samples as Rodney's own writing, authorship would remain inconclusive. All she knew now was that they were written by different hands.

The spiritual leader of the Temple of Brighter Light was leaning back in his chair, his stockinged feet resting on the desk. Hands clasped behind his head, Harold Stedman gazed at the ceiling, speaking in a low voice, words that Claudia could not hear. When he failed to respond to her knock on the open door, she wondered whether perhaps he was praying. Hesitating to interrupt, she cleared her throat. When there was still no response she called his name.

Slowly, his gaze lowered and he turned, staring as if he did not recognize her. Then his focus seemed to sharpen. He sat up straight and removed his feet from the desk. "Good afternoon, Sister Rose. Come in, please. Have a seat." He indicated one of the chairs in front of his desk and rose. "Excuse my casualness. I was thinking about something. 'Lost in thought,' as they say."

Claudia apologized for intruding and handed him the envelope. "My report is in here with the final set of handwriting samples that I'm returning to you. Kelly and I will be leaving as soon as she's awake."

"Are you sure Sister Brennan is going to be ready for travel? She didn't look at all well at lunch. I think you might want to reconsider leaving today. Why don't you stay on for another night and go in the morning, when it's cooler and more pleasant for such a long drive? You're quite welcome to stay here."

She read nothing but concern in his face, and Claudia had to remind herself that Kelly had been surreptitiously drugged and hypnotized, undoubtedly on the orders of this man. It made her want to call him on it, but not wanting to arouse his suspicions she did her best to keep her tone normal. "Thank you, but we need to go. As I mentioned at lunch, I'm needed at home, and Kelly has to get ready for a trial."

And for some reason I don't know, the FBI is about to come down on you.

Stedman slipped the envelope she had given him into the top drawer of the desk. "As you wish. I'd like to—" The phone on his desk rang, interrupting him.

It was the only phone Claudia had seen at the Ark since the first day when she'd had to beg to use the one locked in Rita's desk. Stedman excused himself and answered the call. After listening for a few seconds he put the caller on hold and asked Claudia to wait. He crossed the room in a few strides and opened a door in the far wall, giving her a glimpse of what appeared to be antique bedroom furniture before closing it behind him. So his office and living quarters *were* combined.

While she waited for him to return, she absorbed the

Victorian craftsmanship, which was more noticeable
here than in the other rooms she'd seen. It was evident in
the golden oak corbels that supported the ceiling beams;
in the overstuffed easy chair that had been placed before the ornate cast iron fireplace whose andirons stood
empty and unused in the unbearable summer heat.

She wandered over to the window and discovered
that the angle from the second floor allowed her to view
a large area of the vast Ark grounds. She could see the
women working in the garden and a small group of children walking together on the path. No wonder Stedman
had known she'd been out there the night before. Standing at the window, even in the darkness he could have
easily seen her as she left the path by the vegetable garden and entered the back door below. So much for her
attempt at stealth.

The realization made her jittery with anxiety, unsure
of what Stedman knew or what he thought he knew. She
wished he would end his phone call so she could get the
hell away from the Ark and all that it represented. To
distract herself she began browsing the bookshelves
that lined the office from floor to ceiling; enough books
to fill a small library.

If he had read a small fraction of these volumes, Stedman must be in love with scholarship. A wide range of
Bible translations filled several of the shelves. Eastern
religions were heavily represented, and several were
tomes from obscure denominations Claudia had never
heard of. There were books on psychology, philosophy,
theosophy; books about symbolism, paganism, witch-
craft; even a copy of the Satanic Bible. Whatever she felt
about Harold Stedman personally, his reading materials
were eclectic, to say the least.

She peered through the glass front of a barrister's
bookcase, curious to see what types of volumes Stedman

found worthy of keeping under lock and key. Cracked leather bindings and ornate leather tooling told her that the books on these shelves were undeniably antiquarian. The titles were printed in gilt along the spines: *Nostradamus Quatrains, The Book of Concealed Mystery, The Key of Solomon, The Holy Writ Explained, The Egyptian Book of the Dead.*

"Are you interested in ancient texts, Sister Rose?"

Claudia swung around. Fascinated by the variety of topics, she had not heard Stedman come back into the room. "Yes, of course; my field is written communication. It doesn't matter what language or form it takes, nor how old the text, the principles for analysis are the same."

He came over and stood beside her at the bookcase. "Do you mean to say you can analyze the inscriptions of a monk who lived hundreds of years ago? Or a scribe who lived long before Christ? You would be able to determine something about their personality?"

That strange heat she had felt emanating from him the night before was there again. She edged away, putting a few inches between them. "Oh, yes. The hieroglyphics in Egyptian tombs, for example—it's possible to tell where one scribe leaves off and another begins; each scribe's pictogram displays characteristics, just as writings in the romance languages do. There's no reason why an Egyptian's work shouldn't tell something about his character, too."

Stedman's eyes were alight with interest. "I find that utterly fascinating. Let me show you something interesting." He took a key ring from his pocket as he spoke and began sorting through the many keys until he found the one he wanted. "I think you'll like this."

He lowered himself to his haunches and unlocked a drawer at the bottom of the bookcase. Taking out a piece of old-looking ivory-colored satin brocade cloth bound by a length of ribbon, he held the bundle as gently as a baby. "This is a handwritten translation from the ancient *Egyptian Book of the Dead*. It's quite old."

Claudia stopped listening to him. This piece of immortality—history made alive through the handwriting on the page—drew her in completely. The faded, spidery notes transliterated the original text interlinearly. It brought to mind the image of an elderly translator bent over a desk, carefully deciphering and decoding each word of an ancient papyrus. She read the words to herself:

"'I germinate like the plants. Physical body changes into a sahu—spiritual body ... the soul liveth, thy body germinateth by the command of Ra himself without diminution, and without defect, like unto Ra forever and ever.'"

Stedman's voice came through to her. "... tremendous wisdom."

Claudia nodded, pretending to have heard what he had said. She hoped it wasn't anything that required a response.

"The Egyptians believed in a resurrection to another kind of life," Stedman added.

Claudia wondered whether he was drawing a parallel to the beliefs of the Temple of Brighter Light. "They believed in drinking the blood of their enemies, too," she said. "I think you'd better have a document specialist look at this and tell you how to preserve it. You wouldn't want to lose this. I can give you a recommendation to someone."

"Thank you, I'd appreciate it." Stedman lovingly rewrapped the papers in their cloth cover and tied the ribbon in a neat bow. "The written word has always mesmerized me," he said. "I'll admit my own handwriting isn't the most beautiful—it's a little bizarre, in fact—yes, I realize that. But I do love the feel of a good pen in my hand, drawing it across the page, watching the flow of ink it leaves behind. To me, it's like sharing a truly intimate piece of oneself with the reader."

Claudia could see why people followed him. There was something about him—*charisma*, she supposed. His air of quiet authority made you want to believe him. She nodded understanding. "At least one graphological author has compared the ductus—that's the flow of ink from the pen—to the movement of blood in the body. The ink might be smooth or sluggish, or it might become clogged up in some areas the way blood does as it moves through the veins. The ductus symbolizes the life force, the psychic energy that drives the writer."

Stedman was gazing at her with something like wonder. "I believe you understand that, to me, being able to actually touch these old writings is as intimate as dipping my fingers into the lifeblood of the person whose pen scratched out the words."

Claudia looked back at him, uncomfortable with the allusion, not finding an appropriate response. He didn't seem to notice her silence as he replaced the translated text in the drawer and locked it. "There's something else I think might interest you," he said. "It's a document that I've never shown anyone."

"What is it?"

"A sacred text. I think you would appreciate it for what it is, not just for what it says. It's kept in another area of the Ark, a place where the brothers and sisters can't access."

His offer to let her view a special document was intriguing; especially when he seemed so excited about showing it to her. But the urgency to leave the Ark and allow the FBI to get their operation on track made her think twice. Claudia opened her mouth to decline, but Stedman held up a finger for her to wait. He picked up his phone and punched in a number.

"Good afternoon, Sister Elkins. How is our patient Sister Brennan doing?" He listened for a few moments, then said, "I understand. Thank you, Sister. Her friend will be over a little later to pick her up." He rang off and said to Claudia, "She's still trying to wake up, and Sister Elkins is about to help her take a shower, so it all works out well. By the time we return, Sister Brennan will be all ready to go."

Chapter 20

Harold Stedman led her outside, taking the worn path toward the dining hall. The vegetable garden had emptied at this hottest part of the day. He touched her arm, guiding her to turn right. They were approaching the building that Esther had identified as the bookbindery. With a jolt of surprise, Claudia realized that he was taking her close to the spot where she had hidden the night before and witnessed the appearance of the five hooded figures.

"This is a private area," Harold Stedman told her as they crossed the gravel median and veered toward the building. "Only members of the governing board are allowed access."

As they got closer, Claudia realized that there was an eight-foot wall along the edge of the building, not readily visible from even a few feet away, which hid the entry. As Stedman led her around the wall she was able to see how, under cover of night, it would be virtually impossible to see the narrow opening. That's why the figures had appeared to simply materialize.

The metal door was painted the color of the building, which effectively camouflaged it. When Stedman unlocked it, the door opened with an airtight whoosh. Inside, the twenty-degree drop in air temperature raised goose bumps on Claudia's bare arms, and she couldn't help shivering as Stedman guided her to a sharp turn at the end of a short hallway.

Around the turn was a staircase going underground, sloping beneath low ceilings. Thick-cast aluminum fixtures overhead lit the way with amber fluorescent lights that bathed them in a yellow glow. Stedman explained that the wire-mesh covers were explosion proof.

"So this *was* originally built as a fallout shelter?" Claudia asked.

"Yes. Back in those days the spiritual light had not yet become bright enough for us to see what our true mission was. In the days of the Cold War even the Temple elders bought into the hysteria like so many others did. This shelter was built to house fifty people, and we have others on the grounds. That was shortly before I was appointed as an elder, of course. Now we have learned that the Lord God has other plans for us than to perish in nuclear war, or to burrow ourselves underground like moles. So we use the space for storage and for private meetings of the governing board."

That's what they were doing last night, meeting privately to decide John Talbot's fate.

Claudia visualized standing before those elders and having them pronounce the verdict: excommunication. It must be terrifying for someone who had given their life to the organization to be cast out and left without a support system.

Stedman had descended halfway. He turned and saw that Claudia was hesitating at the top. "There's nothing down here that will harm you," he assured her. "I think you'll find this document of some interest. Just follow me."

"I'm coming," she said, and was mortified to hear a tremor in her voice. The tremor was not caused by fear of Harold Stedman. He was not a large man and despite his powerful speaking voice, there was a frailty about him that led her to believe he posed no physical danger. Her hesitation was prompted by the memory of an earlier time, another staircase; one that had ended in an underground dungeon and sights she preferred to forget.

At the bottom of the staircase she found herself in an arched hallway constructed of cinder block walls. Stedman took her past several closed doors to one at the end of the hallway. He opened the door and stood aside to let her precede him.

The first thing she noticed was the scent of patchouli. In the light from the hallway she could see black velvet-draped walls and a mirror on the wall across from the door. A shelf below the mirror held a half-dozen candles, an incense burner, a glass of water, and a vase of dead roses whose petals littered the floor like pale pink snowflakes.

Stedman lit the candles and closed the door. "I come here to meditate," he said. "It's where I hear the Lord the clearest when he chooses to speak to me."

He took the glass of water from the shelf and dumped it out into a container, then filled it with fresh water from a ewer and placed it on a low table in the center of the carpeted floor. Next, he went to a black lacquer cabinet. A fluorescent light came on inside when he opened the doors and Claudia could see several shelves containing what appeared to be scrolls. Stedman removed one and brought it to the table.

He gestured for her to sit on a floor cushion. "You know that the Bible is called the Holy Writ?"

"Yes, of course."

"There are other documents, authoritative documents that might be placed in that category."

"I thought the Bible was the only one."

"The Bible *as we know it* is made up of sixty-six books. Why not more books inspired by the Lord?" He

looked down at her seated on the cushion and asked
another question. "Do you know anything about automatic writing?"

"I've read something about it. Are you talking about
automatic writing that comes from the unconscious? Or
from an entity outside the writer?"

"Spirit speaks to me through my pen," Stedman
said enigmatically. The candle flames flickered, jump-
ing and dipping, distorting the shadows as he knelt on
the floor across the table from Claudia. In that ghostly
light he could as easily have been an angel or a demon.
He pointed to the glass of water he had placed on the
table. "Water is highly conductive of spirit energy. It al-
lows me to better open myself to receive the messages
that come through. Perhaps you would like to see a
demonstration?"

"I'm not sure."

He smiled at her reassuringly. "I promise, *nothing* will
harm you. I will sit quietly for a few minutes, channeling
my energy."

He unrolled several feet of the scroll and laid it out
so that a blank area covered the table from one edge to
the other. He didn't offer to show it to her, but Claudia
could see that it was filled from edge to edge with some
sort of handwriting.

Stedman got up and came around to her side of the
table. She shifted to make room for him to join her on
the cushion, aware again of his unusual body heat radi-
ance as he sat cross-legged beside her.

He sipped from the water glass, then took a ballpoint
pen from his pocket. Holding it in a light grip near the
tip, he hovered the pen slightly above the scroll and put
one hand on the paper to steady it.

"You can now rest your hand lightly on the back
of mine," he said. "Don't try to guide my hand, just go

along for the ride and see if something happens. It may or it may not." He closed his eyes and drew a long, deep breath through his nose, exhaling through his mouth. The sound of his breathing filled the room. *In. Out. In. Out.* He began to quietly hum, *"Om."*

After a few moments, Claudia began to relax and closed her own eyes. Her breathing slowed to match his. The mind chatter that often plagued her when she tried to meditate quieted, dissolved. All she was aware of was her respiration and his. *In. Out. In. Out.* His hand felt cool under hers.

After several minutes, Stedman's hand started to move. Claudia's eyes flew open and she watched his hand race across the page, back and forth. It was all she could do to keep the contact. She guessed he must have covered fifty lines before he let go of the pen and his arm fell away from her touch.

He seemed to crumple in on himself, panting a little.

"Are you all right?" Claudia asked, concerned. "Do you need anything?"

He shook his head and spoke in a weak voice. "It takes a toll on my energy to make contact with the Lord God."

She looked down at the scroll to see what mysterious messages he might have written there. It looked to her like an EEG printout—rows and rows of jagged lines; peaks and valleys, no discernible words at all. His normal handwriting had been hard enough to read, this was impossible. Stedman had intimated that he was inspired to add to the Holy Writ. This looked more like *un*holy writ to her.

"Can you read what it says?" she asked. "I'm afraid I can't."

Now that he had recovered, his smile had a slightly superior edge. "Of course you can't." He pointed to the final line of writing. To her eyes it was no more legible than the rest. "See here, it speaks of requiring the new blood of the Lamb."

"The blood of Christ?"

"No, no. That sacrifice was already made. This is a new day with new evils. Thus, a new lamb is required."

Claudia felt as though she could hardly breathe. She was afraid to ask, but she had to know. "What does that mean?"

There was an uncanny light in his eyes as he swung his gaze her way. When he spoke, his voice was higher-pitched, overwrought, and she thought he must still be partly in a trance state. "The Lord watches over his people. The light gets brighter and we adjust our thinking as we learn. The end of days is near. We must be prepared."

Whatever was going on here was giving Claudia the creeps. She scrambled to her feet. "Mr. Stedman, I'm leaving now. Will you be all right?"

Stedman blinked at her. "What?" He looked down at the scroll on the table as if seeing it for the first time.

Chapter 21

Without waiting for Harold Stedman, Claudia left the underground shelter and went straight to the infirmary, determined to take Kelly and leave the compound immediately.

Kelly tried to stand on her own but her legs were still rubbery and needed a wheelchair for the long walk out to the parking lot. Martha Elkins protested loudly at every step about letting her patient go in that condition, but she looked secretly pleased to be getting rid of the "outsiders."

Claudia couldn't care less how Martha felt about their departure. She had actually been surprised that no one tried to stop them from driving through the gate, and couldn't stop glancing in the rearview mirror until they got on the freeway.

As soon as she could, she phoned Jovanic and told him they were on their way home.

"You can expect to be debriefed by the FBI," he said. "I've been talking to the agent in charge. We're trying to set up a meeting tonight. We can make it at your house."

"That's fine. I can tell him about Lynn Ryder snooping in my computer, Kelly being drugged, Stedman's paranoia—"

"He'll want to know all of that. Just answer his questions as fully as you can. But remember, you're not sup-

posed to know about their undercover operative. I'd get
my ass handed to me—"

"Don't worry, baby, your ass is safe with me."

He snickered and rang off.

Kelly dozed on and off most of the way back to the
San Fernando Valley. During her waking times, Claudia
brought her up to date on what she had learned from
James Miller about Rodney, as well as her strange visit
to Harold Stedman's sanctum. The drug Dr. Jarrett had
given Kelly seemed to be taking a long time to wear off
and Claudia wasn't convinced she would retain much of
the conversation.

She kept her promise not to breathe a word to Kelly,
but she was worried about the FBI operation and prayed
it would not end up a Waco or Ruby Ridge. Her impression of most of the Ark residents she'd met was that they
were good, decent people. She liked Rita and young Esther a lot. Even Martha Elkins and Lynn Ryder were
just protecting their turf. She would not want to see any
of them come to harm.

She had come to recognize that James Miller and the
rest of them were all true believers, willing to blindly
follow the governing board. That was the one thing she
could fault them for: their willingness to reject *independent thinking* as they had been so thoroughly condi-
tioned to do.

On the other hand, she could fault the leaders for far
worse: brainwashing members, hypnotizing, drugging,
spying. Probably a long list of other offenses, too. Everyone should be free to choose his or her own path, and
it troubled her that the TBL members seemed to have
been misled.

She thought again of James, torn between loyalty to
his friend and his fear of displeasing his spiritual lead-

ers. The conflict in attempting to serve both masters had turned him into a tortured soul. She thought of Karen Harrison, the latest inductee into the Temple of Brighter Light. Karen had happily turned her life over to the elders and accepted their rules for daily living. Yet, Claudia could not deny that overall the TBL members seemed happy and contented.

Reaching into the storage console between the seats she selected a Down to the Bone CD. That should push the Ark insanity out of her head for the rest of the ride home.

It was close to seven by the time they had covered the hundred or so miles to Toluca Lake. They were lucky enough to find parking on the street a couple of buildings down from Kelly's condo.

Gently, Claudia shook her friend's arm. "Come on, kiddo, wake up. I can't carry you."

Kelly opened her eyes and stretched, gave a big yawn. "Wow, we're already here? That was fast."

"Two and a half hours in stop-and-go traffic is fast only if you're snoring through it, old pal." Claudia popped the trunk and got out. She lifted out Kelly's computer bag and handed it to her, rolled her suitcase over to the sidewalk.

Kelly slung the computer bag over her shoulder, staggering a little. "I can't wait to see what kinds of post-hypnotic suggestions those motherfuckers planted in my head. Woo-hoo!"

Claudia steadied her, hoping she would not suffer any aftereffects from her experiences at the Ark. "There's your new excuse for off-the-wall behavior—and, where you're concerned, that covers a lot of ground."

They grinned at each other, both relieved to be far away from the strangeness of the Ark and its inhabitants.

"Maybe I should sue the crap out of 'em," Kelly said. "Or we could just go to a bar and drink Seven-Up, see if we can recruit some believers."

Claudia grabbed the suitcase. "I see the post-hypnotic stuff is already working. Let's get your bags inside."

Erin held open the screen door to Kelly's condo and stood aside to let them in. She looked at her sister with concern. "Kelly, are you okay?"

"Why do you ask that, Erin? Could it be that I look like I've been narcotized and stupefied?"

"What are you talking about?"

Ignoring her, Kelly stumbled inside, leaving her computer bag by the front door. She threw herself on the couch and flung her arm over her eyes.

Claudia stood the suitcase beside the computer bag and collapsed the handle. "Your friends at the Ark got hold of her and we don't know what they did. She's lost an entire day of her life. God knows what drugs they used, or what suggestions they might have given her under hypnosis."

Erin's mouth dropped and her eyes got big and round. "They would never do that. Drug someone? No way."

"Yes, way, Miss Holier Than Thou," Kelly said. "I think they ground up Bible passages and force-fed them to me. I keep wanting to spout Matthew 24:14."

"Matthew 24 is about the end of the world," Erin said.

"Oh, really? Claud, would you get me a Coke? I need a blast of caffeine in a major way."

Claudia went into the kitchen, wondering what Kelly would have to say to her sister while she was out of the room. When she returned a few moments later they were glaring at each other like two angry tigers ready to tear out the other's throat.

Erin turned her back on Kelly and spoke to Claudia. "So, what did you find out? Do you know where Kylie is?"

"Why, yes, I do." Claudia was unable to keep the sarcasm from her voice. She opened the Coke and set it on the coffee table within Kelly's reach. "But first, try this on for size: Harold Stedman thinks your child is the new blood of the lamb. Do you find that at all problematic? What the hell is he thinking?"

Erin waved that off as if it were of no consequence. "That's symbolic. Tell me where she is. Where has Rod taken her?"

"He's got her holed up at some bimbo's house," Kelly interjected, and grinned with malicious pleasure at the shock on her sister's face. "Gotcha, Erin. They're with James Miller's niece."

"James's niece? You can't mean Tabby Barton?"

"Uh-huh, Tabby, like a cat."

"But he *can't* be with Tabby, she's excommunicated! He's not even supposed to say hello to her."

"It looks like your husband decided to do a little independent thinking," Claudia said.

"But that's so dangerous."

"What's more dangerous is wanting to send your child away to live in a convent and never seeing her again!"

Erin gasped. Tears welled in her eyes and she ran from the room. They heard the bathroom door slam behind her.

Claudia turned to Kelly. "Was that too mean?"

"She'll get over it. We've done her a massive favor. I just told her where Kylie is. Now she can go get her back and save her from the damn convent."

Knowing about the planned FBI action, Claudia couldn't help feeling uneasy about the situation. "Do *me* a favor and see if you can get that note back from her. The one she said was from Rodney."

"Why? We're done, aren't we?"

"I just want to check something out."

Kelly started to ask what she was thinking when Erin returned to the living room dabbing her eyes with a tissue. "I don't know how to thank you both for everything you did, going to the Ark like that. I'm so grateful. I hope you can see we're not just a bunch of nut jobs."

"Let's not go there, Erin," Kelly said in a warning tone. "Do you not see me lying on my back with a mondo headache? That's thanks to being drugged by those *nut jobs*—your friends. I may never know what they planted in my head. Hell, I could be a Manchurian candidate and never know it."

"That's totally ridiculous," Erin protested hotly. "I don't believe it for a second. Brother Stedman would never do something like that. He's the most decent, kindest man alive. Why would he want to do that?"

"To get me to hand over my bank account and move in?"

"How can you say that?" Erin sputtered, outraged.

Then Claudia noticed she had her bag under her arm. "Are you going somewhere, Erin?"

"You'd better believe I am. I'm not going to stay here another minute and listen to you two bad-mouth my spiritual family."

Kelly launched herself off the couch and for an uncomfortable moment Claudia readied herself to intervene in a physical confrontation between the sisters.

"What the hell are you talking about?" Kelly shouted. "Are you saying we're lying about the drugs and hypnosis? Thirty seconds ago you were thanking us for finding Kylie. What the fuck's going on here, Erin?"

Erin Powers rushed over to the front door and wrenched open the screen. "I *know* Brother Stedman wouldn't do such a thing. And that means either you're lying or you're just plain wrong! I told you, Kelly, I'm thankful to you for finding out where Kylie is, but that doesn't mean you can talk about Brother Stedman that way."

The screen banged shut behind her. Claudia went to the door and watched her race down the footpath and along the sidewalk. She remembered that Kelly had told her Erin had a car parked around the corner.

"Well, that was more than a little weird." Kelly flopped back down on the couch and let out a frustrated sigh. "I think I've had about enough of being a big sister."

"You gave her what she wanted—Rodney and Kylie's whereabouts." Claudia checked her watch. Jovanic had called back to confirm the meeting at her house with the FBI agent. She would have to hurry if she was to be on time. "Tabitha's not a common name and now we have her last name: Barton. If it's not listed on Google, Joel should be able to get it. I'd like to make sure there's no problem in case Erin shows up over there, demanding Kylie."

Kelly agreed. "Can you think of any other reason than what I said—why the TBL people would do what they did to me?"

Claudia could, but she wasn't yet ready to share her theory. She closed the screen behind her, looked back inside at Kelly. "I'd really like to see Erin's handwriting. Look for notes or anything she might have written while she was here. If you find something, fax it to me."

She was merging from the 101-west to the 405-south when her mobile phone rang. It wasn't one of the special ring tones she had assigned to friends. A quick glance at the screen showed her Unknown Caller. She tapped her Bluetooth and answered.

An unfamiliar male voice said, "Is this Claudia Rose?"

"Yes, who's this?"

"My name is Rodney Powers. I understand you've been looking for me."

Chapter 22

Asshole! She wanted to shout at him: *Where the hell are you? What do you think you're doing?*

Rodney Powers was the cause of everything bad that had happened this week, and here he was, just phoning to say, "I understand you've been looking for me."

But shouting wouldn't get her anywhere, so she pushed the anger down into a hard ball in her gut. "Yes, Rodney, I have been looking for you. I found your note last night in my briefcase."

He was silent for a long moment but she could hear him breathing, so she waited him out. Finally, he said, "I don't know whether I can trust you, but when I heard you were asking about me, I decided I had to take the risk and try to contact you. I have nowhere to turn."

Even through the phone Claudia could sense the desperation rolling off him in waves. She felt her own tension rising in response. "So, why put the note in my bag? Why not just talk to me last night?"

"I wanted to, but . . . Why have you been asking the brothers and sisters about Kylie?"

He hadn't mentioned Kelly, and she could not reveal her connection to Erin. If he found out that she knew his wife, he would assume she was working against him—as essentially she had been. She said, "My only motive is to make sure Kylie is safe." That much was true anyway.

"But why? What's your involvement?"

"Rodney, could we please do this in person? I'm on my way to Playa de la Reina, right now, but I'll be glad to turn around and meet you anywhere you like."

She could sense him thinking hard, but in the end he said, "I have no reason to trust you until I know why you're interested in my family."

"But you already know my name, and you know what I do. Obviously you've got my phone number, and you trusted me enough to call me. You put that note in my briefcase, for heaven's sake. Why?"

"I'm desperate," Rodney said. "But I heard you're working for Brother Stedman." He gave a bitter laugh. "One thing you can count on, nothing stays secret for long at the Ark, which is why I can't be there right now."

Something wasn't adding up. Listening to what Rodney was saying and what he wasn't saying, Claudia tried to figure out what was missing. "I've been told there's surveillance everywhere there. Harold Stedman seems pretty paranoid."

Rodney ignored that. "What were you doing in my office at the Ark?"

"I can't talk to you about that, it's confidential. But I assure you, the work I did for Stedman has nothing to do with you or Kylie."

"What did you tell him about my note?"

She had a strong feeling that the way she answered this question would be crucial. "Not a word. I found it after I'd returned to the Ark from the university, and I had plenty of opportunity to show it to him, but I didn't."

"Who did you tell?"

"I told James about it." She flipped on the turn signal for the Venice Boulevard off-ramp and drove west, toward the beach. She certainly wasn't going to tell him anything about the FBI. "When James told me who

Tabby was, I realized that must have been you sitting next to her last night."

Rodney Powers gave a nervous laugh. "I was afraid someone would see me and think I was *stealing* from your briefcase. But Tabby kept you looking the other way until I had dropped the note inside. Nobody noticed."

So much for campus security.

"Yes, she did a good job. James seemed concerned about you staying with her."

"Poor James. I've worn out my welcome there." His voice held the profound sadness of one who knew he had lost a lifelong friend, thanks to the TBL rules. "I can't ask him for anything more. After he told me about you, I needed to see who you were. I wanted to get your attention; thought you might be able to help."

"You certainly did get my attention. What did your note mean about the evildoing, and that things aren't the way they seem?"

Instead of answering her question, he asked her another of his own. "What have you been told about the reason why I took my daughter?"

That was a tricky question and would require some fancy footwork to keep Erin's name out of it. "I heard at the Ark that you and Kylie are very close. That she's even closer to you than to her mother. Look, Rod, I think I understand now how much of a privilege you believe it is to enroll your little girl in Jephthah's Daughters, but how can you send her there, knowing you'll never see her again?"

"But I'm not!"

"What do you mean, you're not? That's why you ran with her, isn't it? So you can make sure she's ready to leave on her birthday?"

"Remember, I wrote that things aren't the way they seem."

"Then why don't you tell me how they really are?"

"It's my wife who still believes our daughter should go into the program, not me. I changed my mind. I couldn't do it."

Rodney's words and his apparent sincerity lent credence to the suspicion that Claudia had been harboring for a couple of days now. He went on, "Erin is completely devoted to Brother Stedman. He's been like a father to her; he practically raised her. She's always been a favorite of his; she would do anything he wanted her to. He's told us ever since Kylie's birth that the Lord had big plans for her, that she's the Chosen One. At first when he said she would be the next Jephthah's Daughter, we could hardly believe it. It was the thrill of a lifetime." Rodney's voice shook with emotion. "But then, after we got to the mountains, the reality of what it meant set in and I knew there was no possible way I could go through with it. Kylie means everything to me. I could never let her go."

As she listened to what he was telling her, Claudia remembered the strange look in Harold Stedman's eyes when he'd spoken about the new blood of the lamb, and she shivered.

In the background, she heard a child begin to wail. Relief poured over her. It was only then she realized that she'd secretly feared Rodney had gone over the brink of sanity and the child had met with some horrible fate. "Is that Kylie? Is she okay?"

The crying grew louder and it was evident that Rodney was carrying the phone with him as he went to check on his daughter. Claudia heard him make soothing sounds and the crying quickly reduced to whimpers.

He must have picked her up. Maybe she was crying for her mother, and for her stuffed bunny, Tickle. After all the praiseful things Claudia had heard about this child, the sound was somehow comforting—Kylie was a human little girl, after all.

"She's tired," Rodney said. He sounded exhausted himself.

"Does Tabby help you with her?" Claudia asked, doubtful that Goth Girl would show much interest in a toddler.

"She's not a kid person. I'm just grateful she's letting us stay here for a while. I don't know for how much longer."

Claudia gripped the wheel tighter. It was time to decide which one of Kylie's parents was telling the truth. She said, "I need to ask you something important, Rod."

"What is it?"

"Did you leave a note for your wife when you took Kylie away?"

He answered without stopping to think about it. "Of course I did. I wouldn't just take off without saying anything."

"Why did you write that there would be suffering?"

"What are you talking about?"

"Never mind. Would you please tell me what you wrote?"

Now he hesitated and she couldn't blame him. There was no reason for him to reveal so much of his personal life to a stranger. But in the end, he did.

"I told her I loved her, but I had come to realize that I couldn't part with our baby, even though Brother Stedman had said Kylie was the Chosen One, and even though taking her away might mean that I would be excommunicated. Why would you want to know about that?"

What he had just told her bore no resemblance to the text of the note that Erin had showed her and Kelly. If Rodney was telling the truth, and Claudia felt reasonably certain that he was, Erin was lying.

Why would she lie about something that so profoundly affected her family's life and her child's future? "If you changed your mind about sending Kylie to the convent, couldn't you have just told your wife?" Claudia asked. "I know TBL wives are expected to be submissive to their husbands, so wouldn't she—"

"Erin will always obey Brother Stedman before me. That's the way we've been taught—we follow the direction of our spiritual leaders without questioning their wisdom."

"But *you* started questioning."

"Yes. And now my family is torn apart because of it." There was the bitterness again.

"Rodney, what happens to the little girls who go to Jephthah's Daughters?"

He started to answer, but Kylie began to wail again. This time she was right next to the phone and was winding herself into a frenzy.

In the background, Claudia heard a muffled male voice.

Rodney said, "What are *you* doing here?"

Kylie started screaming. "No! No! Daddy, no!"

Claudia strained to hear what the man in the background was saying. She yelled into the phone, "Rod, what's going on? What's happening? Rodney?"

Rodney's voice: "Wait, don't do that!"

The line disconnected.

Chapter 23

The sound of Kylie's screams haunted Claudia as she drove past the wetlands and through the hamlet of Playa de la Reina. The child had sounded distraught. Whose voice had she heard in the background? She kept telling herself that Kylie was just having a tantrum, but deep down was the fear that something bad had happened at Tabitha Barton's house.

She phoned Jovanic and told him what happened. He promised to do what he could to get Tabitha Barton's address and request a welfare check from local law enforcement.

At Tyler's coffeehouse she signaled a left turn. Customers had spilled onto the street and were sitting at sidewalk tables listening to the jazz combo playing inside. Claudia spared a pang of envy for those carefree couples enjoying the pink-and-purple canvas of sky over the Pacific Ocean only a block away.

After her debriefing with the FBI agent she promised herself that she would put the Powers family and their troubles behind her. She didn't fool herself that it would be easy. She hadn't met the child face-to-face, but now that she had heard her voice, Kylie seemed more real.

The nagging question returned: Why had Erin lied to her and Kelly? And the answer: Because she knew that if she'd been truthful, they would not have helped her find her daughter.

What would Kelly say when she heard Rod's version of the story and knew she'd been lied to? She'd spent days cloistered in the blazing hot cult compound listening to propaganda; drugged and brainwashed to unwittingly help her half-sister sacrifice her child to a convent in the Rocky Mountains. Kelly would go ballistic.

Claudia felt as if her own anger was burning a hole right through her chest. Thanks to Erin's manipulations, they had practically delivered the child into Stedman's hands. Her only comfort was the knowledge that Rodney would do whatever it took to keep his wife from handing Kylie over to Harold Stedman. She sighed. Maybe tomorrow night she and Jovanic would stroll hand in hand down the hill to Tyler's and watch the sun fall below the horizon while the music played.

Nearly dusk, the streetlamps on Bishop Street were already lit. Morning seemed a long time ago. Was it really only twelve hours since she and James had made their first trek into the woods? So much had happened in between; it seemed days ago. Claudia turned into her driveway, noting the unfamiliar car parked behind Jovanic's Jeep out front.

The FBI case agent had arrived early and the two men were drinking coffee. They both stood as Claudia came through the door and Jovanic introduced her to Agent Jesse Oziel. Her first impression of the agent was formality in a plain brown suit. Pretty much what she'd expected.

As Jovanic came across the room and took her bags, she observed that his stride was easier than when she'd left town at the beginning of the week, and grudgingly conceded to herself that his workout regimen for the past couple of days might actually be helping in his recovery. He was dressed in casual slacks and a black

T-shirt she'd bought him. He looked so good she hoped the interview wouldn't take long.

Jesse Oziel stuck out his hand and gave Claudia's a firm shake. He looked about Jovanic's age—mid-forties—though he was a few inches shorter, with thinning brown hair and a slender build. He had a prominent nose and vigilant eyes that darted here and there while he was speaking. His speaking voice was dry and reserved.

They all went to sit at the kitchen table and Jovanic brought Claudia a mug of strong black coffee. She hadn't realized how utterly drained she was until that moment when she sat back and took a sip—how relieved to be away from the Ark and everything it represented.

Jovanic told her he'd been able to locate Tabitha Barton's address in Moreno Valley. MVPD had promised to send a patrol car over to do a welfare check.

Claudia was relieved to hear it. "I couldn't be sure when the call dropped whether Rod was dealing with Kylie having a tantrum, or something happened. I heard a man's voice, but I don't know what he said. It sounded like Rod knew him, though. I don't think Erin would have had time to get over there from Kelly's."

"That'd be a two-hour drive on a Friday night. She's probably about halfway there." Jovanic got up and took his cell phone from his pocket. "Let me find out what's going on."

After Jovanic left the room, Oziel took a notepad and pen from the briefcase he'd carried into the kitchen with him. He began the formal interview by stating the names of those present, the date, and the reason for the meeting, scribbling on the pad as he spoke.

"Why did Powers phone you tonight?" Oziel asked.

"He heard I'd been asking about him at the Ark and he wanted to know why."

"How did he know you were asking about him?"

"His friend James Miller. He handles the computers for the TBL." She explained how James had overheard her plans for lecturing at UCR and told Rodney.

Oziel nodded and wrote. "What can you tell me about the time you spent at the Hemet compound?"

Claudia hesitated. She felt obliged to explain that she and Kelly had signed a confidentiality agreement upon their arrival at the compound. "I read the agreement before I signed it, of course, and there was a clause providing for an exception in the event of legal proceedings. . . ."

She figured being questioned by the FBI was probably about as legal as it could get. But while she had plenty of misgivings about the Temple of Brighter Light, breaching confidentiality went against her professional grain. When she said so, Oziel raised a pair of sandy eyebrows. "I'm sure you don't want to obstruct our investigation when it's unnecessary, Ms. Rose."

"Of course I have no desire to obstruct anything. But you have to recognize that officially, Harold Stedman is my client, not the FBI, that's all. My first concern is for the safety of Kylie Powers, but if I know what it is you're looking for, I might be able to help you better."

"Our investigation doesn't directly concern the Powers child, but it's possible that something you saw or heard would relate to what we are looking into."

"Which is what?"

"I'm not going to discuss that," Oziel said in a flat monotone that annoyed her.

"But you expect me to talk to you." As soon as she spoke, Claudia felt herself flush. She softened her tone. "If you could tell me something about what you want to know, I'll be happy to answer."

"Let's do this: I'd like you to tell me everything you can remember from the days you spent at the compound. Anything that comes to mind, regardless of how insignificant it may seem to you, could be helpful."

She wanted to ask him "Why bother?" when they already had someone undercover at the Ark, but she had to protect Jovanic. *"Everything?* That's pretty broad."

"Okay then, let's start with the daily activities, how people are treated. The children, for instance, are they being well cared for?"

"Everyone I met at the Ark seemed pretty happy—more than average, in fact. They were well fed; everyone has work assignments in the garden or the kitchen or the bookbindery, and so on. They have a school, so there must be teachers. I know there were classes for new members because they put Kelly in some of them. I expect Joel has told you that she was drugged and hypnotized."

He nodded. "We'll want to interview Ms. Brennan about that later. Why don't you tell me about the work Harold Stedman asked you to do for him at the Ark. I'd like to hear in detail what it was that he wanted from you."

She explained Stedman's suspicions that some members might be disloyal and that he had given her the handwriting of about twenty Ark members to analyze during her stay.

"What did you find out?" Oziel asked, curiosity pushing through his bureau reserve.

"A couple of the samples had signs of possible deception on specific items, but there were no obvious red flags. No major problems, no pathology. As far as integrity, most of them were in the normal range. The essay that had the most glaring indications of a lie was written by the head of security. How's that for irony?"

Oziel got up from the table, took his mug over to the Mr. Coffee on the kitchen counter, and poured himself a refill. "I agree that's a tad ironic. You're referring to a woman named Lynn Ryder, I believe?"

Claudia nodded. "From the little time I spent with her, she seemed to be a devout member. But from the point of view of a handwriting analyst, it was clear to me that her motivation for being at the Ark wasn't precisely what she wrote in her application essay. And, by the way, the only reason why I knew it was Lynn's handwriting was because she walked in on me while it was lying on Rodney's desk. The fact that it was there really shook her up. I think she was afraid of what I was doing with it. Stedman didn't tell her why I was there, and that bothered her, too."

As she spoke, Oziel continued to make notes. "What about the other one? You said there were a couple of them with signs of deception."

"Someone who identified himself as a dentist. It wasn't that he was directly lying so much as he wasn't telling everything. I believe he was leaving out parts of his story—probably facts that he thought would be detrimental to getting his application approved. The identifying information had been removed, so I couldn't tell you who the guy was. Maybe you have enough information to figure it out." She couldn't think of anything else to tell him.

"From what you observed, who would you say are Stedman's most trusted cohorts? The Ryder woman?"

"He put her in charge of the Ark's security, so she has to be high on his list. Erin told us it was because she used to be a security specialist before she joined TBL. Still, if Stedman wanted me to examine her handwriting, he must have had some concerns or suspicions about her. Unless he was testing me, but I have no way of knowing that. I think he gave me Erin Powers's handwriting, too. He could have been using me to double-check the people closest to him. He's suspicious of just about everyone. His own handwriting certainly had indications of paranoia."

Claudia closed her eyes for a moment while she pondered the question. Opening them she said, "The members of the governing board would have to be at the top of his most-trusted list. They write the literature for all the members—not just for the people who live at the Ark but for those at the satellite branches, too. They write books and pamphlets with all the rules—even what married members can do in bed. It seems to be the governing board who makes the final decisions about what's going to be taught and who gets excommunicated when they break the rules." She paused, remembering the stunned reaction of the members when Stedman made his announcement at lunch.

"Someone was excommunicated yesterday while I was there. Joel probably told you about the people I saw in the yard last night, dressed up in robes, like monks? Some of them went in the direction of the main house. I followed a few minutes later, and when I went up to my room, Harold Stedman stopped me on the landing. He would have had just about enough time to change out of the robe."

"What do you think they were doing out there?" Oziel asked, writing furiously. He was on the other side of the table, which made it hard to see his handwriting, but Claudia could see his hand move fast across the page, which meant he was a fast thinker, too.

"Looked like some sort of secret meeting. I'm pretty sure they came from the bomb shelter Stedman showed me today. The person they excommunicated was a man named John Talbot. I thought they might have been meeting about that."

More scribbling. Finally, Oziel's pen halted and he glanced up, waiting. "What else?"

She told him about the note Rodney had left for her the previous evening and he asked her to produce it.

"The handwriting is different from a note his wife showed me." Claudia showed him the note from her briefcase, along with the one that James had given her. She had already placed them separately in acid-free plastic protective sleeves that she kept in her briefcase. She could hear Jovanic in the living room, talking on his cell phone.

"The writing is also different from the writing on the card James gave me," she went on. "But the handwriting in the note James gave me does match some other writing that I came across in a file cabinet in Rodney Powers's office. What I would like to do before giving a firm opinion is to put them all side by side and compare them. Preliminarily, though, it's my belief that Erin herself wrote the note she claimed was from her husband. She wanted Kelly and me to think he was the bad guy in all this."

"It makes you wonder what motive she might have had," Oziel said.

Claudia refused to speculate on that question. "I don't know her motive, but for some reason she wanted Kelly and me to believe Rodney had written that note. I'd say she was trying to protect herself."

"And you're sure about it being her handwriting?"

"As sure as I can be without physically examining the notes side by side. I'm working from memory, but I'm as reasonably certain as I can be that the handwritings are as I've said. The only way for me to be more conclusive is to get the writing in the thank-you note James Miller gave me authenticated by Erin, and that's not likely to happen." She paused again, asking herself if she was crazy for what she was thinking. "I believe Rodney told the truth: Erin's working with Harold Stedman. She used Kelly and me as pawns to help her get the information they needed to get Kylie back."

One eyebrow twitched. "She set you and Ms. Brennan up?"

"Well, she sent us to the rally, where someone 'just happened' to overhear our conversation. Then, *voilà!* Stedman invites me back to the Ark to work for him."

"That means Stedman knew all along about you and Ms. Brennan."

Claudia felt like a fool for allowing herself to get drawn in the way she had. "I should have charged him more for my services, the bastard. Erin must have told him I'm a handwriting analyst and they used that to get us to the Ark. I suppose if I hadn't given them that excuse there would have been some other pretext to get us there."

"Well, it's not illegal for Mrs. Powers to send her child to the Colorado temple." Agent Oziel clasped his hands together on the table, giving her a serious look that made her queasy. She wished Jovanic would return. What was taking him so long?

"I hadn't planned to share this with you, Ms. Rose, but I'm going to because it may be more efficient this way. But I'm warning you not to divulge this information to anyone." He waited until she gave her assent.

"The bureau has been investigating the disappearances of female juveniles who have gone missing from the welfare system in several states over the past few years. We have reason to believe that some of these juveniles ended up at the TBL facility in Colorado. We have recently obtained the location of that facility and have evidence that ties these disappearances to the Temple of Brighter Light and Harold Stedman."

Claudia cleared the mugs from the table and rinsed them at the sink, then went through the motions of making a fresh pot of coffee. The small activity gave her time to think. "I didn't see anything close to child abuse at the Ark, if that's what you're implying. The children I saw there were all well behaved and happy. They didn't look ill treated in any way."

"There doesn't have to be child abuse; we're talking about kidnapping," Oziel said in his dry way.

"They took Erin in from a shelter and raised her; gave her a much better home than she had, which is why she's so loyal to Stedman. If they took the children you're investigating, they must have been rescuing them from a bad situation."

"If they took the children, they broke the law."

Jovanic returned to the kitchen then and took his place at the table. "MVPD sent a deputy over to the Barton girl's place. Someone came to the door and said there was no problem. No sounds of a child in distress. Nothing for them to investigate."

"'*Someone*' answered? But who? Tabby? Rodney?" Claudia asked, frustrated.

"The deputy didn't say, but he felt everything was okay there." Jovanic turned to Oziel. "You said on the phone that you're close to moving on the Jephthah house in Colorado?"

"Yes, Ms. Rose and I were just discussing that. That's why we wanted her and Ms. Brennan clear of the Ark compound."

Claudia figured she knew what he meant, but said it aloud anyway. "You mean in case there's violence, don't you?"

Oziel turned to her, his expression as bland as vanilla yogurt. "In case there are *any* problems. Now, one more question: Who would you guess might be the most vulnerable person there? Someone we might be able to turn?"

"What about Rodney? He might be willing to talk now that he's left the Ark. Or Talbot, if you could track him down—the man who was just excommunicated."

"We will be making an attempt to talk to Mr. Powers, but he hasn't broken any laws that we're aware of, so his cooperation would be strictly voluntary. His disagreement with his wife is not our concern. What does concern us is the Colorado temple and those missing children."

Jovanic said, "Powers had planned for his daughter to go there; he might know something more about it."

Claudia shook her head. "Every time someone started to mention it to me, they got cut off. It's supposed to be secret from outsiders."

Agent Oziel stood and picked up his briefcase, signaling an end to the meeting. "At least we can question Powers."

Claudia followed him to the door. "Seems like Erin would have to have had a pretty compelling reason to lie to get us into the compound."

"Being instructed by Harold Stedman would probably be reason enough," Jovanic suggested.

Oziel turned, his hand on the doorknob. "These people are under the total influence and control of their leaders. You saw what happened to Ms. Brennan. They'll go to great lengths to get what they want."

"There's an elderly woman at the Ark you might want to talk to. She was complaining about the Jephthah program. Her name is Oka Diehl and I can tell you, she *wanted* to talk."

The two men exchanged a glance. Jovanic said, "Agent Oziel got word this afternoon that Mrs. Diehl passed away during the night."

The news hit her like a sucker punch. "Oh God. It didn't have anything to do with her talking to me, did it?"

"There was a kink in her oxygen tube," Oziel said. "It's a fairly rare occurrence, but it happens. The doctor wrote emphysema as the cause of death."

"She was worried about something; she believed something odd was going on." Claudia pictured the wizened little woman, dwarfed in her La-Z-Boy, and felt sad. Oka Diehl had been a character, but she was a smart woman.

As she told them about George Diehl's involvement with the elders and his wife's concern about the Ark's food supply, Claudia caught Agent Oziel staring at her intently. She knew he was judging every word she said, making a determination about her credibility, and she had no doubt that he would check with his undercover operative to corroborate her statement.

Chapter 24

When the door closed behind Oziel, Jovanic's arms went around Claudia, drawing her to him. He cupped her face in his hands. "I missed you, baby."

"I missed you, too."

They shared a long, deep kiss, and it would have been so easy to just give herself over to the moment. But she knew her thoughts would be far from where they should be, where she wanted them to be. He released her and she stepped away. "Where does Tabby live, Joel? We have to go there. Right now."

He rolled his eyes and gave a resigned sigh. "I *knew* that was on your mind."

"We don't know who it was that came to the door at her house."

"It was probably Powers."

"Or not. The sheriff didn't even say whether the person was male or female, did he? And I bet you didn't ask. Jeez."

"If it wasn't Powers, it was probably Tabby. It's her house."

"Tabby would have been unmistakable with that purple streak. The deputy would have mentioned if it had been her."

"Okay, who else?"

"Erin could have called someone when she left Kelly's. She might have got Tabby's address from Rita or Stedman." Claudia went over to the small table by the front door where she had left her purse and keys. "Everything might be fine, but I just have an intuition about it. . . ."

"And your intuition is never wrong?" Jovanic's cop skepticism wasn't even thinly veiled.

She opened the door. "You don't have to come, but I'm going. Just give me the address."

He took the keys from her hand. "Not so fast, Grapho Lady. I'll drive."

Claudia smiled back at him. "I was hoping you'd say that."

They were speeding along the Pomona Freeway when Claudia's cell phone rang.

Kelly's voice, pitched high, furious. "Erin left some stuff behind in her room. I found a note in the trash signed by Rodney; completely different writing style from the one she showed us   I didn't have to be a handwriting expert to see that. The little bitch was lying to us all along. It was a goodbye note—"

"I know," Claudia interrupted. She told Kelly about her conversation with Rodney, and that they were on their way to Moreno Valley, where Tabby Barton lived.

"Where is it?" Kelly demanded. "I'll meet you over there."

"Stay home, Kel, I'll call you when—"

"Are you crazy? This is *my* sister; *I'm* the one who got the most screwed in this whole deal. I'm gonna throttle her. In fact, that girl's gonna experience some holy *terror.*"

"That's exactly why you need to stay home."

"Listen to me, Claudia. Thanks to Erin's little scheme I slept the whole damned day away and I don't know what's been put in my head. But I'm wide awake now, and in case you couldn't tell, I'm pissed as hell. I'm in my car and if you don't give me Tabby's address, I'm going to the fucking Ark—I'm already halfway there—and I promise you, I *will* find out where she is. Now, give me the *fucking* address."

"Where are you?"

"On the 210. I just passed the Sunflower exit."

That meant Kelly was fast approaching the Orange Freeway, the 57. They were driving parallel, Kelly about ten miles to the north and a few miles east. She would soon be headed south and would arrive at a point where Claudia and Jovanic would pass about ten minutes later.

Claudia looked at the paper in her hand where Jovanic had scribbled the address. She recited it with reluctance. "Promise you won't go in by yourself. Promise you'll wait for us."

"Bye-bye, Claudia."

The call disconnected and Claudia looked over at Jovanic in dismay. It wasn't hard to inject urgency into her tone. "We've got to get there first. I think she's been drinking. There's no telling what she might do."

The speedometer was already at ninety and Jovanic was weaving through traffic with the skill of Steve McQueen in *Bullitt.* "Too bad we don't have lights and a siren," he said. "Hang on, babe, and watch for the CHP."

She could hear enjoyment in his voice as his foot mashed down on the accelerator. The old XJ6 flew; 170 horsepower handling like a brand-new machine. They were passing University Avenue in Riverside when a sea of red taillights ahead was a good reason to hit the brakes.

"Damn it! What's going on?" Claudia switched on the radio. *"Traffic and Weather together on the Fives . . . Fender-bender on the Pomona has traffic backed up past*

Central. All lanes blocked, CHP responding. Expect fif-
teen- to twenty-minute delays."

"Hell. I wonder if Kelly got ahead of that mess."

Jovanic made a derisive noise. "I just hope she didn't
cause it."

Claudia had privately been thinking the same thing,
but hearing him say it out loud knotted her stomach
with anxiety. "Damn it," she said again. She had pro-
grammed Tabitha Barton's address into her GPS and
she now checked the display screen. "We exit at Perris
Boulevard. It's only another ten miles."

"Right now we're doing about five miles an hour. You
do the math."

By the time they had inched up to the accident, two
Highway Patrol cars and a fire engine were in the fast
lane. An SUV was on its side in the center divider. Three
people talking with the cops and no ambulance at the
scene—no injuries. Claudia gave a sigh of relief as they
passed. No red Mustang meant no Kelly.

Once Jovanic was able to fully accelerate again, the
Perris Boulevard exit came up fast. They went south
and followed the GPS directions through a middle-class
neighborhood that deteriorated as soon as they turned
the first corner. Even in the darkness, Claudia could tell
that the homes on this block were smaller and not as
well kept.

"I don't see the Mustang," she said as they made a
pass by Tabby's address. "Thank God she's not here
yet." Lights shone through the undraped front windows
of the house. In the Inland Empire, the evening was still
warm enough for front doors to be left open. A gray
primed sedan with a crumpled hood sat in the driveway
on blocks in front of a closed garage.

"We'll drive around the block," Jovanic said. "Check
out the neighborhood before we go in."

"I wonder what Erin was driving. It was a car from the Ark."

Jovanic parked halfway down the block from Tabby's house. "Let's go see what we've got." He checked the pancake holster he'd worn inside his pants, concealed by an unbuttoned shirt over his tee. "Stay behind me."

"Don't worry, I will." Claudia couldn't help feeling relieved that she hadn't had to do this on her own. They climbed out of the Jaguar and walked along the sidewalk past an old dresser someone had discarded at the end of a driveway; past a freestanding basketball hoop in the street.

Tabitha Barton's small rental house was in the middle of the block at the end of a cracked cement driveway. Jovanic double-checked the name on the mailbox out front on the sidewalk, satisfying himself that they were at the right place. He walked up the driveway, his arms slightly away from his body, staying loose. Claudia followed a few steps behind, making a right on the path, then a left that led to the front porch.

Jovanic mounted the two steps to the front door. Claudia waited below. From where she stood she could see part of the small living room through the screen. The room appeared unoccupied. There was a sofa with slouchy cushions set at right angles to a soot-blackened brick fireplace. A round, low wooden table held a Fisher-Price doll's house and some children's books.

He stood to the side of the door, rapped on the metal screen with his knuckles, and called out, "Tabitha Barton?"

"Did you hear that?" Claudia said quietly. "I think I heard something."

"Shhh." He put his ear near the screen and listened. Then he knocked again and called out, louder this time.

"Tabitha Barton. Police officer." He stepped off the porch; Claudia backed up behind him.

She counted to thirty while he waited for a response. When none came he told her to stay where she was and moved quietly to the front window and peeked inside. He eased around the side of the house, then returned a few moments later, shaking his head. Coming close to Claudia he said in her ear, "Shades are down in the back, but all the lights are on. I'd feel better about this if we had backup."

He went back up on the porch and pushed open the screen. She hadn't seen him unholster his weapon, but there was the Beretta in his hand, next to his leg, pointed at the floor. He moved silently inside.

With a few quick strides across the room Jovanic disappeared down a hallway. Claudia slipped inside and waited by the door. The interior smelled like an ashtray.

A second later, Jovanic called her to come. The urgency in his voice sent her rushing to the back bedroom.

A man lay prone on the carpet, gagged with duct tape. He'd been hog-tied, hands and feet bound behind his back, and he was struggling against his bonds. On the other side of a double bed that took up most of the space in the small room, a cot had been set up. A new-looking baby doll had been discarded on the rumpled blanket.

"No sign of Kylie." Jovanic holstered his weapon and was kneeling on the floor, peeling away the duct tape that had been used to silence the man. He worked slowly to avoid tearing the skin around his mouth, but the man cried out as the last of it came off.

Jovanic set the tape carefully aside, piece by piece. Claudia knew he wouldn't want to contaminate it and ruin any latent prints that might have been left behind. He took a penknife from his pocket and began to cut the cord restraining the man's arms and feet behind his back. The knots could be evidence, so he would leave them tied.

She backed out of the room and hurried into the other bedroom, not wanting to accept what Jovanic had said about not finding Kylie.

As she went, Jovanic's deep voice carried through the tiny house: "What's your name, buddy?"

She could hear the shaky answer: "Powers, my name's Rod Powers. Cut me loose. Hurry, please, hurry!" Rodney Powers's voice rose, close to hysteria. "They took my little girl. Oh my God; they took her."

Knowing in her heart the futility, Claudia checked the bathroom. *Nothing there.*

Jovanic: "Okay, Mr. Powers, if you want me to cut you loose, you'll need to calm down. I understand that you're upset, but we're here to help you."

Claudia couldn't hear the response. *Check the kitchen. Nothing.*

Out of rooms to check and no sign of Kylie. Or Erin. Or Kelly. *Where are they?*

For a moment she stayed where she was, fists clenched, trying to hold in check the fear that threatened to consume her. Jovanic didn't need *two* hysterical people to deal with. When she was feeling more in control of her emotions, she returned to the bedroom.

Rodney Powers was sitting on the edge of the bed, his head lowered. He was taking deep breaths and seemed to be fighting hyperventilation. His breathing got steadier and he began to rub his wrists, stretching his arms and legs; grimacing as the circulation began to return to his extremities. He looked up as Claudia came into the doorway and she saw blood trickling from a cut on his lip. His left eye was swollen nearly shut, though she could see the recognition dawn on his face.

"Do you need medical attention, Mr. Powers?" Jovanic asked. He had his badge out so Rodney could see he was legitimate. "Do you want an ambulance?"

Rodney waved the suggestion away. "No, no, I'm fine. Just get me out of here."

"We should call the local sheriff's office, file a complaint—"

"I don't *care* about that. We have to stop them. We have to—"

Jovanic broke in. "Look, if you don't care, we don't care. No sheriff. Now, you said 'they.' Who tied you up?"

Rodney met Claudia's eyes and she could see the agitation and the fear. "Please," he implored. "You've got to help me. Brother Stedman is planning to kill my daughter."

Chapter 25

"*Kill* your daughter?" Claudia stared back at him, hoping she had misheard, knowing that she hadn't. "You mean at the Jephthah's Daughters ceremony? But that's a symbolic . . ."

"No—yes; you don't understand."

"You've got that right! How about explaining it to us."

"We have to go." Rodney struggled to stand, but when he started to put pressure on his leg he collapsed back on the bed, biting off a cry of pain.

"What did they do to you?" Claudia asked.

"Foot," he gasped. He pushed himself up again, started across the room. Fell to his knees at her feet, sobbing gibberish. "Broken. Broken. Kylie. Don't know what—"

"We'll get you to a hospital."

"*No!* The Ark. Gotta get to the Ark. Tabby's at work. No other way—*Please,* you've got to help me." He grabbed her hands, almost babbling, his words running together as if he couldn't get them out fast enough.

Claudia looked down at the gaunt, desperate face; at the pallor where bruising hadn't yet had time to bloom. He probably hadn't eaten in days. She glanced over at Joel, who nodded. She said, "Okay, Rod, pull it together. We'll take you to the Ark."

Jovanic grabbed his arm and helped him to his feet. "Let's go. You can tell us about it on the way."

Before they left Tabby's house, Claudia returned to the kitchen and dug through the drawers until she found a plastic sandwich bag. She loaded it with ice and wrapped it in a dishcloth for Rodney to use as a compress on his face.

Claudia told Rodney to sit up front and then climbed into the backseat. She pulled up the Ark's address information on the GPS and summarized their route for Jovanic. Hemet was thirty miles southeast of Tabitha Barton's house, the Temple of Brighter Light compound a farther ten miles south.

Jovanic fired up the Jag and pulled away from the curb. "So, you look like shit, Rod. Who did the tap dance on your face?"

"The biggest brother at the Ark—Jermaine Johnson." Rodney switched the makeshift ice pack from his lip to his eye. He seemed calmer now that they were actually in the car and in pursuit of his wife and daughter. "We always call him the gentle giant, but before he joined the temple he was a street thug and—hey, wait! Stop!"

They had turned the corner and Rodney was pointing at an older-model Toyota parked at the curb in the middle of the block. "That's the car Erin and I took to the mountains. She must have driven it here and now she's gone back to the Ark with Jermaine in the car he was driving."

"How do you know it's the one?" Jovanic asked.

"The license plate: ARK004. We keep several cars at the Ark for members to use when they need them. Jermaine got here first and Erin showed up a little later. "

Everyone was quiet for a moment; then Jovanic said, "Seems your wife had things planned out pretty carefully."

"She must have called Stedman as soon as Kelly told her where she could find you and Kyle," Claudia offered. "She was in the bedroom for a few minutes after we got to Kelly's place. There's a phone she could have used."

"Who's Kelly?" Rodney sounded confused.

"Erin's half-sister. After you left with Kylie, Erin came to Kelly looking for help finding you. And because Erin brought a note that she claimed was from you, Kelly asked me to come over and look at the handwriting. I expect that gave Erin a jolt. But, of course, I hadn't seen her handwriting or yours, so I had no idea she wasn't telling us the truth. We went to the Ark to see if we could get any information about where you might be. Then Kelly got suckered into going to a class; they drugged her and, well, it's kind of a long story."

Rodney stared through the windshield for about a minute before he said anything. "Please don't think badly of my wife; she doesn't know what she's doing. Brother Stedman and the elders are—"

"I know." Claudia did not want to hear him defend the TBL leaders. "Independent thinking is a dangerous thing, yada-yada-yada. Honestly, Rodney, I can't comprehend someone believing in a religion where the members are expected to blindly follow what they're told, even if it means casting aside their close family members. Or worse, in this case, doing something that's going to harm a child. Are you *sure* about—"

Rodney twisted in his seat, turning an agonized gaze toward her, and pointed at his already swollen face. "Do you think Jermaine Johnson would have done this to me if they were just going to send Kylie to Colorado? I forgive him for what he did; I know he didn't want to hurt me. My brothers and sisters are a peace-loving people. We don't join in wars, even if it means going to prison for our faith. Jermaine was only doing what he'd been instructed to do. This *isn't* the way we handle things."

"Apparently it is now." The man was suffering and Claudia knew she shouldn't add to his pain, but her anger suddenly flared like a volcanic eruption. "How *stupid* can you people be?"

She caught the look Jovanic flicked her in the rearview mirror, but all he said was, "We're gonna need some backup. Claudia, get Hemet PD on the phone for me."

Claudia got the police department's phone number from Information and punched it in for him, then handed Jovanic the phone as someone came on the line. He identified himself as a detective with LAPD. He told them in cop-speak about the assault on Rodney and the potential danger to Kylie—and requested patrol cars to meet them at the TBL compound.

Jovanic listened for a couple of minutes. He rang off and tossed the phone back to her. "They're not coming."

"What do you mean, 'not coming'?"

"They've already got a bad situation. Gang members crashed a party; a rival gang. Multiple gunshot victims. The desk sergeant already deployed everyone he could spare to the scene, which is on the other side of town from where we're going. It's a small department and there's no one available for us until they get this thing wrapped up."

"But you told them there could be a child's life at stake."

Jovanic caught Claudia's outraged eyes in the mirror. "They'll send someone out as soon as they can, but right now, we're on our own."

In Moreno Valley the 60 Freeway connected the communities east of Riverside. This segment of highway was reduced to only four lanes and was far less traveled than any other route they might have taken. Jovanic punched it, switching to high beams so he could see the dark, twisty road ahead; lowering them when a vehicle traveling west flashed headlights back at them.

He made another call, this time to Agent Jesse Oziel, an effort that ended as fruitless as the call to Hemet PD. The outgoing voicemail message on Oziel's direct number indicated that he was unavailable, which Jovanic said probably meant he had already left for the operation in Colorado.

As they drove, Claudia encouraged Rodney to continue his story.

"He showed up while I was on the phone with you, Claudia." He struggled to keep his emotions in check. "Brother Johnson. He's—"

"Huge," she interjected. She had remembered the name from the badge of the man who had met her at the classroom door the first time she'd attempted to get Kelly to leave the Ark.

"So, this Johnson guy showed up and then your wife," Jovanic prompted. "What happened?"

"Erin said she was taking our daughter with her. She was like a different person." He reached up and pressed his left eye as if he couldn't believe what he was saying and needed to make it real by touching the injured flesh. "I told her there was no way I'd give up Kylie and she started to argue with me. She had this rebellious attitude, completely unsubmissive. I've never seen her behave like that, even in the mountains when the whole issue started. Brother Johnson got between us and tried to persuade me to hand her over. Kylie was terrified. At first she'd been happy to see her mother, but she's smart; she understood something bad was happening. Erin grabbed her out of my arms and ran. Thank God she took her outside before he started pounding on me. I didn't stand a chance against him."

"The man's the size of Paul Bunyan's ox," Claudia

told Jovanic. She couldn't help feeling glad that they hadn't run into Johnson at Tabby's. That would be a confrontation she would not welcome. "Rod, explain what you said before, about Stedman *killing* Kylie."

Rodney sucked in a deep breath and turned to face her. With his left eye almost shut, he had to adjust his seat belt and twist in his seat so he could see her. "Do you know the story of Jephthah's daughter? Jephthah was a judge in the Bible who promised to sacrifice his daughter if the Lord gave him the victory."

"Yes, we've heard about the TBI. program and the temple in Colorado where the little girls go."

He continued, "When a girl child is consecrated and she's being prepared to enter into Jephthah's Daughters, we always have a very special ceremony at the Ark, even if she wasn't born there. Even if her family lives at a satellite facility, they bring her to the Ark for the big event. It's truly a momentous occasion and it happens only rarely. Even though it's something many parents aspire to for their daughters, it's obviously not going to happen every year because it has to be on the third anniversary of her birth."

In the darkness, Claudia could see his eyes shining with zeal as he spoke about the program.

"When a family is preparing for their daughter to go to the temple, the brothers at the Ark get together and build a ceremonial altar. It's a really wonderful thing for a child to enter into the program. The women dress her up in a special gown and fix her hair with flowers. Then she's taken to the altar, where she lies while Brother Stedman says prayers over her and symbolically offers her up to the Lord. After the ceremony we have a big party and then she's taken away to the temple by one of the sisters who lives there, and she's taught to serve the Lord for the rest of her life."

Claudia thought of her conversation with Agent Oziel, and the raid the FBI was planning on the Colorado temple. She wondered when he would receive the urgent message Jovanic had left on his voicemail. It seemed a good time to ask Rodney a question that had been troubling her. "Are you telling us that the girls at the temple are—well, unharmed? There's nothing illegal going on there?"

He was indignant. "Of course they're not harmed. I would never have considered sending Kylie there if I hadn't believed it was the most precious thing we could do for her. Why would we want to harm little girls?"

"Then why did you leave your wife in the mountains and run with Kylie?" Jovanic asked.

"I took her and ran because something different is going on. James Miller called me while we were there, getting ourselves ready for Kylie's consecration. James is like a literal brother to me as well as a spiritual one. He risked his eternal life to call me, but he was so troubled that he felt compelled to." Rodney stopped for breath, as if he needed to consider what he was about to reveal. "James had gone upstairs to hand in a report. When he was outside the office door, James could hear Brother Stedman talking—the door was ajar. He said Brother was praying out loud. He was talking about the end of times—how imminent it is, and . . ."

"Just how imminent is it, Rod?" Jovanic asked, flicking a glance at his passenger when he broke off what he was saying.

In a voice that chilled Claudia to her core, Rodney Powers said, "It's already here."

Chapter 26

"What the hell are we getting ourselves into?" Jovanic muttered as Claudia leaned forward and grabbed Rodney's shoulder. "What do you mean it's already here? What else did Stedman say?"

"James said he was talking about how he had prepared the perfect blood of the new lamb and he was getting ready to offer her up in sacrifice on her third birthday. He spoke about preparing the altar and the"—Rodney faltered over the word—"knife. Sharpening the ceremonial knife. There's *no knife*. There's never been a knife. It was always symbolic—a symbolic sacrifice. Tomorrow is Kylie's birthday." He was beginning to sound panicked again. "Erin doesn't know what Brother is thinking, I know she doesn't. She would never—"

"Wait a minute," Claudia interrupted. "We have to find Kelly. She must have decided to go straight to the Ark and wait for Erin there." She got out her cell phone and gave the voice command for Kelly's number, but it just rang until it eventually switched over to voicemail.

For the next twenty minutes, the ride was tense and silent, each absorbed in thought to occupy the miles. Claudia guessed that Jovanic was mapping out a strategy in his head for what to do when they arrived. He had a weapon and the force of the law behind him, but he lacked Rodney's advantage of being thoroughly familiar with the compound. Even Claudia had a rough knowledge of the layout of the buildings. Some of them anyway. She had not gone past the little village area.

Her mind kept returning to Kelly—wondering where she might be or what trouble she might have run into. She tried phoning several times, but the calls all went straight to voicemail. Either Kelly was avoiding her and had turned off the phone or she was using it. When she got into the hills about five miles before arriving at the Ark, Kelly would lose her cell service altogether.

Jovanic drove into Lamb Canyon with only about ten miles to go.

"We don't have any idea what the situation is gonna be when we get there," Jovanic said. "Rod, forget what you said about being peace lovers. What weapons are there at the Ark?"

"None that I'm aware of, I swear. I truly don't believe there are any. Brother Stedman has always preached Isaiah 2:4: *'They will beat their swords into plowshares and their spears into pruning-knives.'* I can't imagine him suddenly going against that now. It would be completely unlike him."

Claudia couldn't help her retort: "But last week, you couldn't imagine him performing child sacrifice, either. Now he's talking about a knife, and you believed it was serious enough to take Kylie and run. Rodney, how far do you think he might be prepared to go to make sure he gets his way on this? What will he do to protect his plans for your child?"

"God, I wish I knew." His voice cracked. "I just don't know anymore."

Jovanic said, "Rod, I need you to explain the layout of the compound to me. You've got to stay calm and tell me everything you can think of that might be important."

"Yes, you're right. If you have something to write on, I'll draw a map."

Claudia said there was a steno pad and pen in the glove compartment. "There's a gated entry," she explained to Jovanic as Rodney drew. "And a guard twenty-four seven. On each side of the guard shack, there's a hedge at least eight feet high that runs—Rod, does it go all the way around the perimeter?"

"No. In the back, at the far end of the property we have a working farm. The fields are fenced, but not that high. It would be a long hike to get back there from the road; it's better if we go in through the front gate." He pondered for a moment. "I think Brother Martin would be on duty tonight. He's a good friend; we shouldn't have any trouble with him."

Given the circumstances, Claudia was less sure they should count on *anyone* being friendly.

"Inside the gate there's a parking lot, then a Victorian house. That's where the offices are and where the governing board have their apartments. Behind the house is a big garden patch, then the cafeteria and some other buildings—the school, the print shop and bindery, the general store. Like that."

Rodney took up the narrative. "Past the industrial buildings are the residences. We call that area the village. That's where my house is. A little ways beyond the village is the church; and past that, the farm. That's pretty much everything, I think."

"How many people live at the compound?"

"Around two hundred, usually. Around seventy-five or so are adult men."

"Where's the underground bunker you told me about, Claud?" Jovanic asked.

"It's in the area where the industrial buildings are. Rodney, do you know how to get in there?"

"The bomb shelters? Sister Ryder keeps the keys to most of the buildings, but I don't know about the bomb shelters. Brother Stedman might be the only one."

"Sounds like a lot of possibilities to consider," Jovanic said. "We only have one weapon between us, not exactly a lot of firepower if it comes down to a fight. Might be best if we wait for Hemet PD."

In the front seat, Claudia saw Rodney go rigid in protest. "No! We can't wait. We can't risk my daughter's life. I'll go in by myself if I have to. Nothing on earth is going to stop me."

"Face it, Rod, you can barely walk on your own," said Jovanic. "You're not going to be a whole lot of help."

"This is my child! Don't you understand he's going to kill her?"

"Do you honestly believe the members would allow him to actually sacrifice a child?"

He got very quiet; then he said, "One thing I know for certain: whether they like it or not, they will go along with anything the governing board tells them to do."

They had arrived at the narrow access road leading to the Ark. Jovanic made the left turn and drove slowly into the unlit woods. "Shit, it's darker than Bin Laden's soul out here."

"And just as treacherous," Claudia said. "I'll tell you when we get to the last curve before the front gate. Maybe we should park there and walk the rest of the way in."

She gave him the heads-up and he pulled over to the side of the narrow road, switched off the headlights, and killed the engine. Rodney handed him the rough map he'd drawn and Jovanic studied it in the light of the glove compartment. They were still around the corner from the Ark, but there was no point risking drawing attention by using the dome light. When he had finished, they all climbed out to walk the last few yards to the Ark.

As they stepped out of the air-conditioned Jaguar, the heat enveloped them like a blanket, instantly dampening Claudia's forehead with perspiration. She had become accustomed to the late-evening temperature in the hills behind Hemet hovering in the mid-eighties, but tonight the humidity was unusually high.

"Where's the Maglite?" Jovanic asked. Unable to talk Claudia into handling a firearm, a few months ago he had supplied her with a heavy-duty flashlight as an emergency weapon.

"Under the front seat. We're gonna need it behind the house; it's as dark as pitch out there." She felt stupid that she herself had not thought of bringing it along, now that it would have come in handy. Jovanic just nodded as if he knew. He clicked the flashlight on and off to check the batteries.

Rodney was limping badly, but insisted he was fine. "Let me go first. If Jerry Martin is in the guardhouse, he'll let us in without a problem. I'll find out if Erin and Brother Johnson are here."

They turned into the long driveway. Claudia came to a sudden halt. "Oh, Jeez."

Blocking the gate was a red Mustang. Its trunk open.

Chapter 27

"Oh shit, Kelly's car." Claudia's voice sounded quavery in her own ears. "Is she inside?"

"Wait here. I'll see if Brother Martin is on duty." No engine sounds carried on the still night air as Rodney started limping toward the guardhouse.

Standing in the shadow of the trees, they watched him cover the short distance. Claudia noticed that Jovanic kept his hand on the Beretta, and was grateful to have him beside her. She had gotten herself out of a few jams in the past, but having Jovanic there with his weapon felt like the difference between a skateboard and an armored tank.

The guardhouse was not much larger than a tollbooth and had a two-part Dutch door on one side. The top half was open. Rodney was in the small building for only a couple of seconds before he backed out and hobbled all the way around it. When he was finished he waved them over, shaking his head in bewilderment.

"This is really strange. There's nobody here. Someone is *always* supposed to be at the gate. It's never to be left open like this."

Jovanic said, "Let's find out what's up with Kelly's car."

Together, he and Claudia went around to the rear of the Mustang and looked inside the open trunk. The carpet had been folded back, the sheet of Masonite that covered the spare tire left askew. Neither of them spoke; the look they exchanged was enough.

Leaving the trunk they went to the driver's door. As Claudia reached out to open it, Jovanic grabbed her hand. "Don't touch anything . . . just in case."

"You think it could be a crime scene? Oh God . . ." The driver's side window was down. She leaned forward and peered inside, taking care to keep her hands away from the surface of the vehicle.

She could see that the key was in the ignition, Kelly's key ring with the little silver shark attached dangling from it. The key ring had been a gag gift from a former husband—not because she was a lawyer, he'd said, but because she was predatory. She'd been amused.

Her purse lay discarded on the passenger seat; her iPhone on the floor, half hidden under the accelerator. Claudia gave a quick glance back at Jovanic. His face gave away nothing, but she could feel his heightened vigilance; knew he had seen it all, knew he had read the fear in her eyes.

The three of them walked around the front of the Mustang and through the open gate, onto the grounds. In the parking area, the SUVs and several smaller sedans were still parked in the same spaces as when Claudia and Kelly had left the Ark so many hours earlier. There was one difference: a Toyota that matched the one Rodney had pointed out near Tabby's house was parked in front of the Victorian, both doors wide open as if the occupants had left in a hurry.

Shining the flashlight around at the bushes and shrubs surrounding the house, Jovanic strode ahead and checked out the Toyota. When he turned back to them he shook his head, confirming what they already knew. *Not here.*

Up ahead, the front windows of the Victorian were

lit up like the Fourth of July. Only the night lights should have been burning this late. They started up the front steps, Claudia straining in vain to see any activity through the open drapes.

Rodney rushed across the porch, ignoring any pain he might be feeling in his smashed foot, and wrenched open the front door. When Claudia and Jovanic followed him inside, he was still standing in the entry, staring helplessly in one direction, then the other, as if unsure of what to do next.

"Where are they?" Panic made his voice squeak. "Where could they be? Oh, God in heaven, please show me where they are."

The house was hushed with an emptiness that left Claudia edgy. She pointed to the staircase and mouthed to Jovanic, *Stedman's rooms.*

He nodded that he understood and took the lead, motioning them to stay close to the wall. They ascended the stairs with Rodney leaning heavily on the handrail. His breathing was labored as he climbed, and Claudia went behind him in case he needed help. In her view, it was stupid for him to go when he was so impaired, but he insisted and there was no point wasting time in an argument.

On the second floor, light flowed into the hallway from Harold Stedman's open office door. Jovanic stopped several feet short and raised his voice. "Mr. Stedman?"

Aside from his voice and their breathing, the silence was complete. Signaling for Claudia and Rodney to stay where they were, Jovanic moved quickly around the doorway, his weapon out in front of him. He returned seconds later shaking his head: *No one there.*

The door to the guest room Claudia had occupied was also open but no lights were on inside. While she and Rodney waited at the top of the stairs, Jovanic cleared that room and then the bathroom. Two other closed doors—nothing but additional empty bedrooms.

"The governing board members live on the third floor," Claudia said in a low voice, remembering what Rita had told her.

"No!" Rodney insisted. "We don't have time to go up there. They're not here; we need to go to the church."

Jovanic spoke quietly. "Let's keep it low-key. If we're systematic about this, we'll find them. Where's the altar located? The special one you said they were building for the ceremony."

"Behind the church." Rodney started nodding. "The sanctuary. That's gotta be it; that's where we have to go."

They returned to the first floor and were walking single file through the hallway that led to the back door. Jovanic, who was in front, came to a sudden halt. Claudia, on his heels, crashed into him. "What?"

He half turned. "Hand me the flashlight." He squatted into a crouch and pointed the beam at something he had spotted on the floor. Straightened; turned to them with a grim face. "Could be blood."

"Oh, dear Lord God," Rodney moaned.

Claudia swung around. What little color he had drained from his face, and for a moment it looked as if he might pass out. "Lean over," she urged him. "Put your head down."

Jovanic said, "If it *is* blood, there's enough here to indicate serious injury."

Claudia looked past him and saw the dark stain on light-colored floor tile. "Of course it's blood. I can see drops all the way to the back door."

Jovanic turned to Rodney. "Is there any other way out of the building that will get us to the church? We have to avoid contaminating this area."

Rodney slowly shook his head, shock still registered on his face. "Only the front door. We have to go back out the way we came and walk around to the back."

They retraced their route, leaving through the main entrance. With every step to the back path, the words chanted in Claudia's head: *Please don't let Kylie be hurt.*

Overhead, the sky was hazy with clouds that obscured the moon and stars as thoroughly as the gravel obscured further signs of blood. Somewhere in the distance, Claudia heard the rumble of thunder. Summer rain in Hemet was not unheard of, but certainly was out of the ordinary.

They strainined for any sound as they went, but there was only the slight crunch of their footfalls. They had walked about fifty yards when Claudia's ears picked up something else. Jovanic, walking in front of her, gave no indication that he had heard it.

"Joel!" She grabbed the back of his shirt and stopped him with her whisper. "Listen." They came to a halt and let the silence envelop them. Seconds later it came again: a soft groan of pain, followed by a cry for help.

Jovanic left the path and shone the flashlight into a clump of pampas grass that lined the side of the path. He walked around behind the plants and a moment later called to Claudia. She followed his voice. "Is it Kelly?"

"No." He was kneeling on the ground, his body blocking the dark form lying there. As Claudia moved around him, she realized that he would not know if it was Erin. Her eyes followed the flashlight beam over the body protectively curled in on itself to a face streaked with blood.

"Lynn!" Claudia dropped to her knees beside the security chief. "Lynn, can you hear me?"

Lynn Ryder groaned. Her eyes fluttered and rolled

up. "What—what hap—?" She struggled to sit up, but Claudia pressed her shoulders back onto the grass.

"Just stay still, we're going to get you some help." Claudia turned to Jovanic. "Tell Rod to find Dr. Jarrett."

Lynn looked up at her, frowning as if her vision might be blurry. She reached up and touched her head just above the temple; stared at her bloodstained hand. Her eyes seemed to get better focus and she scrunched them as if trying to recall what had happened to her. "Hit me . . . she hit . . . Brenn—"

"Brenn? Brennan? *Kelly* hit you?"

"She was trying . . . take the girl . . . tire iron . . . turned . . . caught my head." Lynn Ryder rolled onto her side with a moan, trying to get up.

Claudia put a hand on her shoulder. "You probably have a concussion. You shouldn't move around."

Jovanic returned from the path and crouched beside Claudia. "Rod's gone."

"What do you mean, *gone?*"

"I mean he's not where we left him and I couldn't see him anywhere."

"Oh hell, he must have gone to the church." Claudia stood and drew Jovanic a few feet away, where Lynn Ryder wouldn't hear. "Lynn's hurt pretty badly, I think. Kelly's missing with a tire iron; Erin and Kylie are missing . . ."

"Tire iron?"

"I'll tell you later. We have to find Rodney before he gets himself into trouble. What should we do with Lynn?"

"We have to take her with us. I'll carry her."

"Joel, you're still recovering from an infection, you shouldn't—"

"I'm fine and we don't have a choice. We can't leave her out here alone."

"Okay. We're not far from the infirmary. We can take her there. Maybe there will be night staff on duty."

Between them, they managed to get Lynn Ryder to her feet and Jovanic swung her into his arms without much effort. Claudia held the flashlight on the path ahead, but her mind was on the church, her heart praying they would find Kylie Powers in time.

As with most of the buildings at the Ark, the door to the infirmary was unlocked. Claudia held it open as Jovanic carried Lynn Ryder inside. As with the Victorian, all the lights were burning, but no one came to the front desk. She opened the door that led to the examining rooms and the room where Kelly had spent the afternoon.

"There's a hospital bed in the back room," she told Jovanic. "I don't think anyone's here, but I think she'll be safe there until we can get some help. There's really nothing else we can do for her."

"We need to get to a phone and call 911."

She helped him settle Ryder in the bed. "As far as I know, the only two landline phones are in the Victorian. One's in Rita's office, locked up. The other is in Stedman's office."

"Shit, we don't have time to go back there." He straightened and the front of his shirt was stained with blood from Lynn Ryder's head wound. "Ms. Ryder, do you remember anything about what happened before you got hit?"

Ryder squinted at them through drying blood. "I just remember—Erin Powers came back with Brother Johnson. She was fighting with that Brennan woman. Why were they—"

"Erin and Kelly are sisters," Claudia said. "Was Kylie with Erin?"

Ryder's eyes clouded with confusion. "Kylie? The baby? No. Not with Erin."

"With who, then? Was Kylie there?"

"Brother Stedman took her. Erin . . . wanted to go and dress Kylie for the con—consecration, but the other one was yelling."

"What about Jermaine Johnson?" Jovanic asked. Claudia crossed her fingers and hoped that Kelly hadn't gone after *him* with a tire iron. She had a sick feeling that to Johnson a tire iron in Kelly's hands would be about as effective as a toothpick.

"Brother Stedman sent Brother Johnson to help . . ." Lynn's eyes suddenly opened wide. "I have to go! The end of time—I have to—"

"You can't go anywhere," Claudia said. "What about the end of time? What's going on, Lynn?"

"It's time. I have to tell my—" Her hand flew up and covered her mouth. "Oh God, what do I do?"

Jovanic got in her face and he looked convincing: "Ms. Ryder, Lynn, listen to me. I'm a police officer." He took out his badge wallet and showed her his ID. "I want you to tell me what you know about what's going on tonight, and it has to be right now."

"You're a cop?" She grabbed his arm with both hands, holding on as if he were offering her a life jacket. "What time is it? Tell me! What time is it?"

He checked his watch. "Eleven twenty-five."

"Oh, no." For a moment, Lynn looked more like a freaked-out kid than the head of security for the Ark compound. Then her voice grew stronger. "You've got to help me. I need to call someone, get them over here."

"Who do you want to call?"

"My—my aunt and uncle. The phone in Rita's office, you can—"

Claudia stared at her, thinking she had to be concussed. "We'll call them for you after we find Kylie. Do you know where Stedman took her?"

"No! I have to call them now. You've gotta let me—" She let go of Jovanic's arm and tried to push herself up; fell back on the pillow, groaning.

Claudia hurried into the bathroom and wet some paper towels. The wound was above the hairline, hard to see in the black hair. She dabbed away the blood from Lynn's face and assessed the damage. She would have one hell of a shiner by tomorrow.

"Lynn, we'll come back as soon as we find Kylie, and you can call your aunt and uncle then. Right now, you have to stay here and take it easy."

"I can't, I've gotta go—gotta tell—"

She was growing more agitated, having trouble getting the words out. Jovanic narrowed his eyes in speculation. "Your aunt and uncle—are they your handlers?"

It didn't seem possible, but Lynn's face paled even further. Her eyes darted from him to Claudia. "Who *are* you? What are you doing here?"

"We just want to find Kylie," Claudia said. "Did Stedman take her to the sanctuary?"

"They were going to Erin's house to get her ready. Please—"

"Which house is the Powerses'?" Jovanic asked.

"Bethlehem. But—"

He started for the door. "We'll come back for you as soon as we can. Stay here until then."

They exited the building and started moving fast toward the village.

"What was that all about?" Claudia asked. "What did you mean, 'her handlers'?"

Jovanic shot her a look. "She's the FBI operative."

"What?"

"It was a guess, but her reaction confirmed it. She's the one. Those people in town, her 'aunt and uncle,' are agents. They're posing as her relatives."

"So, the times she went to see them she was actually reporting in?"

"That, plus an important part of their job would be to keep her deprogrammed, make sure she stayed as psychologically healthy as possible while she was working for them."

"Being undercover for long periods of time has got to be extremely stressful."

"Especially for someone who's just acting as an informant, not an official agent who's trained for it."

"Rita mentioned that sometimes some of the members went with Lynn and helped clean their house because her 'uncle' was in a wheelchair."

"The Feds would have spent a lot of time and effort setting the whole thing up before recruiting her from the group, or sending her in—whichever way they did it—especially considering how paranoid Stedman is."

Claudia thought about it as they jogged along the path together. She remembered remarking to Agent Oziel during her debriefing with him about the irony in the chief of security being the one person whose handwriting indicated lack of honesty. He must have been laughing behind that poker face, aware of the biggest irony of all: that the chief of security was acting as an informant, working with the FBI. Small wonder Lynn's handwriting had showed tension. Small wonder that she had been so upset when she caught Claudia examining her application essay.

Beyond the infirmary, the other common buildings were unlit and the grounds dark. Jovanic carried the Maglite and they ran as fast as the bouncing puddle of light on the path ahead allowed. Claudia could hear small creatures scuttling through the shrubs, and she remembered Stedman's warning about coyotes and other predators. Those night creatures were not the ones that concerned her.

Lights up ahead. A building rose out of the darkness, its interior lights shining like a row of peeping eyes in the night. Jovanic switched off the light. "What's that place?"

"The dining hall." Claudia slowed her steps. "What's with all the lights? Joel, this isn't right. They eat early here. After what Lynn said—" She broke off, not wanting to give voice to her fears.

They were only a few feet away now. Together, they approached the open dining hall door with caution. Then Jovanic moved in front of her and went to look inside. When he turned back, Claudia tried unsuccessfully to read the expression on his face. She pushed past him and stared at the scene inside with bewilderment.

Chapter 28

Row after row of deserted tables. Plates of half consumed food. Seats left unoccupied mid-meal. The rancid odor of tilapia left out too long in the hot room made Claudia's stomach churn.

A slight movement caught the corner of her eye. She swung around. A gray raccoon the size of a small spaniel crouched on one of the far tables, gorging on someone's abandoned fish dinner. Its robber's mask seemed oddly appropriate as it looked up and gave her and Jovanic the once-over before finding them unworthy of further consideration and returning to its meal.

Jovanic caught Claudia's eyes and held them. Neither needed to ask the question aloud: *What the hell is going on here?*

"This is nuts," Claudia muttered. "This is weird." She edged nearer to him, wrapping an arm around his waist, drawing comfort from the bulk of his physical presence and his strength. "I'm scared, Joel. Lynn said Stedman has Kylie; she said it's the end of time. What are we going to do?"

"According to Rod, the altar would be in the sanctuary behind the church. If they've decided to move the ceremony up, as Lynn said, to after midnight tonight, everyone is probably gathered there."

"Still, to leave in the middle of dinner—" She left it

unfinished. "I haven't been to the church yet, but I think if we just keep following the path we'll come to it."

Jovanic consulted Rodney's hand-drawn map. "You're right. The main path is the key. Look, it winds around the houses. Then there's some empty space, then the church. Let's go."

A few minutes later they reached the outskirts of the group of homes the TBL members referred to as the village. Like the dining hall, lights burned through unshaded windows of virtually every home they passed.

"Which one is Bethlehem?" Jovanic asked.

"I have no idea. But it's *interesting* that the Powers family lives in a house with that name, with Stedman calling Kylie the Chosen One."

Jovanic looked at her with skepticism. "You mean he's equating Kylie with Jesus? That's pretty far out, even for this bunch."

"Honey, you don't *know* this bunch. Nothing is too far out for them." She pointed out Emmanuel, the Diehl house, where she had visited Oka. Jovanic swung the Maglite over the door, illuminating a black ribbon that had been tacked up, announcing the elderly woman's death.

They moved quickly from one house to the next, looking for the one named Bethlehem. Each house bore an engraved brass nameplate above its knocker, and on each door a small bound bundle of silvery dried leaves had been tacked up.

"Sage," Claudia informed Jovanic after making a brief detour to check out one of the bundles.

"Why would they put sage on the door?"

She shrugged. "Usually, it's used for smudging."

"Would you like to put that in English?"

"It's a Native American ceremony that's gone mainstream among New Agers. It's for cleaning and purifying a home. You burn sage when you want to get rid of negative energies or entities. But this just feels creepy. It makes me think of the Angel of Death passing over the homes of the Hebrews in the Bible."

"Except that the Hebrews put the blood of the lamb on the door, not sage."

And that made her think of Kylie in the hands of Harold Stedman.

They had nearly reached the end of the row of houses when an anguished cry tore through the night.

For the space of a millisecond Claudia wondered whether she had imagined that the sound had a human origin. Maybe they'd heard a coyote. But she knew better.

In the same instant, Jovanic had the Beretta in his hand. Together, they ran toward the sound.

Someone was coming toward them with a stumbling gait. *Rodney Powers.* About fifty yards from them he collapsed on the path. Harrowing sobs racked him, but Claudia ran past. She ran toward the building he had come from. It had no spire, no stained glass windows, but she knew instinctively that it was the church.

"Claudia, wait!" Jovanic called to her. "Don't go in there."

"Kylie—"

He caught up with her and grabbed her arms, forced her to face him. "Listen to me. You saw Rod back there. Do you think there's anything you can do to help Kylie? I'll go. Let me check it out first. *Stay here.*"

She nodded, watched him go, wanting to call him back—as if she could turn back the clock by keeping him from walking into the church. As if she could change whatever had happened.

Jovanic entered the church and Claudia began counting off the seconds. Twenty. Thirty. Forty-five. Sixty. *What is he finding in there?* Seventy-five. Ninety.

His shadow appeared in the doorway. *Oh God. Oh God. Oh God.*

Claudia's heart was thumping fiercely as she watched him emerge from the building. He had taken off his outer shirt and rolled it into a bundle to cover his nose and mouth. Dropping the shirt to the ground, Jovanic leaned over and put his hands on his knees. He gulped a deep inhale, filling his lungs with fresh air, and she knew he had been holding his breath the entire time he was inside.

When he straightened he was breathing hard, as if he'd run a long way. He stared at her, horror darkening his gray eyes.

"They're dead. All of them. The place is filled with people—families, old people, kids. All dead."

The impact of his words made it impossible to take in the reality of what they meant. But some part of her must have understood because suddenly she was shaking all over. Every cell in her body was being hit with its own little earthquake. She tried to speak, couldn't get the words out. "Wha—how—?"

Jovanic grabbed her in his arms and held on to her, and she could feel him trembling, too. His voice was scarcely above a whisper. "I don't know how. No visible signs. Maybe drugged. Maybe— I've never seen anything like this." He kept talking, as if doing so would stave off the reality that he would have to face with silence. "Not CO_2 poisoning, their coloring would show it; their faces would be—"

Claudia finally found her vocal cords. "Stop! I don't

want to know." She closed her eyes. "What about Kylie? Erin?" Then she realized that he had never seen Kylie or Erin, would not recognize them if he had come across their bodies in the church. "Kelly. Omigod, Kelly . . ."

Jovanic was already regaining control of his emotions. His face had gone hard and expressionless, the way he'd learned to do as a detective when he needed to protect himself.

"I didn't see Kelly, but I just looked to see if anyone was moving. I couldn't hold my breath anymore. If she was in there it's too late for her. I'm sorry, babe, but until we know what it is we're dealing with, we can't go back in there. Let's get back to the main house and find a phone."

Claudia sagged against him, choking back the lump of emotion in her throat. "We found them, but we failed." Jovanic didn't answer, but he kept his arm tight around her as they started walking back.

Rodney raised his head and saw them coming. He pulled himself to his feet and wailed, "James— everyone—they're gone, they're all gone. They left without me."

Chapter 29

Claudia went over and took Rodney's trembling hands in her own. They might as well have been blocks of ice. Stress did that, and there was no greater stressor than what lay beyond the doors of the church. She had no words of comfort to offer. What meaning would sympathetic words have to a man who has just lost everyone he held dear?

She stood there quietly with him until he gathered himself. When he spoke, his voice was thick with emotion. "We've got to find Kylie and Erin."

"I'm sorry, Rod, but we can't go in there," Jovanic said. He put out a warning hand as the other man started forward. "Until we know what killed them—"

Rodney looked at him as if he had grown an extra head. "The gas won't affect *us*. Fentanyl dissipates fast and they've probably been in there for hours."

"How do you know that—what you said about the gas?" Claudia asked sharply.

He turned the look on her. "We *all* know. We've known for a long time how we would travel to the other side. Fentanyl is quick and easy."

"That's what the Russians used a few years ago against the Chechen rebels," Jovanic said roughly. "Only they didn't *intend* to kill anyone. You're saying this is a mass suicide that's been planned?"

"Our departure has been planned, but it's not suicide, it's a passage to a wonderful new life. Everyone gives their agreement when they join TBL."

Claudia shoved him, nearly knocking him off his feet. "If this new life is so wonderful, why were you so hot to rescue Kylie from it? Jesus Christ, Rod, what the hell's wrong with you?"

Rodney's head dropped and he started sobbing again. "James was right, I was weak. I couldn't stand the thought of never seeing her again. And then, it's just—the last few months, Brother Stedman hasn't been himself. Some of the things he's been saying—I was afraid something wasn't right. And when James called me in the mountains and told me what he'd heard Brother talking about—" He put his hands up to his face and pressed them against his eyes as if to shut out what he had seen. His left eye, swollen after his encounter with Jermaine Johnson, was now rimmed in purple. "I don't want him to hurt her. We've got to find them. *Please!*"

Suddenly, Claudia understood what he was saying. "They're not inside the church with all the others? They're not dead yet?"

"No, they're not in there. The congregation had to go first, to prepare the way for the governing board and the Chosen One—my baby Kylie. They're 'over there' now, waiting for her."

Claudia was beginning to think she had gone through a worm hole to some other universe. Maybe all the shocks of the evening had made her hearing suspect.

Jovanic stepped in front of her and grabbed Rodney by the front of his shirt. They were about the same height, but Jovanic's anger made him seem immense. "Do you *know* where Kylie and Stedman are? If you do, you'd better tell me now, goddamn it, so maybe, just maybe we can save your daughter's life."

Rodney took a step backward, half stumbling as he pulled away from Jovanic's grasp. "I was thinking they might be in the sanctuary, but they're not; I looked there. They're not at my house, either. I don't know where else they could be."

Overhead, the sky suddenly lit up like day and a deafening crack of thunder startled them all. Then came the smell of rain and the clouds opened, unleashing a furious downpour.

Claudia had to raise her voice over the noise. "The bomb shelter."

"Those buildings are always kept locked," Rodney shouted back at her. "But Sister Ryder might have a key. She keeps them with her all the time."

Warm rain beat on their heads and ran in rivulets down their faces, soaking their clothing. Thunder boomed again and colossal forks of lightning sent blue-white branches into the sky. Jovanic bent his head against the onslaught. "Claudia and I are going to the infirmary to get the keys. You go to the bomb shelter and wait for us there."

"But—"

"Don't give me any bullshit, Rod. I'm not in the mood. Right now you're a liability. You can't run, you can barely walk. You can't even see with that left eye. Now, do as I fucking told you and we'll meet you in a few minutes."

The rain stopped as suddenly as it began and the air was a sticky blanket once again. By the time Claudia and Jovanic reached the infirmary, their wet clothing was clinging to their bodies like Saran Wrap.

They found Lynn Ryder sitting on the edge of the bed, leaning forward; holding on to the bed railing for support. When she saw them come through the door, she tried to stand. "The phone. I have to call—"

"Not yet," Claudia said to her, gently pushing her back onto the bed. "We need your keys. We have to get into the bomb shelter."

Ryder's hand immediately went to the jailer's key ring on her belt, protecting it. "Are you crazy? I'm not giving you my keys."

There was no time for finesse. It crossed Claudia's mind that shocking Ryder into compliance might be the fastest way to gain her cooperation. "The congregation is *dead,* Lynn. If you don't hand them over, Kylie Powers will be dead, too. Is that something you want on your conscience?"

Ryder had a ready comeback. "We're dead for only an instant. We're immediately resurrected to a new life in another place. Kylie will be fine. We all will."

"She won't be fine if Stedman sticks a knife into her!" Claudia saw the shock in the other woman's face and continued, relentless. "That's what he's got planned. He's going to sacrifice her, literally sacrifice a three-year-old child. Lynn, we know you've been working for the Feds. Why don't you want to help us now?"

"They *made* me work for them. I had no choice; they had something on me. I didn't want to go to prison."

"But when you got here, what? You were taken in by Stedman's preaching?"

"I realized that Brother Stedman was teaching the truth."

"How can you think child sacrifice is okay?"

"That's *not* what we do. It's a ceremonial sacrifice."

"Maybe it was before, but things have changed," Claudia said.

"If it has changed, the directive comes from the Lord God. Brother Stedman would never lie and he would never do anything that wasn't for our greater good."

"I bet you don't tell the Feds you feel that way."

"I did what they told me I had to do," Lynn Ryder said bitterly. "I betrayed my brothers and sisters, and now you're telling me they've gone on to the new world without me. That will be my punishment to bear; I'll still be here when the cataclysm comes. I will be destroyed with the rest of the outsiders."

Jovanic made an impatient noise. He stepped closer to the bed. "We don't have time for this conversation. Now, we can do this the nice way or I can arrest you for obstructing a police investigation. I'd rather avoid the paperwork, so give me the keys now." He moved his shirt aside, letting her see the silver black grip of his weapon in the holster.

Lynn shot him a look of pure venom as her hands fumbled to get the jailer's ring off her belt. Claudia offered help, but she refused.

"Everyone is really dead?" Talking to herself, trying to take it in. She flung the ring of keys at Jovanic. "I was supposed to go with them, I . . ."

Jovanic grabbed the keys as they arced through the air and spun on his heel, heading to the door. Following him, Claudia stopped and turned back to the Ark's security chief. "Why do you want to call your handlers if you expected to 'leave' with the rest of the members?"

"It's what I was supposed to do if anything happened." Lynn sank to the floor and put her arms around her knees. "Stupid of me. There's no point now. It's too late. Too late for everything."

"Rodney Powers is still alive. If there is a God, Erin and Kylie are, too. It's not too late for them."

Lynn Ryder looked up, a flicker of hope alight in her face. "Find them. They'll want to go with our family to the other side. We're going to create a new world together."

Claudia shook her head in disgust. "Not this time, sister."

Rodney Powers was waiting by the bomb shelter door as Jovanic had directed.

"What time is it?" Rodney demanded as they rushed up. It was too dark for Claudia to see her watch. She opened her cell phone. The lighted LCD showed that midnight had passed three minutes earlier.

Oh God, are we too late after all?

"What time was Kylie born?" she asked. The urgency to get the door open and find Rodney's child still alive was almost unbearable. *Alive, but in what condition?*

"It was close to one a.m. Why?" Realization glimmered. "She won't actually turn three until then. Brother Stedman knows that. He won't do anything before the proper time. Hurry! We've still got time to find them!"

Jovanic handed Claudia the flashlight and began inserting keys in the lock. "Rod, you wait here. Claudia, when we get inside, I'll go first; stay behind me. If they're here, I'll take care of Stedman and anyone else. Assuming Kylie's there, you grab her and bring her up here to Rod. If I have to use my weapon, I want you and the kid out of the way." He dropped the key ring, swore at himself, picked it up and tried another key.

Claudia watched him insert one key after another. They worked together in concert as if she could read his mind. He didn't need to ask her to explain what they would find behind the door. She held the light steady on the lock. "There's a short hallway, then around the corner a staircase going down. At the bottom of the stairs, you'll see a hallway with doors on both sides."

Rodney was leaning against the wall. He'd eased the shoe from his injured foot, which had swelled to twice its normal size. Pain and fear were reflected on his face. "What about Erin?" he asked. "You're not going to shoot her, are you? You're not going to—"

"I'd like to avoid shooting *anyone*. If you're right and they don't have any weapons, it shouldn't be a problem, should it?"

The satisfying thunk of the lock retracting in the metal door told them that key number seven was the lucky one.

After the thick, humid air outside, the bomb shelter felt like a refrigerator, making Claudia shiver in her rain-soaked clothes. The stairwell lights were already on, casting Jovanic in their sickly yellow glow as he went down the stairs sideways, the Beretta pointed at the floor. Claudia followed him two steps behind.

When they reached the bottom, they stood in silence while Jovanic got his bearings. He motioned for her to wait for him as he stole along the corridor, soundless in rubber-soled sneakers; stopping at doors, putting his ear to each, moving on to the next one. He wouldn't attempt to kick any door open without a good idea of what was behind it, but Claudia was getting more itchy by the minute—worrying about Kylie, worrying about Kelly. She couldn't make herself care much about Erin after Kelly's sister had put them all in this untenable position. *Kelly*. They still didn't know whether she had been in the church when the fentanyl gas was released. She pushed it all aside to deal with later. For now, the only thing that mattered was finding Kylie.

She began to second-guess her intuition about coming to the bomb shelter. What if Kylie and Stedman weren't even here? What if— She glanced up from checking her watch for the umpteenth time. Jovanic had disappeared from sight.

Chapter 30

Claudia ran toward the shadowed end of the hallway and for the first time realized that it did not dead-end as she had supposed. She was standing in the stem of an L-shaped structure. Jovanic had gone around the corner.

A moment later he reappeared from the arm of the el and came close to her, pressed his lips to her ear. "There's a long incline leading down. At the end there's a curtain drawn across the opening. They're chanting."

Claudia's palms felt sweaty and she found herself gulping air as if she couldn't get enough. "They must have started the ceremony. Joel, we've got to get down there."

"I know." He gave her a quick, hard kiss. "Let's go."

The incline had no lighting of its own, but the amber fluorescents of the hallway behind them glowed eerily into it. Just enough light to see where they were going. Claudia hefted the Maglite. They could not use it for illumination in case it alerted Stedman and the others, but she was ready to use it as a weapon if she had to.

About two-thirds down the grade, she began to hear the chanting. Pleasant alto voices, somber Latin-sounding words. Gregorian, or something like it, muffled by a heavy black velvet curtain. The cloth barrier was all that stood between them and the rite taking place on the other side.

Jovanic got down in a crouch. Slowly, carefully, he moved the edge of the curtain aside and put his eye to the opening for a quick glimpse, then let it fall back into place. He motioned Claudia back up the incline so he could tell her what he'd seen.

"Five inside; four facing away from us. No sign of Kylie or her mother."

Claudia's heart sank. She had been so certain that the chanting would lead them to the little girl. "What do we do now?"

"We wait and watch."

They returned to the curtain. Jovanic had her do as he had done so she could see what they faced on the other side: a large cavern. Rough-hewn stone, the roof above disappearing into darkness. Wall sconces with fat candles, flickering light, dancing shadows. At the far end she could make out four figures in dark hooded garments kneeling before a massive block of natural stone. They faced a fifth hooded figure standing across the structure from them.

As Claudia watched, hardly daring to breathe, the one standing raised his head and lifted his face toward the ceiling. The hood fell back on his shoulders, exposing the balding head and white beard of Harold Stedman. From where she stood his face seemed impassive, but she could imagine the fire burning in the blue eyes.

Stedman gestured with his hands like an orchestra leader in the closing bars of a symphony and the chanting ceased.

Claudia closed the edge of the curtain. "They're getting ready," she whispered. Jovanic nodded. The Beretta looked big and dangerous in his hand. As scared as she was, his cool confidence transmitted itself to her and helped her feel calmer.

Stedman's powerful voice came through the curtain. He was talking about the prophet Abraham and his willing obedience to his God's order to sacrifice his beloved son, Isaac.

"Our Lord God, you stopped your prophet at the last moment because Abraham's sacrifice was a symbol of your own sacrifice—your own lamb's blood. We recall so well, oh Lord, your Revelation, where you tell us of those who have washed their robes and made them white in the blood of the lamb. We have seen your light grow brighter. We have seen you provide a *new* lamb, and tonight we present to you the blood of that lamb so that your servants here on earth may be saved. Our brothers and sisters have gone on before us to prepare the way, and now we, the governing board of your chosen organization, prepare to join them."

Putting her eye to the curtain again, Claudia saw Stedman lean forward and take something from the altar. Something that had been hidden by the bodies of the kneeling men. Her heart began racing on overdrive. In his hands was a leather sheath. The silver hilt of a dagger gleamed in the candlelight.

He raised the sheath above his head and the chanting began again.

How could I have ever thought he was reasonable?

Behind her, Claudia felt Jovanic tense and knew that he wanted to move. But they couldn't risk going in without knowing where Kylie was.

The chanting continued for two or three minutes. Then Harold Stedman said, "Amen," and the cave fell silent. Slowly, deliberately, he lowered the sheath and removed the knife. He laid the cold steel across his hands and displayed it to his companions.

The four kneeling men rose and shrugged off their

hoods. Claudia recognized them from the times she had seen them at the head table in the dining hall. She spared a fleeting prayer for the TBL followers who had given their lives tonight simply because these men had instructed them to. She hoped the fentanyl gas had been quick and painless.

The elders turned to their left and moved single file past the altar, then disappeared from her line of sight. She darted a look back at Jovanic—*What do we do?* He held up his hand: *Wait.*

The next time she looked around the curtain, Erin Powers was entering the cave from the far side, her unconscious child in her arms. Kylie was dressed in white lace decorated with colored ribbons and rosettes, satin slippers on her feet. Her fine baby hair was curled in ringlets and tied with bows.

All dressed up and nowhere to go.

Everything Claudia had been told about Kylie flashed back and she realized that the stories were not exaggerated. Even in sleep this was an extraordinarily beautiful child. A miniature angel. How could Erin do this?

They were at a distance of some twenty feet, but she knew from Erin's glazed look that she was under the influence of something. Drugged and hypnotized like her sister, Claudia guessed. How else would Stedman get her to comply with what he was asking her to do?

Followed by the four elders, Erin laid her child on the altar. Kylie shuddered as her skin came into contact with cold stone, but mercifully, she remained inert.

This is it. Claudia readied herself. It was all she could do to keep from rushing into the cave.

Jovanic touched her arm. *Now.* She stepped aside and he pulled open the curtain.

His voice echoed loudly in the chamber. "Drop the knife. Harold Stedman, you're under arrest." He had the Beretta pointed at Stedman's heart.

Harold Stedman flicked a disinterested glance at him and continued to raise the knife above his head. He began to intone: *"Benedicámus Patrem et Filium cum Sancto Spíritu."*

Erin stood at the end of the altar, frozen in place, staring straight ahead.

The four members of the governing board had frozen, too. They stared at Jovanic, horror mirrored in each of their faces.

"Throw it on the ground, Stedman," Jovanic ordered again. "Now!"

"—quemádmodum sperávimus in te. In te, Dõmine, sperávi . . ."

Claudia edged along the wall, preparing to grab Kylie and run. Her eyes were glued to Stedman's hands, still above his head, the knife poised in his fist.

She was nearly parallel to the altar now. How long would he be able to hold the knife aloft?

Then everything got crazy. Several things happened at once:

A guttural cry pulled everyone's attention. *Kelly!* Her eyes wild above her duct-taped mouth. Leaning against the wall at the place where Erin had appeared, she strained to push herself along toward the altar. Hampered by the tape binding her ankles, her hands behind her back.

She's alive!

Distracted for an instant, Stedman jerked his head in Kelly's direction. Claudia dove at the altar, felt the icy stone surface against her midsection.

Stedman started to bring the knife down. Claudia grabbed for the child's legs and pulled.

Erin screamed, "No! She's the Chosen One!" She threw herself across Kylie, not to protect her from Stedman, but to stop Claudia from taking her.

The knife plunged.

Gunshots exploded like thunder.

Chapter 31

Claudia could hear nothing but the echoes of the gunshot. The splash of hot blood on her skin made her recoil. Erin's blood on her arms. Stedman's blood on her face. She wanted to scrub it off, but she had to attend to Kylie first.

Erin. Oh God, Erin. Lying on the ground, struggling for air, grabbing at the dagger that protruded from her neck.

Stedman, fallen behind the altar, a bullet in his heart.

Kelly had passed out.

Jovanic was shouting at the elders, ordering them to lie on the floor, hands behind them. He grabbed a fistful of plasticuffs from his pocket and began to secure them.

There was nothing Claudia could do now to help any of them. She forced herself to turn away from the scene in the cavern, seized the still-unconscious child from the altar, focused on one thought: *Get an ambulance.*

Claudia ran, still nearly deaf from the gunshots, yelling for Rodney, not knowing how loud her voice was. She was in a nightmare, running forever. Kylie's unconscious body heavy in her arms; the incline steeper, the hallway unending. She had reached the staircase when she saw on the landing, looking down at her, his frightened face. Saw his lips form his daughter's name.

"What about Erin?" Rodney took his daughter gently

and held her tight against his chest. Tears streamed down his cheeks. "Where's my wife?"

Claudia was still trying to shake the ringing in her ears. "I've got to get to a phone, Rod. She got in the way of Stedman's knife. Let me go and get her some help."

He was still asking questions, trying to make sense of it all, but Claudia was still running. By the time the Victorian came into view, she had a stitch in her side and was short of breath. She had taken Lynn Ryder's keys from the door to the bomb shelter. She stumbled up the steps to the back door, trying to decide which might fit Rita's desk.

She hurried into the front office and found someone already there. Lynn Ryder was sitting at Rita's desk. She swung around when she heard Claudia, a cordless phone in her hand.

"I know where Rita keeps her keys," she said in a monotone, answering Claudia's unasked question. "I've already called my people. They're on their way over."

"Call 911; we need an ambulance. I think Stedman's dead and Erin needs help."

Ryder shook her head and handed her the phone. She put her head down on the desk. As Claudia took the phone and dialed the emergency number, Lynn began to sob.

It was two days later before Claudia was allowed to see Kelly, who had been hospitalized for observation.

She entered Kelly's room with a small bouquet of yellow roses and gave her friend a hug. Kelly couldn't stop crying for a long time, but finally she managed to give Claudia her account of what had taken place on Friday night.

"On the way to Tabby's house, after I talked to you, I got so worked up—I kept thinking how Erin had betrayed us. I was furious and, you know how I am—when I get mad, I drink. I felt like I had to fortify myself before I confronted her. But as usual, one drink turned into two; and by the time I got back on the road, it made sense to just go straight on to the Ark. I was sitting outside in the car half asleep when Erin and that ginormous Johnson dude got there."

"When we got there your car was blocking the gate," Claudia said.

"Someone had left the gate open and the guard was gone, so after Erin and the big dude drove through, I parked at the gate so they couldn't get out. The only weapon I could think of was the tire iron in the trunk, so I got it out. I followed Erin into the Victorian. Lynn Ryder was there, rounding people up, sending them over to the church."

"Is that when you hit her?"

Kelly's lips twisted. "I didn't mean to hit her. It was a mess. I was yelling at Erin, and Kylie was crying. Then Lynn Ryder showed up. Seeing her pissed me off all over again about being drugged and all that. She's the last person I remembered talking to, so I thought she probably had something to do with it. I was asking her about it . . ."

"*Asking* her?"

"Okay, fine, I was accusing her. Then the big dude stepped in and got all threatening. He reached out and tried to grab me, so I swung the tire iron. He ducked out of the way and Lynn Ryder was standing there, so . . ."

"I get it."

Claudia had spent some time thinking about Ryder and wondering whether she would be held liable for any of the events at the Ark compound. There weren't many members left to share blame. It seemed ironic that she had been recruited by the FBI and blackmailed into being placed inside the cult as an operative, but something in their teachings had struck a chord. She had been so thoroughly taken in by Harold Stedman's charisma and his promises, she became a true believer.

Stedman had bccn so convincing.

Chapter 32

A week after the suicides.

Claudia and Jovanic were spooning in her bed, safe together, and for now that was all she asked for.

"The coroner's report came in on Harold Stedman," Jovanic said. "Turns out he had a brain tumor."

"A brain tumor? You mean, that's why—"

"The likely cause of visual and auditory hallucinations."

"That explains his twisted thinking," Claudia said, remembering the odd handwriting he had showed her. "And his channeling automatic handwriting. If that had been authentic, at least some of the words would have been legible." The strange body heat she'd noticed must have been a result of his illness, too. Despite everything she couldn't help feeling sorry for the man and wondered whether he had somehow managed to meet up with his followers "over there."

"I talked to Jesse Oziel, too," Jovanic added.

"You've been very busy, Columbo. Is that where you went today? To the office?"

He grinned. "Hey, babe, I'm done eating bonbons and watching soap operas. The doc's releasing me." The grin faded. "Now I just have to get past the review board." Firing his weapon while on leave meant facing a board of inquiry to justify his action.

"They should give you a commendation for what you did."

"I'll be lucky if I get to keep my job."

"You saved Kylie's life, which ought to be worth a lot." She scooted closer and Jovanic folded her in his arms, his cheek resting against hers. "What did Oziel say?"

"You already know that his team got to the Colorado temple just in time to prevent another mass suicide. They've started processing the kids they found there. Oziel admitted they were all well cared for. I think he was actually regretting having to return them to the welfare system."

"A system that's already failed them once."

"It's the law, babe. He's sworn to uphold it, just like I am."

A great wave of sadness washed over Claudia as she remembered the young members of the Temple of Brighter Light—Esther. Magdalena; her sister, Rachel. She remembered all the others, too—Rita, the Treadwells, the Diehls, and all the rest. Good, decent people, she was certain of it, but lemmings who had followed their leaders off a cliff. Well, maybe the lemming thing was a myth.

This is what rejecting independent thinking gets you.

She sighed and he kissed the top of her head, held her a little tighter.

"Are you thinking of Erin again?" he murmured into her hair.

"She was so young, so completely taken in by Stedman. They all were. Why? Why were they so gullible?"

"You're the psych major, babe. You tell me."

"I suppose most of them were missing something from their lives. Maybe they were like Erin and didn't have good parenting when they were growing up. Or they lost something along the way and were looking for guidance—for authority figures, so they were willing to do whatever they were told. They were so desperate for a better world that they went along with Stedman's bullshit, and now they're dead. Nearly two hundred people, wiped out in a few minutes."

"At least it was fast and supposedly easy."

"The bastards gave it to Kylie in a lollipop. Thank God she survived."

They'd Googled fentanyl together and discovered that the drug was a painkiller a hundred times more addictive than heroin. It had been pumped in gas form into the air vents at the church. The elders had a supply in the cavern ready to use on themselves after Kylie's sacrifice. The mass suicides had long been planned.

"How's Kelly doing?" Jovanic asked.

"It'll take a while for her to get over it all. She blames herself for Erin's death, though she couldn't have changed anything."

Rodney and Kylie were staying at Kelly's condo until he could figure out what to do with the rest of his life. He had begun to question the TBL teachings, but as indoctrinated as he was, it would likely take a long time for him to let it all go, assuming he ever could. But before he was able to move forward in any way, constructive or not, he had some grieving to do.

"I think we need a vacation," Claudia said after they had discussed it all over again.

Jovanic laughed and stretched to kiss the tip of her nose. "I think it's about time I went back to work and got some rest. Chasing criminals is a lot less exciting than hanging out with you, Grapho Lady."

THE MYSTERY SERIES STARRING
FORENSIC HANDWRITING EXPERT
CLAUDIA ROSE

POISON PEN
A Forensic Handwriting Mystery
by
Sheila Lowe

Before her body was found floating in her jacuzzi,
publicist-to-the-stars Lindsey Alexander had few friends,
but plenty of lovers. To her ex-friend—forensic
handwriting expert Claudia Rose—she was a ruthless,
back-stabbing manipulator. But even Claudia is shocked
by Lindsey's startling final note:
"It was fun while it lasted!"

It would be easier on the police—and Claudia—to write it
off as suicide. But Claudia's instincts push her to investigate further, and she quickly finds herself entangled in a
far darker scenario than she bargained for. Racing to
identify a killer, Claudia soon has a price on her head—
and unless she can read the handwriting on the wall,
she'll become the next victim.

**Available wherever books are sold or
at penguin.com**

THE MYSTERY SERIES STARRING
FORENSIC HANDWRITING EXPERT
CLAUDIA ROSE

DEAD WRITE
A Forensic Handwriting Mystery
by

Sheila Lowe

Handwriting expert Claudia Rose heads to the
Big Apple at the behest of Grusha Olinetsky, the
notorious founder of an elite dating service whose
members are mysteriously dying. Drawn into the feckless
lives of the rich and single, Claudia finds herself in a
twisted world of love and lies fueled by desperation.
But is one among them desperate enough to kill?

Claudia must find clues in the suspects' handwriting
before more victims are scribbled into the killer's
black book...

**Available wherever books are sold or
at penguin.com**

THE MYSTERY SERIES STARRING
FORENSIC HANDWRITING EXPERT
CLAUDIA ROSE

WRITTEN IN BLOOD
A Forensic Handwriting Mystery
by

Sheila Lowe

The widow of a rich, older man, Paige Sorensen
is younger than—and hated by—her
stepchildren. And they're dead set on proving
that she forged their father's signature on his
will, which left his entire estate, including the
Sorensen Academy for Girls, to her. Claudia
admits she's intrigued by this real-life soap
opera, and breaks her first rule: never get
personally involved. But she's grown attached to
a troubled Sorensen student—and when
disaster strikes, she'll realize that reading
between the lines can mean the difference
between life and death…

**Available wherever books are sold or
at penguin.com**

Also Available from
Karen E. Olson

The Missing Ink

A Tattoo Shop Mystery

Brett Kavanaugh is a tattoo artist and owner of
an elite tattoo parlor in Las Vegas. When
someone calls to make an appointment to
get a tattoo of her fiancé's name embedded
in a heart, Brett takes the job but the girl
never shows. The next thing Brett knows, the
police are looking for her client, and the name
she wanted on the tattoo isn't
her fiancé's...